TO SPELL & BACK

FATE WEAVER
BOOK THREE

REGINA WELLING

ERIN LYNN

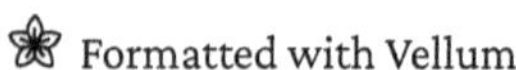 Formatted with Vellum

CONTENTS

TO SPELL & BACK

CHAPTER
ONE

"Get away from him." Sylvana's scream cut the air like a knife, her voice edging toward hysterical. "You vicious old witch. Leave him alone."

White fire lanced from her fingertips, arrowed toward her mother's body. Clara batted the sizzling flame away with as much attention as she would have paid a fly buzzing around her ear.

While her daughter raged, Clara's attention remained focused on the man who was at the crux of this fight. Or, technically, the minor deity: Cupid. The one and only god of love who carried a bow and heart-tipped arrows, but was as far from a winged cherub as a donkey is from a goose.

Chiseled perfection from head to toe, there was nothing baby soft about him. It was no wonder Sylvana had fallen for his...charms. Had that been all there was to it, the three of them might never have come to this moment. Or rather, the four of us.

I'm Lexi Balefire, daughter of Sylvana, granddaughter of Clara, and Cupid? Well, he's my dad. I know, it shocked me, too, when I found out.

While the fight raged, I was the squealing infant tucked into a carry basket and left forgotten on the grass. Paradoxically, I was also the time traveling interloper watching the biggest mystery of my past play out before stunned eyes. Not your typical Wednesday, I'll grant you.

This was the pivotal moment that would leave me virtually orphaned, send my mother to hell and my father to who-knows-where. In a few minutes, nothing would be left but a black scar on the ground, my grandmother's body turned to stone, and me; a crying infant who would grow up with the stigma of having hailed from wicked witches.

Or a murdering witch, if you want to get technical. When my faerie godmother found me, she assumed my grandmother had killed my mother—a supposition I recently learned was a total mistake. Now I would find out exactly what happened that fateful day.

I wasn't sure I could watch, but I knew I couldn't look away.

"She doesn't know what you did, does she?" Clara Balefire's wrath curled around Cupid like a living thing that might strangle him if she gave full reign to her temper. "Just how many lies *did* you have to tell to get my daughter to let you put a baby in her belly?"

More white fire arced from Sylvana's direction, to be deflected with a twitch of Clara's finger while my father's burning gaze rested on my grandmother.

"Of course he told me." Looking at my mother at this age gave me a shiver. Peaches and cream complexion, wide green eyes under thick black lashes, and ruby lips. Except for the teased-to-the-max '80's hairdo, we could have been twins. Okay, maybe the hair *and* the clothes.

She wore artfully torn leggings under a ruffled mini—both in black—and a hot pink cropped top. Half a dozen bangles clanked together every time she lobbed another ball of witchfire at her mother. Madonna would have been proud, or maybe dismayed at her effect on my mother's sense of style.

"Didn't you, baby?" Sylvana purred at Cupid, then spat at her mother, "We don't keep secrets."

Cupid declined to comment, and even from a distance, I could see the secrets in his eyes. Blinded by her infatuation with him, my mother would never admit my father's intentions might have been dishonorable even if she'd known truth. Not that I would have expected anything different—he's a god, for freak's sake. They don't play by human rules.

"The child has promise. At the right time, I will teach her how to make the most of her gifts." His voice reminded me of a French horn; tenor with a deeper resonance underneath. His glance strayed toward the baby, and I had trouble wrapping my head around the fact that *she* was *me*.

"This one carries the potential to be the strongest of her kind. I would not allow her to take on that burden without guidance."

"How very noble of you." Clara's sneer turned the

words to knives. "Do you even know her name? Or is she just a thing to you? Something to mold and shape."

Cupid's lack of interest deflected the cuts as surely as if he'd worn forged armor.

"You presume too much, Clara Balefire. I protect what is mine and Alexis," he placed emphasis on my name to prove a point, "is mine."

"Like you protected Beatrice and Reginald? Like you would have protected my sister if she'd been stupid enough to let you have your way with her? Alexis would be safer if she never realized that potential. You're willing to put a target on her back out of a sense of inflated ego."

Unwilling to allow my attention to slip from what I was watching, even for a second, I didn't have time to ponder who Beatrice and Reginald were, or that I had a great aunt I'd never met.

"He loves us." Sylvana leaped aside to avoid a spell that boomeranged back on her when Clara, without even looking in her direction, deflected the curse with a single finger. "We're going to make a family together, and we don't need you to be part of it. Just leave him alone and let us go."

"Did he tell you that in so many words? Did he tell you how he's been trying to bed a Balefire woman for centuries? First my mother, then my sister, and now my daughter, and who knows how many before that? And all to make a new and more powerful Fate Weaver."

Sylvana thought about it for half a second.

"Shut up, you old cow. You're wrong about him—he

loves us, you'll see." My eyebrows rose toward my hairline at Sylvana's harsh criticism; an old cow isn't at all how I'd have described my grandmother, nor would I have dared to blithely show such disrespect to a family member.

Then again, growing up without my true family had given me a different perspective on its sacred nature.

My mother and I had both inherited our looks from Clara, and I wasn't complaining. The Balefire women carry good genes, and I'd bet Clara had heard the tired line about how she and Sylvana looked like sisters from more middle-aged men than it would take to fill a country club.

Eyes trained on my father, Clara slammed a barrier to close Sylvana out of the conversation. "Are you even capable of love?"

Cupid faced away from me and even leaning sideways I caught nothing more than a glimpse of the curve of one cheek, half covered by the edge of the Bow of Destiny. All gold and shining, the weapon's string chimed soft notes against the light breeze.

"Love is my business." The bow looked like a liquid blur practically leaping into his hands, the strings screaming a tune of willingness. What's more, the compass around my neck shrieked to life. Okay, shriek may not be the best word, but saying it broke into song turns this story into something straight out of a Disney musical, and let me tell you, this was not one of those.

Dark was the bowsong, with honed edges that cut and sliced. I only got a glimmer of it from the echo of the compass, which seemed to be acting as some sort of speaker system; my father is the one who took the brunt of the onslaught coming directly off the weapon in his hand. My instincts told me the bow was warning Cupid against rashly taking action. My head rang with a dizzying sound that turned me weak. How on earth could Clara just stand there like she saw nothing happening?

"My daughter's happiness is mine." Fast as a striking snake, Clara crossed the space and before my father realized her intent, snatched the bow, fitted arrow to string, and took aim. "If your will is what makes this thing work, then my own should remove the blinders and help her see her way clear."

She dropped the barrier and dodged as my father made a grab for her.

Silence fell like a balm when the arrow flew straight and true on a course for Sylvana's heart.

Faster than a human can move, my father covered the distance between himself and Sylvana. Clara's arrow slammed into his backside with a solid sound that made me blanch. Did I mention I'm supposed to wield that same bow as Miss Fancy-ass Fate Weaver, or whatever title it is the gods want me to carry? Was I supposed to shoot people with that thing? Nope. Not on my list of things to do.

Clara's triumphant shout ended in a roar of, "Nooo."

The force of the blow slammed my dad into my mom, and she hit the ground hard enough to knock the wind out of her. Staggering and struggling to regain his footing, Cupid yanked the arrow out of his flesh.

"Stupid witch. Do you have any idea what you've done to me?" He grabbed the bow from Clara and then tossed it away as if the bright gold had turned to searing flame. Whether it burned or not, the bow did something to Cupid he hadn't expected. His face altered from robust perfection to a haunted pallor so quickly it reminded me of watching a movie on fast forward.

By the time he turned and walked away without so much as a backward glance at Sylvana, my father had become a shadow of his former self.

My mother, however, seemed to gain all the strength her lover lost.

"Look what you did." Sylvana practically levitated off the ground, fury oozing from every pore. Almost absently, her hands formed magic like I'd never seen before.

Black fire ate daylight and grew between her palms to a crackling mass so large she could barely hold it. I'm not sure whether a trick of the light made it seem so, or if her eyes actually turned black, but I knew I had to take action.

"Stop. You have to stop this right now. Look what you're about to do to each other. Look what you're about to do to *me!*" I jumped into the middle and shouted until my throat burned, but it made no difference. Neither of them could see me. There was nothing left to do but watch in horror.

The moment drew out long and pregnant with magic while Sylvana railed and cursed Clara with every filthy name she could pull to her lips.

"Think what you like, I only want you to be happy."

Clara's statement, quietly made and sincere as far as I could tell anyway, sent Sylvana fully over the edge to the dark side. Everything after that happened at high speed.

Sylvana let the seething magic go with all the force she could muster. Clara spoke a few short words, but I could tell she'd reacted a half-second too late.

The Bow of Destiny went up in a cloud of smoke. Knowing where it ended up, I assumed my grandmother had wasted precious seconds ensuring my father's legacy wouldn't be found until I searched it out either twenty-four-odd years in the future or a couple of days ago depending on whether I was counting back from my present or forward from the past I witnessed now.

"Ligabis, Ostium, Carcere." Clara's second spell rippled through the air and turned to a set of shadowy ropes. A binding spell.

Halfway between the two women, Sylvana's crackling, ebony flame crossed with Clara's spell and I saw something I never thought possible. The two spells—well, mingled isn't exactly the right word, but it's the best one I can find.

Sylvana's witchfire absorbed the binding spell and hit Clara, who tried to throw up a shield but failed. Face fierce, hair floating on the breeze created by the force of Sylvana's intent, I watched the spell bust through the feeble beginnings of a barrier and turn my grandmother to stone. Inch by painful inch.

Sylvana's moment of glee quickly turned sour when the evil she'd sent out bounced off the feet of the stone effigy and returned to her before she had time to duck. A flash, a sizzle, the scent of ozone, and a scorch mark on the earth—I'd heard the story so many times that seeing the aftermath in person felt surreal.

Well, except for the cries coming from the basket. Those were so real that her—my—terror at being left utterly alone punched me in the gut.

How could my mother have been so naive? Then again, she hadn't seen that same look on Cupid's face when he walked away from my half-brother Jett and his mother, and I had. My father's wanton ways had resulted in a number of demigod children; I didn't even want to know how many half-siblings I had floating around out there—the one I'd already met was enough to sour me on making a family connection.

Whatever Clara had done to Cupid, he'd had coming, and Sylvana certainly hadn't pulled any punches with her ball of evil fire.

I walked over near the basket and stared at my scrunched up face, red from crying.

"Shh, it's going to be all right. Tru..." I bit the end of the word off. Never again would I utter the phrase *trust me*. "Terra's coming, and she'll take care of you....us."

This conversation took the concept of talking to yourself to an entirely new level.

The baby ignored me since, to her, I only existed in some amorphous form, and another few minutes passed in an eternity of helplessness before my faerie godmother and two of her sisters came to the rescue.

"Hello. Can you see me?" I waved my hand in Terra's face, but she didn't so much as bat an eyelash, so I settled in to watch what happened next.

Terra cast a shrewd eye over the scene, recording it for the future when she would describe it for me in great detail. A graceful hand, tipped with ruby red, speared through her hair.

This Fae woman would go on to become the next best thing to a mother I could ask for, and after a lifetime of living with her, I could have sworn I knew her every expression. Happy, angry, sad, or vengeful—she can be one scary faerie—all her faces are heartbreakingly lovely.

In that moment, with chocolate-streaked cascading locks spilling over cheeks the hue of a mountain sunset I watched Terra as though seeing her for the first time. The leaves in her hair, the soil on her cheek spoke of wild adventures and a carefree spirit that might have remained untamed if not for me. One crystalline tear pooled before love spilled over her and sent it to trace a path down her face.

"Poor baby," she cooed into the basket, wiping my tears away and cupping my tiny cheek with her gentle fingertips. She gazed into the faces of her sisters, Soleil and Evian, and I could tell she'd made up her mind after that one simple touch.

Time Traveler me gasped; I'd just witnessed the moment when Terra evolved from a faerie with an affinity for the earth element into the true Earth Mother I'd come to know and love.

"What are you thinking, Terra?" Soleil demanded, the edge of suspicion in her tone so recognizable to my trained ears I would have smiled if I wasn't mesmerized by the scene unfolding before me. Her short mane of unkempt hair streaked all the reds and oranges of a brilliant flame contrasted starkly with pale, freckled skin and lips the black of a cooling ember.

Evian, the third of the trio I knew would take me home and raise me as their own, mimicked her sister's swipe down my chubby baby cheek with mirror-tipped fingers that had always reminded me of the surface of still water. "You want to keep her, don't you?" Eyes the color of a tropical sea flicked up to meet Terra's, and I saw no resistance in them at all.

I'd always assumed an argument of some kind had preceded Terra's insistence on taking me in—after all, most witches don't ever get to meet their faerie godmothers. It takes a lot for one to step in, and even then there are limits to how much interference they're allowed to run.

That my cries called Terra to me made up a miracle in and of itself. That she, Soleil, and Evian had snubbed convention even further and taken me under their care spoke of kindnesses I could never repay and costs I might never have counted before.

"I don't know what, but something tells me this is what we're supposed to do," Terra responded, her eyes pleading with her sisters for support.

"Sounds like fun. I mean, how hard can it be? It's one baby, right? We can take her home with us; she won't take up too much space." Soleil and Evian were already staring at my innocent face, speaking in baby talk, their minds made up, while I gazed up at their impossibly beautiful smiles with a look of pure wonder.

Apparently, it had been love, at first sight, all the way around.

"You can't be serious," Evian scoffed at Soleil's suggestion. "If we're doing this, we're going to have to stay in her world." The look on her face said she thought it would be worth it. "I'm in. What's the plan?"

"The Balefire house is right there; I remember it from my orientation visit."

And with that, my fate was sealed. They—we—all walked away, leaving adult me alone with the evidence of how my family's greatest shame hadn't exactly happened the way I thought it had. What was I supposed to do now? Click my heels three times? Or wish upon a star? It would be just my luck to end up spending the rest of my life as a ghost in my own past—in my jammies, no less.

The thought of that made me want to pull my hair out. In fact, my hands were already heading in that direction when I caught a flash of light near one of them. Before I had time to wonder what I'd seen, a rush of motion sickness hit me, and I came back to myself huddled on the window seat in my room.

CHAPTER

TWO

Taking only long enough to get dressed, I made my way to the bench in front of Clara. She looked the same as ever: long hair flowing in the wind created by magic, hands outstretched in the final, fatal casting. I'd come here hundreds of times over the years to look at the face that could have been mistaken for mine if not for the faint traces her years had left behind.

They say hindsight is 20/20 and I couldn't fault the adage because today her face looked completely different to me. Blinded by an untruth, I'd taken her fierce expression as one of evil intent. Now, with the true vision of her history fresh in my mind, I could see the pain written in every tense muscle.

Tears burned while I imagined Clara, granite crawling through her veins, watching Sylvana celebrate a victory. The scene played through my mind again, and I shivered in helpless horror now as I had when I'd watched the creeping stone take her over. Bit by bit it swallowed shoes, dress, arms and hands, the amulet around her neck, and finally her face.

I would see that scene in my nightmares for many years to come.

The punishment when one witch kills another is literally set in stone. Or would that be figuratively? I can never remember. Either way, any witch who kills another turns to stone. There's no judge, no jury, no trial. Just a swift and final sentence followed by a new statue in the world.

When Terra found me in that basket, she and her sisters assessed the crime scene and assumed my grandmother had killed my mother. As a result, I had lived with the stigma of rising from wicked beginnings since before I was old enough to understand what that meant.

I should have suspected something when my mother, Sylvana, turned up right after Beltane—very much alive and not at all forthcoming about the events leading up to Clara's current state. Gullible fool that I am, I fell for the convenient lie that Clara probably killed someone else after banishing her daughter to a portal on the edge of a hell dimension.

How many times had I sat in this spot and self-righteously ranted at my grandmother for choosing the evil path and leaving me alone in the world? And why do we find it so comforting to speak to our dead? Is it because they can't carry our secrets away with them or because they can?

"It was never you. I know that now. Mag gave me the ring, and I went back to the day you...she...what Sylvana did to you; to us. I know you can't hear me, and I don't deserve your forgiveness for jumping to conclusions, but I'm sorry. I'd have liked the chance to get to know you."

Witches aren't supposed to cry, but then, I'm not like most of my kind. Or maybe I am.

Depending on who you talk to, it is believed Fate Weavers—half witches and half children of Cupid—are nearly extinct. My familiar, Salem, says I'm the last, but Delta, a bounty hunter from Olympus, disagrees. According to her, there are more like me out there somewhere.

As far as I can tell, we're cosmic cogs in the wheel that determines the balance between good and evil. No pressure there, or anything.

All I can do is keep orchestrating matches between soul mates much the same way I have since long before I had any idea that what I *was* had any bearing on what I did for a living. Just my way of being one up on those who prefer wreaking havoc and tipping the scales toward chaos. Such is the way of human nature.

I'd go looking for others like me if I could, but I'm also the Keeper of the Balefire flame. A sacred job handed down from the very same grandmother whose stoned body currently loomed over me and a job only I could do. One that kept me on a short leash.

The Balefire, once a wild and mighty thing, now warmed the hearth of my home. My magic fed the flame and the flame gave magic to all witches. Seems like a circular situation now I'm thinking about it. I'll admit to being a little fuzzy on the exact details, but one thing was certain, my job didn't come with either paid or unpaid vacations. I stayed put, or the fire went out. Simple as that.

Besides, the Bow of Destiny, currently concealed in a box in my magical sanctum, had shattered into three pieces during the godmother's attempt to wrest it from Sylvana after she betrayed me and tried take my birthright.

Yeah, my mother, what a peach.

Sylvana had planned, I could only assume, to use the bow in some nefarious scheme to find my father. A plan we'd foiled, but I'd still have to fix the weapon before I could wield it, and I had no idea how to go about repairing a tool of the gods.

While my brain tried to chase down the technical term for a fixer of bows, a flutter of red at the base of the statue drew my focus. One and then another blood-colored rose burst into bloom. Feather-soft petals sent their fragrance into the air like a gift, and I snapped my gaze back to Clara's face, searching for any sign of movement or change. She looked the same as ever, except knowing she might still be alive inside that stone prison made my heart ache.

"I *will* figure out a way to free you, Grandmother, that's a promise." Between trying to figure out how to repair the bow and embrace my Fate Weaver heritage, it looked like my life was about to get even more complicated than usual.

My mixed heritage had come as quite a shock. I'd always known I'd tend the Balefire flame, and that I had an affinity for putting couples together, but I'd taken both of those things for two sides of the same coin, and it had a witch on it—not a god or a heart-tipped arrow.

Descended from wicked, murdering witches had colored my life with a truth I'd come to accept, and now it looked as though I'd been wrong about that, too. Perhaps, fate wished me plagued by unanswered questions and erroneous assumptions.

Every truth I knew about Fate Weaving would fit neatly in a thimble and leave room for two pieces of pocket lint and a fingertip—most of it being hearsay even if it had come from trusted sources. As much as Salem and Delta tried to help, there were gaps in their information big enough to drive a truck through.

Learning that Clara had not supported my father's wish to train me as a Fate Weaver raised concerns I couldn't properly define. If I succeeded in reversing the spell that incapacitated her, would she accept the decision I had made to follow in Cupid's footsteps? You know, once I figured out how to find them.

Or would Clara, who had missed out on the debauchery of the last couple of decades on earth, perhaps come to see that the world collectively stood in line to buy tickets for a trip. To Hades in a hand basket.

I was still contemplating the ramifications of my visit to the past when the present intruded in the form of a white van with colorful advertising splashed down the side. The vehicle I had dubbed the Faerie Van of Party Planning rocketed down the street and missed tearing the bumper off a Jeep by a narrow margin. My faerie godmothers were home, and it was time to tell them what I'd seen.

Stepping into the house, I heard excited female voices punctuated by one with a deeper tone drifting toward me.

"Hi Honey," my boyfriend, Mackintosh Clark met me in the hallway looking a little pale after his ride with Evian at the wheel. He hugged me and whispered in my ear, "She's a maniac. How long has she had her license?"

"Don't ask." I pulled his head down for a kiss and a moment of peace before I broke the news of my latest escapade. At least they couldn't peg me for being impetuous since my trip to the past had been completely unplanned. I mean, come on, if I'd meant to go wandering through time, I'd have at least put on a decent outfit.

Growing up with three—and now four—women who crawled out of bed looking breathtakingly gorgeous had forced me to develop a healthy body image. Otherwise, I'd have found a rock to live under and never shown my face in the light of day.

As mere mortals go, I do all right in the looks department. It's a family thing, apparently. We Balefire women seem to run to a particular pattern and we're cut from pretty cloth.

Kin earned about a million boyfriend points by not appearing dazzled whenever the godmothers were around—and another million for working with them on the music portion of their newly hatched business, Enchanting Events. Initial concepts for the

Martinez/Kirkenbaum wedding were the focus of the day, and I hated to bust up the excited chatter, but I had big witchy news.

I lived in the same house where prior generations of my family have kept the Balefire flame alive. Once I hit the age where most people move out on their own, it would have been the expected thing for my faerie godmothers to return to the Faelands. Had I come into my magic at the age of fourteen like every other witch, perhaps that would have been the case, but I was a late bloomer. Heck, I was almost a non-bloomer. A dud flower.

It had taken ten long years and a gift from my returned-from-the-dead mother—who waltzed into my life in disguise, no less—to trigger my Awakening. Shock number one in a series of changes that left me reeling. My ring-assisted blast from the past probably wouldn't be the last of them, either. My life had gone from slightly boring to totally crazy in a matter of weeks.

The godmothers choice to stay and protect me meant my smallish house had become home to three larger than life personalities. As a concession, they had added their own wing onto the back which, you'd think, would have granted me a modicum of privacy. You'd be wrong.

We all shared the kitchen—which was a lie we conveniently chose to believe because that area of the house was not where my talents lie. Consequently, it fell under faerie domain and was the most frequented area in the house.

All our most important conversations happened there,

and so did the bitterest of battles. I've lost count over how many times the faeries have nearly demolished the room during one of their epic fights.

My current news shouldn't set off any sort of faerie apocalypse, but you never knew about these things. I let them have a few minutes to fuss with the makings of a light meal before I dropped the bomb.

"I used a time traveling ring to go back to the past and watch what happened the day you all came to live here."

The four faeries froze in an approximation of Clara's stoning, except with bugged out eyes and slack-jawed shock riding their faces.

"You did what with a what, now?" Recovering the fastest, Vaeta, the newest addition to the household demanded answers while the other three continued to stare at me like I'd grown a second head.

I guessed I should have eased them into it.

"My grandmother had a time traveling ring, and I used it to go back to the day when she fought with Sylvana. Accidentally." I slid onto a stool at the breakfast bar and added that last bit to help soften the blow. "And I learned a lot about what happened that day."

Kin took the seat beside me and when his leg brushed against mine, I felt the tension in his muscles. It wasn't hard to figure out the cause when the air had gone heavy and warm.

Did I mention the godmothers are elemental faeries? Each held dominion over her own element—earth for Terra, Soleil was fire, and Evian controlled water.

Rounding out the foursome, Vaeta's affinity with the element of air was probably the culprit in the looming feeling in the atmosphere. The most recent addition to our home, she carried the nickname Airy Faerie—one I wouldn't recommend using unless you've always had a deep desire to see what the inside of a tornado looks like.

After taking a deep breath, I launched into my story and gave the most salient point first.

"We already knew Clara didn't kill Sylvana, but she didn't kill anyone else, either."

Kin stroked my right hand with his guitar-string calloused fingers the whole time, squeezing gently whenever he felt my muscles tense. Like I said, best boyfriend ever. Golden blond curls that looked even cuter since he'd let them grow out a little tumbled above deep-set, chocolate brown eyes, full lips, and a strong jawline. It got even better further down, but I couldn't let myself get distracted by thoughts of his body during an emotional conversation, so I averted my gaze.

"They fought, and Cu...my father was there to make it worse. Magics got tossed around, and then Clara grabbed the bow and tried to shoot Sylvana, but he jumped in front of her and took the hit instead. It did something to him and he took off right before the two women wound up for the final salvo."

Compared to the magical fights the three, and now four, sisters indulged in from time to time, the one that took my family had been tame in comparison. Still, it was odd that not a one of them offered a comment. Worse, they all had on their best closed-off faces so I couldn't tell what they were thinking. Instead, I just blurted out the end and waited.

"Clara tossed what looked like a binding curse at the same time Sylvana shot black witchfire. The spells crossed, and bing, boom, bang. That was a few minutes before you guys showed up and saw the results."

The air cleared enough to make breathing easier while I waited for a response.

"How does one accidentally use a time traveling ring?" Uh oh. Terra had gone all lofty on me. Not a good sign.

As patiently as I could, I explained what had happened and then turned the conversation back on her.

"Since we're being candid with one another, can you explain to me why Clara's faerie godmother didn't step in before it went that far? I know for sure if I'd been in that situation, you would all be there to protect me. Isn't this the type of cataclysmic event godmothers are supposed to prevent?"

Soleil and Evian exchanged a look, then turned their eyes to Terra. "Explain it to her. It's time."

Terra sighed. "You're right. Lexi, please forgive us for not being completely honest with you, but there are certain things we're not supposed to talk about. We've broken enough rules that I suppose one more is just a drop in the bucket." She settled back into her chair, and I mimicked her action even though the tension in my shoulders turned to knots and refused to budge.

"What you saw; us taking you in like that—is forbidden."

"Forbidden? By whom?" Was there a council of faeries somewhere who made the rules? Despite the seriousness of the conversation, I indulged in a brief mental image of the three of them standing in front of a group of their peers trying to explain why they'd chosen to raise a witch and worse, why they'd thought she needed a pink unicorn for a pet. "The faerie police?"

Taking my humor for snark, Terra flashed me a warning look, and I zipped it. The next one might be dirty, and Terra's version of dirty looks tended to be literal; I didn't have time for a shower right now.

"This kind of thing just isn't done for reasons too numerous to share. We've been in and out of hot water ever since."

Soleil ran a hand through her fiery hair, "Tuning our magic to the Balefire was a big no-no." Then she wrinkled her nose when her sisters shushed her.

"I don't understand. The Queen of Faerie is a Balefire witch, for heaven's sake. Why would Esmerelda punish you for taking care of me?"

"It's not Esmerelda, dear." Soleil interjected, "It's just that for us the whole of witchkind is new. I know it seems like an eternity, but in Fae terms, a few thousand years isn't all that long. We're still settling in with our role in your lives."

Evian raised an eyebrow, "You know it's not a godmother's job to prevent all harm from coming to her charge. We don't have the power to alter a witch's will. Otherwise, we'd be no better than the Unseelie, making decisions for others, taking matters into our own hands. That decree came directly from Esmerelda; we were given leniency and allowed to raise you, but only if we agreed to certain conditions."

"And we did, for a while anyway," Terra looked chagrined, "but then you took that spill off the roof the year you were eight, and I set the bone in your leg before it even occurred to me to take you to the hospital. That started the downward spiral."

"What exactly *can* you do, then?"

"We're allowed to protect our charges, but only from certain types of danger—outside forces and the like. Your mother and grandmother ended up where they did strictly through their own actions. Two spells crossed—badly intentioned spells from what you described—and intention is not something we meddle with. It's a fine line. Like I could assist you with that eaflock you summoned because you didn't mean to call a faebeast. It's just, well—"

Evian, never one to keep quiet for long, cut Terra off, "Typically, a godmother isn't allowed to show herself; she'd intervene without her charge ever knowing she had been there. Make it look like an accident or just good luck. It's our mission to stay out of sight and perform our little miracles anonymously. We don't grant wishes, we don't send Cinderella to the ball, and we don't live with our charges. Those Grimm brothers muddied the waters for all of us even if they did get some of the basics right."

With hindsight, I could see the times the faeries had brazenly and unapologetically broken the rules to be the best parents they could. It hurt to know how often I'd taken for granted the knowledge that Terra was just a whisper away? I asked of them so many things, never realizing each act carried a price. I owed an overwhelming debt, and I knew they'd never allow me to attempt to pay it back.

"I'm so sorry. You will not put yourselves on the line for me anymore. I mean it—all of you. The best thing you could do for me is to stay safe yourselves. No more protection; no more of anything you're not supposed to be doing."

Terra pursed her lips, "Whatever you say, dear." Yeah, like I believed that.

"I'm serious, Terra. I won't have you paying for my debts."

She steadfastly avoided my gaze and returned to the topic of my trip to the past. "Well, I think I speak for all of us when I say it's a great relief to know the truth. I guess it's a good lesson in how evidence can be deceiving. Or about jumping to conclusions."

A tender smile curved Terra's lips and I looked up to see it mirrored on her sister's face as well, "If you're asking us whether or not we are sorry for how we handled things, though, the answer is no. You, Lexi, were worth the cost at any price. We'll help you however we can. I'm not crazy about sharing you with anyone else, but that's selfish—so if you're able to restore Clara, we'll just have to figure out how we all fit together."

Unshed tears glistened at the corners of my eyes, and I was beginning to think I'd better start carrying a bottle of water to replenish my fluids if I was going to continue to cry that much.

"It hurts my heart we didn't discover the truth sooner," Evian added solemnly.

"How could you possibly have known? It looked like what it looked like and knowing wouldn't have changed the outcome. At least now I know what happened to Clara, and I might even have a shot at restoring her."

I dropped that bomb on them and turned to follow Kin up to my bedroom with only one thought in my head —that the potentially awkward conversation had gone better than expected.

Okay, maybe there was one more thought as I watched Kin's backside amble up the stairs.

CHAPTER

THREE

Ducking down the wide alley between French Street and Hinge Avenue triggered a mild case of déjà vu I deftly brushed aside. The last time—technically the first time—I'd passed through the portal to the Fringe, I was following my mother down a primrose path, never knowing she was the snake hiding under the petals.

This time, I was alone, and my rose-colored glasses lay in shards on the ground. If I'd been raised to hate, Sylvana would have made a convenient target given the extent of her betrayal. My heart had been more trusting that day, and now I could kick myself for missing all the signs. And the lies flitting from betwixt her lips like butterflies on a hot summer day.

I'd definitely pulled losing tickets in the family lottery. A treacherous mother, an absentee father who dropped a load of responsibility on my shoulders before walking away, a grandmother I might never get a chance to know, and a half-brother named Jett Striker who hated my guts. Plus, there are who knows how many half-siblings out there, considering my father was known for heating up the sheets at every opportunity. I'll pass on attending the family reunion, thanks.

A line of debris marked the spot where a single step would take me to a different world, and I wished I could leave my family drama behind as easily.

I only hoped the portal was open, and there wasn't some magical access code or password required for entry.

The Fringe, according to my research, occupied the space where many worlds met. Like a train station or a hospital waiting room, most people were just passing through. Still, a train needs a conductor and a hospital needs nurses.

Probably not the best analogy for the people who lived there full-time, but I imagined those types had a great need for refuge, and perhaps the Fringe was the safest place for them.

Squeezing my eyes shut tight (as if that would help me at all), I stepped toward the solid brick wall in front of me, took a deep breath, and walked forward. Wind—redolent with the smell of cotton candy—gusting around me, the heat of the sun on my face, and the sounds of the carnival warned me I'd made it through before I even opened my eyes.

A midway, teeming with people from all sorts of worlds, stretched out in front of me, beckoning me to throw a dart at a balloon. Or, in a twist from the expected version of the game, try my luck guessing the weight or age of various volunteers—none human. Growing up with faeries who never seemed to age made that game a losing prospect. When fifty and fifteen hundred look the same, the chances of guessing wrong skyrocket. Plus, the price for playing was way beyond my means.

Instead, I took a deep breath, kept my eyes to myself, and vowed to explore later. I knew the path at the opposite end of the Ferris wheel would lead me to Mag's house —the Mudwitch, Sylvana had called her, and I still had no idea what that title meant. Last time I'd come here, I'd downed an invisibility potion, been charmed with the ability to walk through walls, and poked my head inside Mag's hut while searching for my father's Bow of Destiny.

Mag had not been happy with me.

I hoped politely knocking on the door might garner me a bit more cooperation, especially since Mag was the one who had given me the time travel ring in the first place. I had an apology ready, but I was wearing a pair of running shoes, just in case.

I trudged across a short field and had to use a pair of nail clippers (that I'd tossed into the bottom of the gym bag-cum-witch hunting kit slung across my back) to wrest what appeared to be an entire skein of yarn from where it stretched back and forth between two thin birch trees and blocked the path toward Mag's place.

Ahead, a line of smoke coiling skyward, glimpsed from between two gnarled branches put a spring in my step. Mag was home, and that meant I had a shot at getting the answers I needed. Ducking into the trees, I shivered as their shade eclipsed the sun and the warm embrace of its rays. The deeper I went, the darker it got; and the darker it got, the louder my footsteps thundered across the forest floor.

My imagination supplied a giant case of the creepies and made my shoulders twitch.

If the carnival was full of supernaturals of indeterminate origins, I could only imagine what creatures might be waiting for me in the woods. I quickened my steps and let the magic flow across my fingertips, ready to strike at a moment's notice if the need arose. Cooperation between species was expected in the Fringe—Sylvana had warned me of that—but it never hurt to be prepared.

When the trees finally began to thin again, I could see the break I knew would open onto a small clearing surrounding a tiny wattle-and-daub cottage that looked both quaint and creepy enough to satisfy Snow White and the Gingerbread Hag simultaneously.

Except it wasn't, anymore. There, I mean. At least not all of it. Half the thatch roof still smoldered, which explained the smoke I'd seen earlier and was the only recognizable piece left of the hovel Mag once inhabited. It looked as if a meteor had landed in the middle of the kitchen, pulverizing most everything in a 5-foot radius. My heart sank.

The gossiping chickadees a few branches above my head were of no help to me, nor were the lazy, blarping bullfrogs croaking away on the base of a nearby tree.

Had Mag been in there when the place was blown up? What could that tiny old lady ever have done to deserve such violence? A little voice inside my head reminded me that when I'd met her, Mag had rendered me incapable of using my magic or controlling my own body. I'd been trapped, quite helpless, and would probably still be inside scrubbing her floors if Sylvana hadn't intervened.

Sylvana. Could she be responsible for this? It was clear she hadn't cared for Mag, but that's a long way from homicidal. Then again, I hadn't thought she was going to let my boyfriend plummet to his death or use me to find it so she could steal the Bow of Destiny the first chance she got, either. And all of those things happened. Not to mention, I'd seen firsthand what she'd been willing to do to her own mother.

As much as I didn't want to, I sifted through the ashes looking for bits of fried witch. What I would have done if I found any, I can't say for sure, but I suspect I would have ended up needing fresh pants.

Thankfully, since I hadn't packed a change of clothes, I found no evidence Mag had been inside when the blast hit her house. The only thing to have survived was one of the fancy plates I remembered seeing propped up on a shelf. I blew the ash off it as best I could, stuffed it in my pack, and turned back the way I had come. Maybe someone at the carnival knew where Mag was, or what happened to her. I can't even describe how happy I was when the sun once again shined on my face, and the joyful sounds of music and laughter filled my ears.

The midway was clogged with foot traffic. I passed a pair of nymphs—wearing clothing for once—buzzing around the honey stall, raised an eyebrow at a group of dwarf children who appeared to be on a school-sanctioned field trip, and almost tripped over a fat golden lab puppy who looked up at me and said, "Excuse you!" when my shoe grazed his hind paw. A snappy retort caught in my throat as I noticed the sign floating in the air beside the door of a tent across the way.

When my mother first approached me after her escape from the same nexus where Vaeta had been trapped (Sylvana still didn't know I was responsible for her escape, and I intended to keep it that way)—she'd disguised herself as the proprietress of a magic shop near my office. By some twist of fate, I now stood in front of a tent made from at least six different pieces of patterned canvas carrying the same name: Athena's Attic.

My heart caught in my throat when I wondered if Sylvana joined the ranks of those poor, refuge-seeking souls I'd speculated about on my way in here.

Only one way to find out. Suck it up, Lexi, I said to myself, and pulled open the door flap like I was expecting a rabid hell beast to jump out and bite off my face. Instead, I stepped into an emporium of magical supplies housed in a lavishly decorated space I wouldn't dream of referring to as merely a "tent."

The interior defied all logic as well as the laws of spatial dimension by being many times larger than the exterior.

Gleaming mahogany shelves spiraled from floor to ceiling in a circular space at least fifty feet in diameter and three stories high. A complicated series of ladders suspended on rails allowed for access to thousands of books on the third floor. Foot after shining foot of brass hardware sparkled as though freshly polished, and the whole system made the one in my sanctum at home look like a box of generic shredded wheat.

I thought I'd be stocked with spellcasting supplies for the rest of my life the first time I walked into the cavern behind the fireplace in my parlor, but as it turns out, eye of newt is a necessary ingredient for an awful lot of potions and my supply was running low.

Athena's Attic's second floor offered a full line of amphibian parts along with every other ingredient I'd ever heard of or read about. I itched to start rifling through the shelves for hard-to-find herbs—after I resolved the worry that my mother might be skulking around.

It was a good plan, except I hadn't counted on getting distracted by the magnitude of items for sale on the first floor. Ritual tools, crystal balls, wands, cauldrons, and potion bottles—all the typical supplies a witch could want—occupied only a small portion of the store.

The rest was taken up by more unusual wares: full skeletons hung like clothes on a rack, and not all of them were human; premixed potions guaranteed to grant your heart's desire glittered along half of one wall. Precious gems tumbled out of elaborately crafted boxes, and even those were for sale. A locked glass box case a single scrap of parchment that rested on a padded display made from purple velvet, and when I got close enough, I could see that the precious artifact was an autograph. Merlin. *The* Merlin. That's something you don't see every day.

But I wasn't about to pay my left arm for it.

A whole area near the back of the room was curtained off like the dirty movie section at the video store. I wondered what the owner of this place thought was so taboo it couldn't be shelved near a narwhal's skeleton and walked hesitantly closer. Big mistake. There must have been some kind of ward on the material because I could not get within five feet of the place. Every time I tried, I found myself some distance to the side and facing away.

Three times I made an effort before giving up. I must not have a dark enough soul to pass the barrier. There was some small comfort in knowing that.

There were so many things to see; I had a hard time focusing on any one of them as I made my way toward the gilt-trimmed counter in the center of the room. Before I could stop myself, I plucked a pair of glasses from a cardboard—I'm not sure why I found this odd—display that was labeled Clear Vision and tried them on. There was barely time to tell if anything looked different when an elven woman stood up from arranging something on one of the lower shelves, and I exhaled the breath I didn't realize I'd been holding.

"I'm Athena. Can I help you find anything?" she asked in a thick accent. Decidedly not Sylvana and I didn't even need the glasses to tell me that. The energy Athena emitted matched that of an elf who used to babysit me when I was six or seven. One of Terra's friends, she would carry me through the treetops on her shoulders, so far up in the air, I grew breathless but never frightened, secure in the trust only a child can so easily extend. Even in glamour, Sylvana could never convey authentic Elven energy.

"I'm trying to reverse a spell. Any suggestions?" Until I heard the words come out of my mouth, I'd had no intention of asking for help, but I got caught up in my memories, and it slipped out. Or maybe I was sick of everything happening *to* me and was willing to swallow my pride if I could take control of at least one aspect of my life.

My grandmother had been cursed while trying to protect me, and all I'd done since I could learn to talk—and was allowed to cross the street—was rant at her stoned form and condemn her for a crime she'd never committed.

Now it was my responsibility—no, my privilege—to figure out how to bring her back. And if there was something in this shop that might assist, I certainly wasn't going to find it on my own. Talk about a needle in a haystack. More like a needle in a needle stack.

"It depends on what type of spell needs reversing."

I wasn't sure how much I was comfortable revealing, but if I was going to get answers, I'd have to spill the details. "I'm not really sure. All I know is that two spells collided—one witch got banished to a nexus, and the other turned to stone. I'm trying to bring the stoned one back to life."

You'd have thought I'd answered *yes* to *do you want fries with that burger* the way she didn't bat an eyelash at my response. I'd expected more of a reaction; a gasp, perhaps, or at least a pinch of concern, but this Athena remained completely neutral.

"There are two ways to go about lifting any curse or reversing any spell: you either need to know the material components used to create it in the first place, or the specific intentions of the caster."

Of course, it would boil down to intention. Salem was always harping on me to clear my mind before working any magic. I could replay his diatribe in my head verbatim; *you must focus your intention, Lexi. Your spells will never work the way you want them to if your intention is unclear, Lexi.* Blah, blah, blah.

Except it wasn't nonsense—I just insisted on tuning out and using inexperience and my late blooming as a crutch. Excuses, Salem would say, and he'd be right. Not that I'd tell him that to his face.

I couldn't begin to imagine what Sylvana's motive might have been for cursing her mother. I doubted it was spur of the moment; it seemed far more likely that years of resentment had built until it boiled over in the most malicious act Sylvana had ever committed. At least, I hoped she didn't have dirtier skeletons residing in her closet. Regardless, I'd seen what she lobbed toward Clara, and I had Salem and the Book of Shadows on my side. Surely we could figure out exactly what type of spell it was and brew an effective counter.

"I don't think the intention method is going to work for this." Mainly because I couldn't fathom the level of intent to harm it must have taken. I shook my head at Elf Athena's expectant smile, "but I might be able to figure out what elements were used to create it. I'd have to do some research. In the meantime, I'll just browse if that's all right."

"Of course, as you wish." Athena waved in the direction of the upper floors, "I'll be in the stacks if you need any help."

An hour or more passed while I filled a basket with must-have items. Prices were marked in at least a dozen different currencies, some of which shocked me. Depending on the degree of purity in your Fae heritage, you could use strands of hair, nail clippings, or eyelashes to purchase items from some of the shelves. It was probably not a good idea to say, *I'd give my left nut to have that* because at Athena's it just might be the price. The one currency she did not accept was plastic.

My wallet weighed considerably less, and my pack weighed double by the time I paid what I owed.

"One more thing." Curiosity was burning a hole in my brain. "Do I look familiar to you?" Sylvana had chosen to name her shop Athena's Attic, and I wondered if there was a connection.

"You look like your mother, Lexi Balefire." And while I processed her knowing my name, Athena disappeared behind the curtain I could not pass.

FOUR

Exiting Athena's, I mentally cataloged the items I hadn't been able to buy and vowed to come back with more cash next time. Distracted, it took a minute before furtive movements pulled my focus toward my mortal enemy, Serena Snodgrass, skulking around the rear flap of a sketchy-looking black tent.

Color me shocked. I didn't think she had enough magic in her to handle the trip through the portal.

Normally, I wouldn't care two cents what Serena was up to, but I hadn't laid eyes on her since Jett's unfortunate disappearance (i.e. his banishment to the Faerie dimension courtesy of my best friend, Flix). And since my brother had the poor taste to date my mortal enemy, I was pretty sure she had some type of revenge planned for me. I'd been wondering just what that might be, and now I was being handed the perfect opportunity to find out, right in front of me on a silver platter.

Not my first time stalking someone—I'm a matchmaker and sometimes that requires me to scope out potential matches in their natural habitat. But for some reason, sneaking around after Serena made me feel dirty. Or maybe that was just the stench of her rotten heart.

Once upon a time, Serena had been my best friend. Back then, she'd been a chubby beauty with a perpetual smile on her face.

Serena was the only other witch I had known who wasn't already a grownup. Inseparable in our early years, I couldn't remember what caused us to drift apart, but I knew she'd turned on me.

Maybe it wasn't any single thing, but by the time our fourteenth birthdays rolled around, and Serena achieved her Awakening to witchhood while I watched in jealous fascination the split was a done deal.

Turns out, those who were once the best of friends make the strongest enemies. The pretty little girl I remembered had become a stick-thin, white blond, Goth witch who hated me enough to have her family spread nasty stories about me to the rest of the magical community—turning my Beltane duties into a rather awkward night each year.

We Balefire witches have the enviable job of tending a magic fire—the Balefire, hence my last name.

Once a year, on Beltane, witches flock to my home to light their own twigs and branches from the flame in my hearth. Then, like the Olympic torch, the witches pass the flame on until it spreads across the land. Yeah, I know it has that Santa Claus flair to it, but this is my life. I am Keeper of the Flame.

A job I nearly lost when my witch powers threatened never to Awaken. Most witches get their power when they turn fourteen. For some, it takes a little longer, and then there are a few witches for whom it never happens at all. It looked like I was going to fall into that last category when I was just days away from turning twenty-five—the witchy cut-off date—and still hadn't gained my majority.

That was when Serena got the cockeyed notion she would be the next witch tapped to guard the Balefire, even though that's not how it works. Sure, the duty would have fallen to the next, most qualified witch if my long-lost mother hadn't shown up and given me the one element I'd been missing. the Stone of Blood heirloom pendant every Balefire witch had used to Awaken for centuries. I doubt Serena was up to the task, but I've since learned more about my family history and now I know it was never that simple.

I wasn't certain whether Serena hooked up with my half-brother just to stick it to me, or if she had been stupid enough to actually fall for the jerk. Since I hadn't known he existed until well after they had already begun playing Bonnie and Clyde, it seemed more likely Jett had purpose-fully sought her out because she hated me, too. No doubt she blamed Jett's current predicament on me, and I had no illusions about the dark and terrible ways she was currently plotting revenge.

Jett was only in this situation because he'd tried to steal the Bow of Destiny before I could get to it, and I was sure that if he *did* find his way back to our realm, it would be the first thing he'd go after. Over my dead body.

Of course, if that's why she was here, the miserable little wench was taking her sweet time. Nearly half an hour passed before the flap of the black tent popped open and Serena emerged with a tight-lipped expression on her pointy face.

"What are you doing here?" She hissed when she spotted me.

"The question is, Serena, what are *you* doing here?"

"None of your business, you traitorous bitch!" She sauntered toward me, her face mere inches from mine as she spit the last word.

"Traitorous? You mean, as in not loyal to the brother who *tried to kill my boyfriend?*"

"Kin attacked Jett first! Jett was just trying to get to what should have been his all along! That bow *belongs* to him, not you." I'd given up the bow to save Kin from the long drop into a deep pit Jett intended for him. Flix had taken things a step further and used the magic of his fae heritage to provide the offender with an epic time-out.

"It's not like he'd have much use for it in the Faelands." A slip that gave her more information than I intended. Serena brings out my irrational side.

"The Faelands? You're telling me that *halfling* had enough juice to send Jett to the Faelands?" Her voice had become so shrill I expected to find a pack of angry dogs circling us by the time she finished. "I must go to him. He needs me." Drama queen much?

"Serena," I stated calmly, even though inside my head I was screaming at the top of my lungs, "Jett was using you. It's time to move on, get over it. Abandon whatever little scheme you're plotting and let it go. Don't be stupid enough to follow after that idiot. You don't have what it takes to survive in the Faelands, and if you try, someone or something *will* take you out."

"I hate you, Lexi Balefire." Old news and too often repeated to have any effect on me.

"Run along now, Serena."

Surprisingly, she did run along. Throwing me a *wish you were dead* look over one shoulder, she slithered back into the same tent she'd just exited. When I turned around to head back home, another familiar face caught my eye, this one wearing a rueful expression as she eavesdropped on my conversation.

"Adriel?" I asked, as though there was any doubt. Trust me; you'd recognize Adriel in a hot second if you ever saw her.

Tall, fiery red hair, creamy skin, and emerald eyes that pierced the soul, Adriel—or should I say former guardian angel Galmadriel—had one of those faces that stick in your memory. Especially after seeing her take on an upper-level demon—or rather, a faerie godmother posing as one.

I met Adriel when, using a fledgling guardian for bait, Vaeta had staged an elaborate ruse to break free from the Underworld. When the dust had settled on that fiasco, I'd gained another faerie roommate and freed my mother from prison. Drawing lines from that day to this, I had Adriel to blame and to thank for my current situation.

"Alexis. Are you here alone?" Adriel was at least a foot

taller than me, so she didn't need to crane her neck to look behind me. "No faeries with you today."

I gave her a cheeky grin, and she offered to buy me lunch. Since I was out of cash anyway, I let her. Once we settled at a picnic table at the edge of the midway, I caught her up on all the changes since our last meeting. I even told her about my part in releasing Sylvana from her prison in the Nexus—and about what I'd seen on my first trip back in time.

Even though she was locked out of her world and stranded in ours, Adriel had mad skills of her own, and I wondered if she might have advice for me about how to break the spell on Clara.

"Sorry, there's nothing I can do to help you. Even when I was a Guardian, it was only within my power to help humans. What about Clara's faerie godmother? She would be the closest counterpart to the type of work I used to do." A quirk of her lips indicated Adriel missed being a guardian.

"Not an option, according to Terra. Something to do with intentions and not saving a witch from her own actions."

"Ah, yes. I'm familiar with making those kinds of distinctions." A tinge of bitterness flavored the sentiment and, not for the first time; I wondered how Adriel had come by her status as a *former* guardian angel. Something told me there was an interesting story there.

And then I told her the rest.

"Cupid's daughter? That must have come as a shock, though it makes sense given your affinity for lovers."

"Not as big a surprise as when my dead mother turned up—not dead. You have no idea." I shook my head, still having a hard time accepting the situation myself.

"I do have some experience with handling sudden life changes." Adriel's eyebrow quirked and I realized she was right; falling from grace after serving as an angel for an eternity certainly made my family issues seem a bit trifling.

"So now, I'm supposed to repair the Bow of Destiny, but I don't have a clue where to start and there's no one I can ask. Is there anything you can tell me about Fate Weavers?"

Fingertips tapping on the tabletop, Adriel fell silent for a minute. "I know someone who might be able to help you with the bow. He might also have information for you about Fate Weavers, but you'd have to ask." She gathered the trash from the table and stood. "I can take you to him now if you have the time."

This day just kept getting better. Well, except for the part about Mag's house. And seeing Serena.

Adriel's long legs ate the ground so fast I had to step lively to keep up with her, and by the time we crested the short hill, my calves were feeling the strain.

"There," she pointed to a striped tent. "I'll introduce you, but then I have to go."

"I can't thank you enough."

"It's nothing. Come on, and be warned. Lamiel can be a little cranky at times."

"Lamiel? Is he a former guardian, too?"

"Something like that." I'd have preferred a less cagey answer. Still, if he could help, it didn't matter to me what role he played in the larger scheme.

I'd been prepared to meet the male version of Adriel. Tall, handsome, angelic.

Lamiel looked more like an accountant than a messenger from above. He stood when we entered the tent, and proved himself shorter than me. Dark, expressive eyes flanked the long nose he lifted in the air disdainfully.

It's not easy to look down your nose at someone when you have to look up to see them, but he managed it. He pressed his lips into a straight line, and not a single mousy hair on his head was out of place.

"This is Alexis Balefire. She needs information about the Bow of Destiny," Adriel explained after introductions were out of the way, and then she excused herself. I wondered if she would be waiting once I left the tent.

I took the chair he indicated and cleared my throat. "Specifically, I need to know how to repair it."

"Repair it? How on earth did you break it?"

The question I hoped he wouldn't ask. "I didn't. My faerie godmother did. When she took it away from my mother." How's that for a dysfunctional family dynamic? That last I kept to myself, and still his eyebrows shot nearly up to his hairline. "It's in four pieces at the moment."

"Living gold." Lamiel nodded as though the cryptic statement should be enough of a clue.

"Living gold?"

Lamiel went into lecture mode.

"Living gold is the subject of many myths and is said to pave the streets of Heaven. I can neither confirm nor deny the assertion. Certain pieces of knowledge I am forbidden to reveal. Few humans—witches included—have ever had the power or ability to work living gold. Both magic and fire are required in the forging process. However, it has been used to create a number of powerful objects that you would recognize if you paid attention to your legends."

"Fire and magic? What about a magical fire, then?"

"Ah, yes. Adriel did say you were a member of the Balefire clan. It might be possible were there any living gold left to be found."

"What does that mean?" It sounded bad.

"There was an incident involving a golden crown that fell into the hands of a corrupt ruler, and so, for the good of humanity, all the living gold was gathered up and taken to Olympus for safe-keeping."

Olympus. Great.

"Can't I go there and get some? I'm Cupid's daughter; I should be able to go to Olympus, right?"

"Even if you survived the trip, you would not be

allowed access. Unless you have a time machine, I'm afraid you are out of luck." A time machine? Hmm.

"And I can't use the Balefire to, I don't know, melt the broken places, so they re-attach?"

"Once forged, living gold cannot be smelted a second time. Your intention to repair, but not alter the bow might be enough, but I can't promise more than that."

"Well, thanks for all your help." I started to stand, then settled back into my chair, "What can you tell me about Fate Weavers?"

"Probably a lot less than you want to know. My dealings with them are peripheral at best—different deities, different rules." Leaning back in his chair, Lamiel steepled his hands and began to recite as though by rote.

"Fate Weavers. The progeny of Cupid—sometimes known as Eros—and a blood witch; gifted with the ability to discern and affect nuances of human fate specifically through the pairing of proper bloodlines and fostering True Love's Kiss."

The pinched lines around his mouth made me think Lamiel wasn't a fan of my process. Maybe he thought it gave a semi-mortal too much power. Maybe he was right.

But you knew most of this already, didn't you?" Lamiel's eyes scanned me like an emotional x-ray that left my every secret laid bare before him, but kept all of his safely behind glass.

"I did." Since there was nothing left to hide, I went for broke. "My father seems to have dropped off the map and my mother is convinced he is lost in some way. Do you know where he is?"

From mild displeasure, Lamiel's face went to looking like he was sucking on a sour pickle and he didn't even bother to spit out the no, so I asked one more question.

"Are there others out there like me?"

Eyes shifting to the papers littering the table, Lamiel admitted, "Over time, there have been a fair few."

Getting information out of him was like trying to pry the lid off a can with a wet noodle, but I gave it one last shot. "Can you tell me where I might find another Fate Weaver?"

"I'm sorry, but no. Goodbye, Miss Balefire." And that was his final word on any subject, so I left feeling largely unenlightened, but hopeful from learning I was not alone in the Fate Weaver world.

Adriel had not waited for me outside the tent, and it was getting late when I began to make my way back toward the portal with a thousand errant thoughts whirling through my head. Instead of leaving the Fringe, though, I spun around in the direction from which I'd come and headed back to the creepy tent Serena had been so interested in earlier.

Curiosity. I know, it can be a killer, but I was seduced by the need to know.

This tent was nothing like the one where Athena's Attic was housed; though a similar engorgement charm had increased its square footage considerably. As I pulled back the folds and stepped inside, the musky scent of sandalwood made my nostrils flare in appreciation—but another awareness, this one tickling my sixth sense, set the butterflies in my stomach stirring. There was a faerie inside if I wasn't mistaken—and I definitely wasn't.

She wore a long robe of black that shimmered with what I hoped wasn't faerie dust (a single speck of that stuff could turn you into a toad faster than you can say *croak*) and her face was just as beautiful as any of my godmother's, save for the fact that it was twisted into an expression of disgust that only partially abated when she greeted me.

"May I help you?" The faerie asked as though I had no right to be there at all. Maybe I didn't, but that wasn't going to stop me from finding out what I wanted to know.

"I was hoping you could tell me what my friend Serena was here for…" I trailed off, realizing a second too late that I'd made a cardinal mistake.

"Friend, you say? That conversation you were having outside didn't sound very friendly to me." Not only can faeries smell a lie from a mile away, but they can also hear one, too.

I shifted uncomfortably, "You're right, we're the opposite of friends." Now that I was waist deep, I might as well dive all the way in. "Actually, she's a psychopath with a grudge against me."

"Ah, the truth at last. At least, *your* truth. Was that so difficult?"

I wasn't exactly sure how to answer that question, so I remained silent.

"It wouldn't be fair for me to divulge the personal details of a paying customer, would it?" She rubbed her thumb and first two fingers together, eyes twinkling.

I sighed and dug around in my bag for anything she might accept. The only thing of value I could find was a small diamond that had fallen off my birthday tiara. Don't laugh, but I've heard you can cut glass with a diamond, so I thought it would be a good thing to have in my back pocket, just in case I was ever, I don't know, stuck in a glass box.

Hey, I'm a witch, weird things happen.

If I'd have found it at Athena's earlier, I'm sure I would have spent it already, so fate was looking out for me.

I offered the bit of sparkle to the faerie, "There, now I'm a paying customer, too." She tucked the diamond into a pocket and cleared her throat.

"The other witch wanted to know how to get in contact with her faerie godmother."

Not remotely what I had expected, that's for sure. "And is there a way? I mean, how would one go about doing that?"

"There is a way, but it's unpleasant. And that's all I'll say. Besides, you don't need that information; you're already quite familiar with your own, aren't you Lexi Balefire?"

I dodged the question, and, wondering whether *every* supernatural being in the Fringe knew my name, made my way out of the tent.

FIVE

When I reached my hand into the Balefire flame and grasped the lever positioned at the center of the fire, a thin membrane of magic kept my fingers at a normal ninety-eight point six. Without it, they'd have been charred to the bone. The fireplace rotated, creating a large enough space for me to walk unimpeded into the space behind.

Looking at the blueprint, you'd think Soleil's room was positioned on the other side of the wall, but by some charm I sincerely hoped I'd have the power to one day cast, the hearth opened instead into a cavernous space I had dubbed my "sanctum."

That's some serious magic.

Half again the size of the house, the room existed in its own dimension. Filled with everything a witch could ever need—shelves of books on witch lore, cauldrons of every size and shape, and enough ingredients to whip up practically any potion—it had become my personal sanctuary.

In the center below an impressive domed skylight lay a casting circle and a podium holding the Book of Shadows handed down to me from my grandmother. The only thing I'd never found was a broom to ride on...not that I knew how to ride one anyway, and I hadn't dared to ask Salem about it in case it was one of those myths that he would tease me about later. Sounded like fun though, unless riding a broom gives one a wedgie.

After having spent a little time at Athena's Attic number two, the bulk of items I'd once believed would take a lifetime to sort through suddenly seemed paltry in comparison. Salem must have been worried sick about me, because he was pacing across the stone dais positioned in the center of the space, tracing the five-pointed star pattern of a pentagram set into the stones.

When I opened my mouth to greet him, he threw me a look that made me shut it again and give him some space.

While he pulled himself together, I made myself busy straightening the shelves even though I really wanted to unpack my recent purchases and add them to the stores. Another glance at his expression reinforced the decision to not flaunt my illicit shopping.

"Why didn't you tell me you were going to the Fringe? I could have come with you, you know, made use of my contacts, shown you around. Will you ever stop thinking of me as a pet?"

Salem was in his human form, which to me, by now, wasn't much different than his cat form. While true enough to have become a cliché, the stories about witches and black cats lacked a few important details.

Familiars are blessed (or perhaps cursed) with nine lives, each corresponding to nine witches he or she will serve during their lifetime. With each witch's passing, the familiar is reborn—until the ninth life is extinguished and true death is met. As if the weight on my shoulders wasn't already threatening to break my back, it was my honor to serve as Salem's ninth and final witch.

For some reason, he was worried I'd meet my end too soon. Go figure.

Oh, and to dispel another myth, not all familiars are black. Salem is, save for a patch of white hair on the top of his head. In human form, his ebony skin is just as supple as his meticulously-groomed fur, and he sports one blue eye and one green. That shock of white translates to a head of platinum hair.

As for *serving* me, that was a relative term. Think of it more like him punishing me for failing to Awaken for so long. An unavoidable situation that left him stuck in cat form and relying on the garbage bin and the kindness of strangers for anything besides the kitty kibble I gave him. I hadn't meant to torture the poor thing; I just didn't know any better.

"I'm sorry. I promise, next time you're my wing man." Salem still seemed a bit annoyed, but when I broached the subject reversing the spell on Clara, he perked right back up. "I'm hopeless by myself, Salem. Please?"

"Oh, all right. Tell me everything you remember about the spells Sylvana and Clara used against each other." Salem pointed toward the sofa, and I took the hint that it was time to settle down and spill the details.

I squeezed my eyes shut and focused on replaying the final scene between my mother and grandmother,

"Sylvana made what looked like a ball of black witchfire—except it was black witchfire on crack—all lightning and sparks. It crackled between her fingertips while it grew. Clara had something brewing of her own, but there wasn't any physical manifestation. Then I heard her whisper an incantation."

"Do you remember what she said?" Salem stretched in a distinctly cat-like manner and practically oozed into a position opposite where I sat.

"Not exactly. I do remember the spell looked like a ball of ropes—which is why I assumed it was a binding spell. That's something, right?" Salem's level stare cautioned against being overly self-congratulatory. "Anyway, the two spells met in the middle and sort of...I'm not sure how to describe it."

Frowning, I tried to frame the description so Salem would get a visual. "They didn't combine, but each one picked up elements of the other. Does that make sense?" Without even waiting for an answer, I continued, "Sylvana's spell took effect first, and even though Clara threw up a shield, it was too late." I described the horror of Clara slowly turning to stone and Sylvana's explosive exit while Salem listened intently. "Do you think we can restore my grandmother?"

As much as I knew it might be futile, I'd begun to hope and with hope came something more; a conviction that took me by the throat and demanded I make this right. My grandmother had not deserved her fate, and while I was in no position to win any medals in the good decision

Olympics, this one was a no-brainer. If there wasn't a way, I'd make one. I'm a Balefire; we're handy like that.

"Well, there are two ways to reverse a spell." Salem began to lecture. "Intention and ingredients."

"Yeah, yeah. I know." I ignored the annoyed vibe. "And I don't see how either of them will work," I explained my concerns about pinpointing Sylvana's intention, "whatever she meant to do to Clara, I don't think it was turning her to stone. I don't think either of them got what they wanted, actually. All that negative energy probably lit the fuse of a reciprocity firecracker, and they both got burned."

"I'd be willing to bet the power of threes played a role, yes. Betraying blood ties packs a punch, and the effects tend to show themselves immediately."

While it might seem amazing, having enough power to bend the world to your will is not all sunshine and roses, let me tell you. We witches live by a code: harm none, do what ye will. And not just for the protection of those we might hurt—oh no. Whatever a witch puts out in the world will come back to her threefold.

Salem explained it better, but what it boils down to is this: all of the energy in the world is connected, and whatever type you choose to work with is what will surround you. And what will come back around to either bite you in the butt or pet you on the head. Could be good, could be bad; but eventually your intention will make its ring around the rosy, and will likely have brought some friends along for reinforcement.

"I still don't see how knowing the ingredients is going to help us. The magic came from *within* both of them. There were no ingredients."

"Once again, you're wrong. And this is exactly why—"

"I know, why I should be focusing on our training sessions. You do realize that being snarky is going to circle its way back to *you*, right? I'm focusing now, so just instruct." Salem's eyes widened and then slid away from mine—cats tend not to dwell in guilt, and Salem was no exception.

"Er, sorry. But it's not as complicated as you think. All spells have a signature, and just because you didn't see her mix a potion doesn't mean Clara didn't gather a variety of components to create the desired effect."

He rose to prowl the room.

"We're talking about the use of all three branches of magic at the same time here. Everything around us is full of different elements; not just earth, air, fire, and water, but the chemical material all matter is made of. There's your Elemental component; as for the Mental, she used telekinesis to pull all of those molecules together; and of course, the acts of binding and enchantment affect the will of the spell's target, so there's your Arcane branch."

"Okay, I get the theory, but how does that help us figure out what was going on in her head?" I said.

"What would help is if you could remember what colors came off the witchfire. The sparking type is powered by the essence of a deity, which means Sylvana invoked a particular god or goddess to help do her bidding. I'm guessing it wasn't a benevolent one."

"Got it. I distinctly remember purple and white." I grinned, proud of myself for having retained something helpful, but my smugness was short-lived.

"Now if you can tell me what words Clara spoke, we might have a shot in Hades."

My heart skipped a beat, and my face fell, "I wish I could, but I was a little distracted at the time. I'd know the words if I heard them again. Maybe there's something in the Grimoire."

I approached the podium where the large, weathered, leather-bound tome rested. As always, I ran my fingertips over the embossed pattern of the Balefire family emblem. An intricately-wrought tree with flame where the leaves and branches should have been.

I laid my hand over the top of the book and called on the power of the Balefire. Blue flame leaped across the room, danced upon my outstretched palm, and strengthened my desire to locate the phrase Clara had uttered. Nothing happened, not even a flick of the pages.

"I guess I'll have to do this the old-fashioned way," I sighed, settled into an ancient, tufted settee, and began leafing through the pages.

Several hours later I'd scanned every last page, and the headache building in my temples was now carving out a space to squat behind my eyes. I pinched the bridge of my nose and set the book back down carefully. Had it been a less sacred volume, I might have chucked it clear across the room.

"It's hopeless. We'll have to figure out another way."

"Not necessarily," Salem stroked his chin, "there's one final option, but it's advanced magic. Something we've never tried before."

A long silence followed Salem's statement as I looked at him expectantly.

"The bond between a witch and familiar goes deeper than what we've explored so far. I am tied to you and you alone, and the same connection that allowed me to find you all those years ago can be used to share a memory."

"Sounds intrusive."

Salem shrugged, but not in a way that made me think I had been wrong.

"What are you planning to do, pull the words out of my subconscious?"

"Sort of. It's all there somewhere, but this way I'll be able to hear and see it along with you. I'm going to use a form of hypnosis to guide you to the information, and then hitchhike with you on the trip." Sounded simple enough that the reticence in his voice seemed out of place.

"I don't see the problem. Let's do it."

Salem rolled his eyes, but his expression softened. "Usually, tethering takes training and practice, but you've excelled at so many disciplines with only intuition on your side that I'm willing to try off the cuff. You trust me, right?"

"Always." Having come into my powers ten years late,

and without the benefit of a mentor's wisdom, Salem's word and what I could glean from the books lining the workshop shelves were all I had to go on. Trusting him wasn't a choice, but a necessity.

At Salem's instruction, I lit five white candles and walked clockwise around the casting circle, placing one in the center and at each of the star's four shoulders to represent earth, air, fire, and water. "Calling the corners helps keep our energy confined to the circle—where we need it," he explained. I invoked the deities representing each of the basic elements in turn, under my breath and at a speed the guy from the Micro Machines commercials would have envied.

"Cardea, Aradia, and Nuit of the east, the primordial goddesses of air. Isis, Aphrodite, and Marianne to the west, representing the water element. Vesta, Hestia, and Brigit in the south, with your connection to fire. Persephone, Rhea, and Ceres, who hail from the north and identify with the earth element! Heed my humble plea and lend your aid." Each name felt as familiar as an old friend's on my tongue, and I wondered if after centuries of invocation I might consider them as such.

A whoosh indicated the closing of the circle, and an iridescent dome of magic ran around the band connecting the five points of the star. I stood in the center and called on the element of spirit. With one final *click*, the protective barrier shimmered to translucent silver and became tactile. When I ran my finger along its curve, the dome expanded slightly before snapping back into place like a rubber band.

Salem and I knelt on the floor, about two feet apart and faced one another. "Take the other end of this string," he instructed, handing me a piece of thin, white twine, "close your eyes and focus. Play through the memory in your mind's eye. Listen to my voice, and close your mind to distractions."

Of course, as soon as you're told to not think about something, that's the first thing that comes to mind. I struggled for a few moments but finally forced myself to concentrate. I thought about Clara's stoned figure and how maybe she'd been cognizant this whole time—forced to watch life pass her by, trapped for no good reason other than she tried to protect her family. The notion sobered me, and I began to relax, allowing Salem's steady voice to lull me into a trance state.

I replayed the events of that day in as much detail as possible, several times until finally, automatically, at Salem's persuasion I paused right before Sylvana wound up the black ball of power. I opened my eyes and willed the next part of the memory out through my fingertips and watched a flicker of bright cerulean blue work its way across the twine and into Salem's outstretched hand.

"Ligabis, Ostium, Carcere," he repeated the words that were now forever etched into my conscious mind—I certainly wouldn't forget them a second time—while I basked in the high that always comes when I use my power in a new way.

"That was so cool, Salem!" I grinned, and he beamed.

"See, sometimes I'm useful."

"Ligabis, Ostium, Carcere," I repeated the spell. "What does it mean?"

"It means your grandmother wasn't fooling around. She meant to put Sylvana into a position where she wouldn't be a danger to anyone."

"A prison in the underworld?" That was harsh, even for Sylvana.

"Well, she probably didn't mean to send your mother to hell's nexus specifically. That one's probably on Sylvana for funneling darkness into her witchfire. And now we have what we need. It's a good thing, too, because we'd never have figured out which goddess your mother invoked—though it should have been obvious, I mean, she turned Clara to *stone*. Duh." Salem hopped to his feet and began scurrying around the sanctum, gathering ingredients while he mumbled and ranted.

"Hello, lost over here." I waved my arms exaggeratedly.

"It's the Eye of Ra. Egyptian Goddess Tefnut. Presides over humidity—and also the lack thereof."

In a twisted way, it made sense. Drying out a witch might look a lot like turning her to stone.

"You're not going to make me call on her, are you?" I wasn't thrilled about handling certain potion ingredients, to begin with; the thought of calling up some scary-ass Goddess turned my knees wobbly.

"What? No. We're going to use..." Another cabinet

door slammed open. "Canary feathers!" Salem's cuss-words cracked me up sometimes.

"What's wrong?"

"We need Van Van powder, and you used the last of it when we put together that batch of Fae-proof laundry soap." Things get magically messy when the godmothers engage in one of their famous battles. When five washings with mundane products failed to render my favorite pair of jeans wearable again, I'd resisted asking for help and hit the Sanctum to put together something with a little more kick. Worked like a charm (no pun intended), but used up my entire stock of powder. So much for hiding my impromptu shopping trip from Salem.

"Good thing I went to Athena's." Reaching into the corner where I'd stashed it, I grabbed my pack full of goodies and rummaged around to find the bottle of Van Van, which was not only good for cleansing but for drawing out negative energy. Those hoodoo priestesses really know their counter-curses. "I just happened to remember we were out."

"How you manage to suck up and gloat at the same time is beyond me." The bottle landed on the table with a thump. Salem moved fast when he was annoyed. For the next hour and a half, he had me pounding, grinding, slic-ing, and dicing ingredients for the spell before he was satisfied we were as ready as we would ever be.

Dipping low on the horizon, the sun tipped the trees with fire and bathed Clara in a warm glow. I've always loved the time of day when everything looks magically warm and pink. Mother Nature—who, by the way, Terra swears is the biggest gossip in all of the Faelands—knows how to paint a pretty picture.

"Breathe into the magic," Salem instructed after I'd downed the potion. For once, it tasted halfway decent—like herbal tea—and proved wrong my theory about how all potions were designed to taste awful to discourage witches from getting addicted to them. Two minutes after the liquid hit my belly, though, it also proved there's always a downside to drinking potions. This one functioned to, shall we say, create water—and create, it did. Sweat shot out of my every pore, and I've never had to pee so bad in my entire life. In fact, I wasn't sure I could build a ball of witchfire with my legs crossed.

"Lexi! Control yourself." Akin to a ruler on the back of a hand, Salem's schoolmarm voice worked the same. I snapped out of it and concentrated on the spell I was supposed to weave.

Witchfire grew from the spark I carried in my heart, arced between my outstretched hands, and built to a roiling ball of yellow flame with occasional glimmers of green. When the time felt right, I opened the floodgates (pun totally intended) and let the liquid pour from me into the golden flames. The sweat dried in an instant and my bladder did a happy dance when the burden eased.

Wet fire. Whodathunkit? Technically it was pee-sweat fire, but that can be our little secret.

"Now." Salem's voice rang in my ear, and I let the fireball fly straight at my grandmother's head where it hit with a splat and sizzle. I hoped she'd forgive me for pelting her with the disgusting mess.

For a minute, I thought we'd done it. Expelled by my fire, moisture left a dark stain as it crept across Clara's face and down over her neck, shoulders, and arms. Stepping closer, I watched the liquid draw into the stone and waited for it to plump up her skin, her muscles, her bones. I guess my face was roughly six inches from the end of her pointed finger when something finally happened.

With about the speed and velocity of a high-end shower, the water erupted from her finger, hit my forehead, and fountained off every which way. Salem, who hates getting wet as much as the next cat, stood right in the path of the spewing liquid and was drenched before his agile reflexes could carry him out of the line of fire. Or, more technically, the line of water.

Hissing and spitting, he glared at me balefully and, even though I was upset that our spell had failed, I pressed my lips together to hold back a laugh. "Don't blame me; this was your idea."

Knowing what I needed to find to fix the Bow of Destiny, and having the first clue where to find it were two very different things. I should have asked Lamiel for more detail. Stupid me.

With no obvious next step ahead of me or any new ideas on how to free Clara, I turned to my business for a distraction. I'd owned FootSwept Matchmaking for several years, and in that time, amassed an inches-thick book of wedding photos to prove just how potent my Cupid-given abilities were, even before I Awakened as a witch—or knew how much my heritage had brought to my work.

The broom and stars logo and the tagline *Get Swept Away* was a nod to my heritage. An inside joke among those in the know. I hadn't intended to tell Kin my deepest secret until— well, the twelfth of never seemed appropriate.

About a minute into our relationship, I'd found myself without any other choice.

It probably would have come out eventually, as truths tend to do, and better he heard it straight from the witch's mouth rather than catching me in the act of spellcasting.

That kind of shock is enough to send a person running for the hills, or even worse, pushing a shopping cart up Main Street while wearing a tin-foil hat and muttering things that could get him committed.

Thankfully, the cat's out of the bag, and I can at least attempt to keep Kin safe from any other curses that might wind up floating his way as a result of spending time with me. One less thing I have to worry about, especially since I was about to be distracted by a whopper of a *shit*uation. At least this one was work related. For the most part.

Even when business gets so crazy that I have back to back first meetings lined up, I love my job. Flix, my BFF and business partner, runs a salon out of a room adjacent to the office. He started out fixing up FootSwept's most needful clients just for fun.

By the time most people get to me, they're hanging on to the threads fraying from the knot on the end of their dating rope—and some have already begun to wind it around their necks. A little pampering helps lower their defenses, and sometimes a simple makeover can inspire the level of confidence they need to put themselves back out there. Mostly, I just want to give the battle-weary souls something to smile about.

The problem was, once Flix's magical (literally) hands touched a client, they were hooked. Half-Fae and full-on stud muffin, Flix's most potent power was his ability to empathize. If you've ever seen a gaggle of women at a salon, hanging out all their dirty laundry, you can imagine what the back room of my business looks like.

Between Flix's area and mine was my den of designer delights: clothes, shoes, and accessories to give my Cinderellas—and the Cinderfellas—the full-on makeover experience.

On the side, I made time to sit in on job interviews for a few local, and a couple of internationally-recognized department stores. My ability to match employees to employers was an asset in great demand. Corporate head-hunting, while lucrative, never gave me the same buzz as matchmaking—even before I knew love was in my blood.

Instead of money, I took my payment in deep discounts on designer clothes. Extremely deep. As in free. Overstock, samples, whatever they wanted to send my way went into the closet.

Ever since Flix had blasted Jett into who-knows-where, my business had increased exponentially. Meddling with my work for several months, Jett's hatred of me had affected dozens of couples, pairing incompat-ible matches all over the city. His banishment had the fortunate result of breaking whatever spell he'd cast, and now the miss and mister wrongs were all looking for their rights.

My process worked more like a cross between a fairy tale and a feel-good romance movie. For each new seeker of love and something—instinct or magic—clicked on my internal love detector. Provided, I assume, by my father—you know, considering he's Cupid and all.

I wanted my clients to have a great story to tell their grandkids about how they met, and one that didn't have me or my business figuring into it. So, I did my homework and figured out a "meet cute" for each set of clients.

Finding the right scenario can be a lot of extra work, but it's worth it. One of my favorite meets was an off-the-cuff thing where I just shoved the woman into the guy's lap in a coffee shop. Crude, but it seemed like the only way to get his attention. They'll always have a good story to tell.

For once, Flix had beaten me to work. I caught him swooshing around the salon in a nearly invisible flash, sweeping and straightening until you could eat off the seat of the chrome barber's chair and his gold shears gleamed.

Fae-born on his mother's side, his natural magnetism drew clients to him like bees to honey. After all, who better to do your hair than the hot man with the tight butt and perfect mane?

Our halfling heritage, while not the basis of our friendship, was a point of commonality, though I was more comfortable with my status than he was with his.

Lately, though, he seemed less angsty, and there was only one person to thank for that: his new beau, Carl. Let me tell you; the man has crushed countless female hearts by his non-interest in the fairer sex.

"Hey Lexi, how are you feeling today?" Yeah, he was still wearing kid gloves when dealing with me, just like everyone else since the incident at Shadow Hold. I suppose expecting me to have a nervous breakdown after being betrayed by my once-thought-dead mother wasn't a completely ridiculous notion. I'd had a lot thrown at me in a short period of time.

"Everything's great. You know we've got four appointments this afternoon alone. It hasn't been this busy since the week before Valentine's Day."

"Too many matches, too little time. I'm not sure how you'll pull it off, but you always do. You know what would make things easier around here?" He hedged.

"What?" I asked, already knowing the answer. Flix had been trying to get me to step away from my paper and lists and embrace the digital age for years.

"A computer with a database for all our clients." Once matched, my couples stay that way, so I don't get a lot of repeat business. I needed a database like I needed another pair of shoes. Wait, strike that, there's always room for another pair of shoes. But, I saw no use for a computer.

"You know how I feel about electronics; I don't even like using my cell phone, but it's a necessity I can't do without. I'm perfectly fine with my lists and my date planner." I wasn't about to tell him it was getting harder and harder to find the paper version of those every year—another casualty of the digital revolution, along with cassette tapes and actual books.

"You know you could link the computer with your phone and make it that much easier to stay on top of things. Did it ever occur to you that it might make *my* life easier, too? Salon business has also increased, and since you don't pay me, maybe you could give a little. I get why we can't have an assistant in here, or even a receptionist, at least consider doing *something* to help lighten the load."

"Cheap shot. I've offered to pay you how many times now?" One of Flix's cars cost more than FootSwept netted in a year, and he could drive a different one every day of the week if he wanted to.

Flix grinned because he knew he was going to get his way. It was one of his gifts. "Several, but that's beside the point. Come on, Lexi, do it for me." His eyebrows lifted and his perfectly sculpted lips began to turn down into an irresistible pout. "You never know, you might like it."

How many times had he heard that from women?

I couldn't help but soften; FootSwept had been Flix's brainchild, and since he never asked me for anything I figured I owed him one. Especially since it would take approximately half a gazillion clients to pay Mister Moneybags what he was worth.

"I'll think about it," I replied, refusing to make eye contact and knowing he'd take my response as a definitive *yes* whether I meant it as one or not.

A knock on the door interrupted our conversation, and in stepped my eleven o'clock appointment. My eyes roved over him before I could stop them—hey, I'm taken, but I'm not blind. This should be an easy match. You know how some men are handsome and some men are charismatic even though they're not particularly attractive? Like Kevin Bacon—not exactly good looking, but the way he carries himself—the swagger in his step—is enough to make you follow him into a dark alley? Well, the man who lowered himself into the chair across from my desk had both; unbelievably gorgeous with that certain *je ne sais quoi*—he looked like sex on a stick, and I could practically hear the drool dripping off Flix's chin into a puddle on the floor.

Dark everything—eyes, hair, artful stubble on a strong chin—could have passed for brooding good looks except for the cheeky smile on his face that took him from Heathcliff on the moors to Heath Ledger (and I was still mourning that loss) in 10 Things. If this guy was having trouble getting women, something was clearly wrong with the entire female population in a hundred mile radius.

Flustered, I looked down to check my schedule again.

"Hello, Mr. Owen. I'm Alexis Balefire." Even now, I'm not sure why I said that—I *never* called myself by my full name, it was Lexi all the way—or why my tongue rolled over the L's in a husky tone. Well, I *do* know why and it just made me feel dirty. I had a perfectly handsome and sexy man of my own, who I loved to the moon and back. Maybe I was ovulating or something.

"Nice to meet you, Alexis. Please, call me Joshua."

I made an effort to tattoo Kin's face to the backs of my eyeballs, vowed to order him a lovely dinner that night, and became all business again. "This is Flix, my business partner. Don't you have an appointment in the salon?" I asked Flix pointedly and received a dirty look in exchange.

"Sure do. Nice to meet you, too, Joshua. You're in good hands." Flix waggled his eyebrows at me from behind Mr.

Hottie's back. His goofy expression brought me back to earth, and I continued my usual spiel about how things work at FootSwept without further incident.

"So tell me a little bit about what you're looking for, Joshua." I've learned that open-ended questions of a general nature typically elicit more honest responses than pointed ones.

"Truthfully, I'm not looking. I'm here to satisfy my mother, who thinks I'm going to turn into one of those lonely old men who sit on benches outside the super-market drinking cheap whiskey out of a brown paper bag. Her exact words. I'm only thirty-two, but she wants grandchildren and was hoping you'd work some kind of magic on my love life."

Then again, maybe this wasn't going to be as quick and simple as I'd thought. It's one thing when someone *wants* to be matched; it's quite another if they're forcing it, even for noble reasons. I wasn't getting my usual tingle, which said a lot.

Plus, the minute he spoke his truth, all that lovely attraction I'd been feeling turned to dust. Smelly dust, too. Like the kind left behind in an old moldy house. It's rare to run into someone in my own office who gives off the jerk vibe at full blast like that. My player radar—my *play*dar, if you will—automatically keeps men like him from regis-tering with my gut-driven, magical love-finding system. I have a theory that both parties have to be looking, or at least open to finding a mate before one of them is beckoned to my door.

"And what kind of women do you usually date?"

Joshua shifted in his chair and looked me straight in the eye. "Women like you. Beautiful, confident, self-sufficient." His lips curled into a smile I'm sure he thought was alluring, but all it did was threaten to elicit my gag reflex and a tiny little fantasy of punching him.

"Well, thank you for the compliment, *Mr. Owen*," I'd give him the standard number of strikes, and he was definitely at an 0-2 count, "but let's see what we can do to find you someone *unattached*." He couldn't be all bad if he loved his mother enough to show up in my office, right?

Still, if Joshua wasn't ready to settle down, I explained there might not be anything for me to offer. Halfway through that conversation, the singsong hum I'd heard before from the golden compass turned to a jangling cacophony in my head. After my last experience, I assumed the device was channeling the bow to help me somehow, but this racket wasn't at all useful.

It sounded like a pair of parakeets chattering away at each other—at the tops of their lungs—and a little bit like the teacher from the Charlie Brown shows. Wah-blah-wah-blah-wah.

Just once, if someone could tell the whole story when they talk me into doing something, it would be nice. Delta never mentioned the Bow of Destiny was sentient. Maybe I should have guessed because of the living gold. After all, the word *living* is right there in the name of it.

Pushing the distraction into a corner of my brain, I concentrated on the man sitting across from me. Fixing the bow before it drove me crazy jumped to the top of my list. With stars and red arrows surrounding it.

"No, I promised my mother I'd give you a fair shake, so you do your thing, and we'll see how it goes," Joshua said.

It came off as though he was doing me a favor by allowing me to help him and that rubbed me the wrong way. I pitied the woman who got tangled up with this guy. What I wouldn't give to have one of those signs that said I could refuse service at any time. Not that I would. Probably.

"Ought to be fun to try, right? I like the dating part. How many women will I get to meet?"

Another burst of frustrated sound rocketing through my head triggered a flash of me leveling the Bow of Destiny and taking aim at Joshua's heart. The vision was so full of sensory details, the world turned pink for a few seconds, and I felt the arrow quivering between my fingers.

Well, okay then. I gave in to the demand that at some point in time, I would make this happen and the dream state poofed—taking the screeching in my head with it.

"I'll pay extra if you can hook me up with an even dozen."

Really? Had he listened at all when I told him how this works?

"We'll see. Listen, thank you for coming in, but I have another appointment. Give me some time on this, and I'll get back to you as soon as I have a potential match." *Or half an hour after hell freezes over.*

"You're welcome, *Alexis*." His tone matched the one I'd used when I'd first introduced myself, and I wished that stupid ring would work again so I could go back and smack myself in the face—not that I'd feel it, anyway, but it would make my present self feel much better.

I wondered what kind of woman might find him worthy, but somehow that felt a bit like passing judgment and that wasn't my job. Who was I to assume he lacked even the most basic level of romantic decency?

What the hell, arrogant jackasses have matches, too.

"And that was just my first appointment of the day. I wish I could say it got better from there, but I think Josh might have been the high point." I sighed and looked across the cozy candlelit table for two at Kin, who had been wearing a sympathetic expression until I mentioned being hit on by a client.

"I'm sorry, babe. Do you need me to take him out for you? I'll bring the big guns." He puffed out his chest and flexed nicely toned arms in what would have been a menacing manner if not for the hint of a smile playing around his lips.

"Something weird happened, though."

In my world, weird was a relative term, and one Kin took with a grain of salt. Pink Himalayan salt—a chunk as big as my fist—to be exact.

"Weirder than usual?"

"Does an inanimate object talking in my head qualify?" I told him about the bow making noise every time Joshua Owens spoke. "I think it was trying to tell me something, but it sounded like a lot of blah, blah, blah to me. To top it all off, I spent two hours last night trying to get Clara's ring to work again, and all I got was the beginnings of a callus and a terrible night's sleep."

"That's what you get for sleeping by yourself. Should have shacked up with me." Kin wiggled his eyebrows just as Flix had earlier, with an entirely different effect.

I let the day slide off my back with a laugh and reveled in the delicious tingle of skin-on-skin while Kin gently stroked the back of my hand with his fingertips. Imagining those slow circles on other, more sensitive parts of my body kicked my breathing a little faster. Under the table, I slid off one shoe and ran my toes up his leg; Kin's eyes darkened, and I knew he was thinking the same thing I was. If the waiter hadn't picked that exact moment to show up with a bottle of wine, we'd probably have skipped dinner entirely.

Letting the promise of *later* show in my eyes, I leaned back in my chair and knocked back a swallow of smooth, sweet Riesling. Kin had made reservations at my favorite restaurant in the city, and the atmosphere was part of its allure. With only a handful of tables large enough to hold more than two people, lights so low I wondered how the wait staff maneuvered without dropping their trays, and an aphrodisiac-filled menu, it was no wonder Gentile's was considered *the* dinner destination for couples in love.

In fact, I had spotted Harry and Lemon Tart across the

dining room and specifically requested a secluded table out of their line of sight. Unfortunately, we were located too close to the dessert cart, and when Lemon got distracted by a slice of airy, chocolate mousse cheesecake on her way out of the restroom, she spotted us and dragged Harry over to say hello.

"We had the most amazing time in Cozumel; talk about the perfect honeymoon destination!" Lemon exclaimed once she'd settled into the table next to us and asked their waiter to bring their plates because, yes, thank you, they'd love to join us. Bloody hell, why did the Faeries raise me to be so polite?

Newlywed bliss must have softened Harry who, last I checked, didn't care much for Kin after the debacle with Lemon right before the wedding. My darling half-brother, Jett, had cursed songwriting legend Skip Stark's guitar—which at the time belonged to Kin—to cast a love spell over any woman who heard it played. Lemon had gone bonkers for Kin, turned into a groupie, and convinced herself she was going to run off with my boyfriend. Jett's spell also bound Kin's soul to the guitar, forcing me to come out of the broom closet and reveal myself as a witch to save him. All I'd needed was true love's kiss, but I didn't know that until the last minute.

Before the dust settled on that situation, I'd talked the godmothers into helping me put on a wedding to replace the one Lemon had all but canceled. Now, I wasn't sure whether to blame her or thank her for being the launchpad of their new party planning business.

Talk about a whirlwind relationship. I'd gone from just starting to date Kin to knowing fate bound us at breakneck speed. My life already had fairytale aspects and being raised like a Disney princess made the transition a bit easier, as did Kin's easygoing, accepting nature and unflappable nerves. Both of which were getting quite the workout right now.

"So when are you two lovebirds planning on tying the knot?" Lemon asked, her wide blue eyes conveying a spark of mischief beneath a facade of innocence. I pasted a smile on my face and deftly avoided the question while shooting looks at Kin to see his reaction and trying to figure out some way to get us out of there.

"Lexi, I'm *really* not feeling well. Do you mind if we get a doggy bag and just head home?" I didn't know how he managed to make his face look green around the gills, but it worked. In less than ten minutes we had escaped to the street to collect Kin's vintage Corvette from the valet.

"Good job, babe, you played that perfectly!" I exclaimed, depositing a kiss on Kin's cheek. Fortunately, he turned in the opposite direction to vomit, so it didn't end up all over my face. Or, more importantly, my shoes. They were really nice shoes.

"Oh, you weren't faking it, were you?"

"Definitely not." He squeaked.

"Let's go back to my place. The godmothers will fix you right up. I'll drive." I knew he needed one of Terra's home remedies when he didn't protest to me driving his precious Betty.

I dragged Kin inside and dosed him with the Faerie version of Pepto Bismol, relaying how our evening had played out while Kin's coloring returned to normal.

"We're going to have to start going out of town for date night if things like this keep happening." Kin commented ruefully. "We can't go anywhere anymore without seeing someone you've set up. I love that they love you, but an evening without interruption would be nice."

"Why bother? You don't need to go anywhere—we throw the best parties right here in the backyard." Soleil rolled her eyes toward the rear end of the house. "What more could you ask for on a Saturday night?"

"Date night isn't supposed to be a party. It's supposed to give us a little alone time in a romantic setting. I like a good party as much as the next guy, but…" Kin might as well have uttered a sentence made of nonsense words given the lack of attention Soleil paid the ones he did say.

"You need to relax, and I know just the thing…" Soleil bounced with excitement, which set things jiggling and cost Kin the will to disagree. Bouncing breasts tend to do that to a guy, and how could I begrudge him for it? They were excellent breasts.

"Hot tub." Entering the room, Evian tagged on the tail end of the sentence. "Perfect."

"Lovely. I'll grab the wine and tell the others." Soleil dissolved in a puff of red smoke and Kin shot me a questioning look. As much as I loved him, it hadn't even been an hour since he'd tossed his cookies at my feet. Faerie remedy notwithstanding, I could use a little time soothing in frothy water to wash away that visual.

"One hour and then we'll kick them out, I promise. I'll wear that bikini you like," I waggled my eyebrows at him, and he gave in without a fight. If the possibility of seeing any one of the faeries in a bathing suit had anything to do with his decision, he hid it well. Even though we all appeared roughly the same age, thinking of the godmothers as mother figures was a well-ingrained habit that Kin lacked the history to understand. Plus, since we were in the middle of the great no-fighting-party-planning compact, he remained blissfully unaware of their true nature. Talk about a honeymoon phase.

Back in my room, Kin ousted Salem from the polka-dotted beanbag chair at the end of my bed and settled in to watch my hunt for clothing ritual. Every week I added organizing my clothes to my master to-do list, and every week, it topped the unfinished items column. Instead, I preferred to rummage through the jumble of clothes jammed into my drawers and closet. Faerie magic kept the rest of the house neat and tidy, and I allowed Terra just enough access to clear up dust and grime twice a week, but I refused to let her go through my drawers. A woman needs her privacy. Using my magic for housekeeping smacked of personal gain, even though I did bend that rule just enough to have charmed my workshop into a dust-free zone.

"Is Lover Boy spending the night again?" The transition from cat to man ended with a naked Salem lounging against my pillows.

"Put that thing away and stop talking about me like I'm not here." Accepting that Salem was a cat in human form had not been easy for Kin. And Salem's habit of forgetting to put on clothes when he morphed failed to speed up the process in any measurable way.

"Yes. There you are.." Considering Salem's role in putting me together with Kin in the first place, I knew his annoyed tone had more to do with being kicked out of my room at night than anything else. Kin is a prince among men, but he draws the line at making love to his girlfriend with a man/cat lounging at the foot of the bed. Don't tell Salem, but I'm totally with Kin on that one.

"Found it." I spied a bit of purple material peeking out from under a disordered pile of tank tops and yanked the bikini to light. "We're doing hot tub night, Salem. You're welcome to join us." The sweetly phrased invitation was met with wide-eyed horror. Salem's run-in with Clara's water fountain was still fresh in his mind, and he shuddered at the thought. Served him right.

"No? Okay then." I grabbed a towel.

"What am I supposed to wear?" As often as I slept in Kin's bed, he'd only just begun spending the occasional night in mine. I really did need to prioritize the clothing storage project so he could have a drawer of his own.

"Your undies will do."

"Men don't wear undies. Or panties. It's not manly. We wear boxers."

I snorted. "Manly? Your boxers have Yoda on them, and you're calling that manly?"

He had no reply, so I pinned my hair up, tossed him a towel, and led him back downstairs to watch the transformation in the back yard.

Because she considered this a party, Terra went all out calling the earth into her desired configuration. A circling hand hollowed solid rock into a basin complete with seats while the other drew white sand from some sun-warmed beach. She completed the oasis with a pair of palm trees and a Bird of Paradise plant. Delicate flowers bloomed from hardy New England plants that had adapted to survive harsh winters, not carry such fragrant beauty.

Evian's contribution—water from a green-blue sea—shot into the basin where Soleil added enough heat to coax wisps of steam, tossed a few sparks under the surface to make a gentle glow and sent more glittering embers to circle the trunks of the trees.

"Now that's what I call a set of fairy lights." Kin said.

With a flick of her fingers, Vaeta added the bubble and froth.

I had one anxious moment when I feared all four of them might strip naked in front of Kin and give him a heart attack. They've done worse. But, tonight, modesty was in order. One piece suits skimmed other-worldly curves closely enough to turn a man's head but covered all the bases.

Soleil had been right; this was just what I needed.

We spent a little more than the hour I promised, but before long, Kin and I were alone in the wet heat.

"Finally." His voice turned husky, and he leaned in close to trail a line of burning kisses from my neck to my lips while his busy hands slid under the water and did things that shortened my breath.

When he stopped to ask, "You don't think they're watching, do you?" I wasted no time setting his mind at ease. Calling the image of an enclosure firmly to mind, I satisfied Kin's modesty by releasing enough intention to make it so and turned my attention to spending some well-earned private time with my man.

"What are they doing in there?" I put my green tea and strawberry smoothie down on the table and checked my watch. The ring still wasn't working, the office phones had been ringing off the hook for days, and I'd finally hit my limit. Flix talked me into meeting up with Kin and Carl after their kickboxing class for lunch and a much-needed furlough from the chaos.

We'd have been better off simply dealing with clients, but there are limits to patience, and I'd reached mine around the time the third cup of coffee had cooled to tepid before I'd managed more than two sips. Flix had increased his efforts, campaigning hard for my blessing to hire an assistant, but given the supernatural nature of our business, that sounded like a problem waiting to happen unless we could find a nice witch in need of a job.

What would that wanted ad look like?

"Is Carl one of those long shower types? Kin is a speedy washer."

My comment elicited a pained look from Flix. "Too much info," he said. "Way too much info."

Funny, I don't remember him ever censoring details

about *his* conquests. Carl was turning Flix into a bit of a prude, which was saying something, coming from me. I'm not into smut or toilet humor, and I don't understand why some girls think it's cute if they can belch the alphabet. But that doesn't mean I won't share some details with my nearest and dearest. A tiny sideways grin let me know he was only joking.

Half an hour had passed while we sat in the café-style seating of the juice bar attached to the health club. "Can you go check on them? I have another appointment in an hour, and if they don't hurry, I'm going to have to skip lunch." I drummed my fingertips on the table.

With a sigh, Flix skirted the table and made his way toward the locker room/shower area. While he was perfectly willing to pitch in when I needed him and give me a hard time when my life got in the way of work, Flix lacked a certain sense of urgency with regards to deadlines and appointments that probably came from being long-lived. Most of the Fae in my life tend toward a *this-too-shall-pass* attitude, which isn't always a good fit for the human world. They adjust and adapt, but they never really understand how a shortened life span makes things operate on a finite and foreshortened scale.

Witches can live for centuries, so my perspective falls somewhere in between the human and Fae, and well closer to the human side of the equation considering I'd only recently resolved my null status and hadn't expected a long lifespan. Consequently, I was feeling the strain. Plus, I was starving, and it was all you can eat shrimp day at Jericho's. Visions of succulent pink yumminess weren't improving my mood.

Less than a minute after he'd left, Flix's solemn face appeared in the doorway leading to the showers. He motioned for me to come quickly. I met him in the section between the men's and women's separated areas.

"What's wrong?"

"Spell. You need to come see."

"I can't go into the men's shower room." I felt the flames of embarrassment wash my face with redness. "There are naked men in there."

"You are familiar with the concept," dry tones did not hide the amusement at my discomfort.

"Shut up. Of course, I am. It's just that it will cause a scene if I waltz in there like I don't know any better."

In answer, Flix waved his hand, and I felt the tingle of a glamour settle over me. "Fine, now you look like a dude. Can we please go now?"

Keeping my eyes focused forward, and well above waist level, I followed him into the men's locker room— and guess what? It didn't look like anything you've seen on TV. There were no towel-snapping fights going on; the men weren't all oiled up and flexing. The scent of athlete's foot spray mingled with whatever the latest craze in men's body spray happened to be at the moment, and a faint whiff of something else I recognized but couldn't place.

I could also hear a commotion coming from around the corner where I guessed, from my trips to the mirror-image ladies' room next door, the showers were located, "What's going on?"

I followed Flix, who declined to answer, as Kin and Carl's raised voices met my ears.

"Well, so that you know, your butt doesn't look as good as you think it does in those stretchy pants you like so much!" Kin had his arms crossed in front of him, his jaw clenched, and he was glaring at Carl with an expression of barely-contained contempt.

One of Carl's hands landed on his hip, the other hand raised in an *oh no, you didn't* gesture, forefinger extended toward Kin's nose, "Well yours really does look amazing in those jeans you wear when you strut around on stage!" Carl countered, "Wait, that's not what I meant to say!"

"What's going on?" I asked for the second time, my voice approaching a shrill tone that didn't remotely match the male face Flix had given me. Carl's eyes widened, and Kin nearly jumped out of his skin.

He glared in my direction with suspicion in his eyes, "Lexi? That's incredibly disturbing, and I'm not sure I'll be able to get the image out of my head later tonight when we're..." Kin clasped his hands over his mouth, eyes wide with shock as he realized what he had just stopped from coming out of it. Flix waved the glamour away, and I was back to looking like my regular self. Their argument must have driven everyone else out of the locker room anyway, because the four of us were alone.

"What happened to you two? I smell magic—and cheap perfume." Suddenly, I realized the scent I couldn't place before had been copious amounts of knockoff Chanel No. 5. "You know who this was, don't you? Serena Swampgrass." I turned to Flix, putting the pieces together before either Kin or Carl could answer my question.

"You're sure?"

"Oh, it was her, all right. What did she do to you?" I asked again.

"Truth serum," they both said in unison.

Flix and I looked at one another, sharing a look of panic.

"What did you tell her?" I directed my question at Kin.

"That you have no idea how to get to the Faelands. And that you're trying to fix the Bow of Destiny," Kin looked down at the floor, refusing to meet my gaze, "and that your godmothers aren't currently welcome in Faerie."

Carl piped up before I could express my feelings about Serena knowing another one of my secrets, "She asked me the same thing—I told her I didn't have any details. Now I understand why you've been so unwilling to talk about it. If I'd known more, I'd have spilled my guts. Fortunately, Serena heard the door open and climbed out that window." He pointed toward a pane of glass barely big enough for a teenage girl to squeeze through. Good thing Serena was built like one.

With a shudder, Carl added, "It was like watching my grandmother trying to put on skinny jeans."

I suppressed a giggle at the unkind image. Serena always brought out the worst, snarkiest side of me. "Well, she's long gone by now. Speaking of which, is there another way out of here?"

None of us were getting through the window, and traipsing through the gym with two men suffering from verbal diarrhea would attract unnecessary attention. "We've got to get them home and let it wear off. Neither of them can go back to work, and really shouldn't be out in public."

"I'll check." Flix was gone a long time while I sat between the two anxious men and held onto Kin's hand for reassurance. He and Carl were both attempting to keep a lid on it, and I resisted the urge to ask a few questions of my own. When Flix returned, it was from the same direction we had entered the first time.

"Side door for employees only, and it's closer than going all the way back to the main parking lot, so I pulled the car around and circled back. You'd better cancel your afternoon appointments." Controlled fury put a chill in Flix's voice that I knew wasn't aimed at me even though it probably should have been. It was more my fault than his that Carl had become a target in Serena's game of revenge.

When Flix sent Jett to the darkest region of the Faelands, it had been for my protection, and I don't think either one of us considered Serena much of a threat. Though I doubted there would be any lasting effects from the serum. If anything serious happened to Carl, Flix would make the gawky witch wish she had never been born.

"She hurts Kin and I'll hex her so hard her kids will feel it," I muttered darkly.

Not content to let either man leave our sight, we led Carl and Kin out the hidden exit and settled them in Flix's convertible Jaguar. My hands were shaking from the roller coaster of emotions I'd just experienced: fear-fueled adrenaline had hit the second Flix motioned for me to follow him into the men's room, morphing into confusion and then amusement and relief.

Now, all I could conjure was anger that Serena had summoned the nerve to strike when Flix and I were mere feet away from the scene of the crime. Either she was gaining confidence or becoming increasingly desperate.

Serena had just taken a step over the line, and as I canceled my afternoon, it was with one part of my mind playing out scenarios for dealing with her. The woman had already driven me to the brink of my dark side once, and even though I'd vowed never to lose control like that again, she'd been the one to pull out the can opener. I was more than happy to supply the worms. Or the whup-ass. Or both.

I made the calls and reshuffled my schedule to free up the rest of the day, debating, for the hundredth time in the past few weeks, whether Flix was right. Maybe there was a way I could hire an assistant without them finding out too many of my secrets. Probably not, but I'd listen more intently the next time he broached the subject.

"Nice car, man," Kin said.

"And he doesn't even need to compensate for the size of his..."

Flix managed to stop Carl from finishing that sentence, but only just.

"It's pretty. Just like you." Kin continued as though no one else had spoken. "But not as pretty as my Lexikins." Now it was my turn to blush red.

Of course, when I come home looking for a little peace and quiet, I'm more likely to find a swamp in my foyer, but when it would be convenient for at least one of my godmothers to be there, elsewhere is the place to find them. I rummaged through my purse for the faerie godmother equivalent of a panic button and pulled out one of the seashells that made up Evian's direct communication hub. White as snow outside with a pale pink interior, it was pretty as well as useful.

"Evian," I spoke clearly into the shell.

"What's wrong?" Her voice boomed back.

"Tone it down a bit. I'm fine. That's why I didn't call Terra directly." Had there been a real emergency, she was only a whisper away. "Serena hit Kin and Carl with some truth spell or potion. Trying to find out how to get to Jett. We're at home now, and I thought maybe one of you could check them over, make sure I didn't miss anything." One of Terra's tonics wouldn't go amiss either—not that a tonic would lift the spell; that would have to wear off on its own.

"We'll be right there." The shell went dead in my hand.

"You sure you didn't just stir the pot?" Flix knew first-hand the weight of faerie godmother wrath.

"Just trying to keep the lines of communication open. They're going to find out anyway, might as well bring them in early, save me a headache later, and keep the faerie freakouts to a minimum. I can't tell you how nice it has been to come home and not step into the seventh level of hell. I thought a dinosaur was the worst they could do until I came home and found a dragon burning down the backyard."

"The party planning is going well, then?"

"So far." Prone to taking out their aggressions in both magical and epic ways, the four faeries made a no-fighting pact when they started their party planning business. I still wasn't sure if the agreement only covered business related issues, but since they'd sealed the deal with an enchanted vow, it seemed to be working for petty grievances as well. Or maybe they were just too busy to argue. Either way, I wasn't dumb enough to look a gift unicorn in the mouth. Well, not a second time, anyway. Unicorns absolutely hate having their dental hygiene called into question, and their hooves are pointy when they kick.

"We're going to have to do something about her, you know." Flix and I lingered in the entryway, speaking in low tones while Carl and Kin took seats in the parlor.

"Based on what I learned that day in the Fringe, all she wants is to be with Jett. She's willing to co-opt her faerie godmother to make it happen. That's crazy in my book." My living arrangements notwithstanding, trying to coerce a Fae was right up there with jumping off the Empire State Building and expecting to land on your feet.

Never going to happen.

"She wants to be with Jett so badly; I've got no problem sending her to the Faelands." I heard her doom in his voice and didn't want to be a party to the disappearance of another person, even if getting Serena out of the way would be a huge relief and one more thing off my plate.

Jett's chances for survival were double hers based on his parentage and truth be told; I would not have opted to send him there, either, had I been given a choice. Serena's demise, though it figured in my more creative fantasies at times, was not something I wanted to bring about on purpose. Even if she wouldn't thank me for the consideration.

"Tempting, but no. I'll deal with her in my own time. At least we know what she wants, not that it was ever a burning question. But why go after Kin and Carl? Neither of them have magic, so how would they know how to get Jett back?"

"You're seriously asking me to parse the intentions of the stupidest person I've ever had the misfortune to meet? For all we know, her intentions could have been for something entirely different to happen. She's not exactly gifted when it comes to spellcasting."

"Or choosing boyfriends," I said ruefully. "I think Jett only kept her around because she was biddable. You could tell he was the one calling the shots. How sad is that, though, when *he's* the brains of the operation? Makes me that much more thankful we've both found ourselves amazing men. I mean, considering the secrets that could have come to light today, I think Carl's appreciation of Kin's butt is pretty far down the list of things to be concerned with."

I couldn't help the little smile that often came when I thought of Kin and all he meant to me. The long list of husbands on the genealogical page of the Grimoire combined with knowing the mothers and grandmothers had enjoyed a longer lifespan, led me to dismiss the men in my history as less important than they probably were. In the meantime, I was in this relationship—all the way in —and if Serena thought she could get away with taking aim at my man, she had a nasty surprise coming her way.

With the faerie invasion imminent and two men trading truths like baseball cards, my grandmother's ring sparking back to life seemed like impossibly bad timing. Or, in other words, par for the course.

This time I vowed to be better prepared—my second trip to the past would not be clothing optional. To make sure I didn't take any more accidental journeys, I left the ring on a shelf along with the compass and the Stone of Blood pendant I'd been wearing since the day my mother gave it to me. Without the constant weight of the two symbols I carried, my neck felt strangely barren as I added a generous amount of lavender oil to the bathtub—more than was needed for a ritual cleansing but enough, I hoped, to soothe the jumpy places inside me.

There hadn't been time to get nervous before the first time leap, but this one was different. Fixing the Bow of Destiny depended on the outcome and I wanted to give myself every chance to succeed. A lot was riding on my success—if I had known exactly how much at the time, I don't think all the warm water and lavender oil in the world could have calmed me.

The sound of that arrow striking my father's flesh was still as clear in my mind as the first time I'd heard it. No one ever asked me if I wanted a job that involved aiming pointy things at people and, clearly, no one cared that my answer would have been no.

I'd rather groom goats or scrape gum off the sidewalk, thank you very much.

Not even my dislike of Joshua Owens was enough to make the idea of firing a weapon at him palatable.

"Quit lollygagging in there," Salem yelled through the doorway.

"Come in here and say that." I didn't want him to, and I knew he wouldn't. He knew I wasn't above splashing him if he annoyed me.

"What happens to your body when you leap? Does it stay or go?"

I thought about it for a second and gave the snarky answer. "Yes."

"Helpful, Lexi. Real helpful. Hurry up; I'm dying to see what happens."

"You know I can't guarantee anything will happen, don't you? I'm not even sure exactly what I did the first time."

"Oh, come on, you turned the ring on your finger while thinking of where you wanted to go. It's witch 101, even if it was an accident."

"Thanks for reminding me," I yelled.

There would be no more relaxing with him in this mood, so I got out of the tub, dried off, and dressed in the comfortable clothes I'd picked out. Jeans so well-worn they were soft as butter, a knit tank, and just in case it got cold, I tied a sweatshirt around my waist.

I slipped the ring on my finger, and clasped the compass around my neck, then stood looking at the Stone of Blood. Its connection to my mother made it feel tainted with her betrayal. Before I could wear it again, it too would need a good cleansing, but for now, it could stay on the shelf.

"Are you ready?" I've seen kids in a candy store less excited than Salem as he practically bounced from one foot to the other.

"As I'll ever be." We made our way down to the room my grandmother would have called the front parlor, but in modern times was referred to as a living room, and I reached into the blue flame of the Balefire to pull the handle and enter my sanctuary behind the fireplace.

I'd added a few personal touches to make the sanctum my own, including some comfy pillows and throws on the old sofa which was where I settled now. Just me and the pterodactyl-sized butterflies zipping around in my stomach. Salem would stay because it's his job as my familiar to aid me in my magical endeavors. He calls them escapades, which I think is the equivalent of a familiar slur, but I can't prove it.

However, if he made that sniffing noise meant to hurry me along too many times, his butt—furry or not—would be out in the kitchen with the rest of them.

"Think happy thoughts."

"I'm not Tinkerbell."

I took a deep breath, fixed my mind on the desire to find what I needed to repair the Bow of Destiny, and twisted the ring around on my finger. Once, twice, and at the third turn, I felt a pull behind my navel, and then the sensation of falling. Colors and shapes spun past in a haze of nauseating motion that lasted just long enough to send a scream bubbling up in my throat.

My heart beat so hard and so fast that for a minute, I could hear nothing except the glug and thump of it—like a metronome keeping time. A deep breath filled my nose with the scent of pine pitch, its odor sharp and clean in air unpolluted by industry. I opened my eyes to the sun and a wash of sky so blue it nearly hurt to look at it.

Something about the horizon seemed both familiar and alien.

There wasn't time to ponder, though. I had come here for a reason. To find living gold and figure out how to use it to repair my father's bow. I spun in a full circle to try and get my bearings and only succeeded in reawakening the clammy sickness in the pit of my stomach.

"Easy, Lexi." And now I was talking to myself out loud. "Get a grip." I did it again.

Somehow, I hadn't expected to end up in the middle of a forest with no idea where to look. Nothing Lamiel had said during our short conversation led me to think there would be living gold just lying around loose on the ground no matter what period of history I'd been dumped in. If that were the case, there would have been a lot more items like the bow and compass.

The compass.

I'd completely forgotten I had it with me—the trip

here must have scrambled my brains. Yanking it out from under my shirt, I held the shining instrument in my palm. The same polished golden hue as the bow itself, the compass had guided me to its counterpart when the bow was still hidden inside Shadow Hold. About the size of a silver dollar and attached to an intricately-woven chain, with a rendering of the Bow of Destiny engraved on the back side, it felt warm to the touch and full of energy.

The needle swung wildly, and my heart sank. I'd placed a lot of hope on the compass being attracted to the material from which both it and the bow had been worked. A logical assumption on my part, but you know what they say about making assumptions.

Please, I sent up a plea to whatever deity might be listening. *Please.*

I felt a vibration and then a click when the compass homed in and my prayer was answered. Turning in a half circle, I began to walk in the direction the needle pointed —and promptly measured my length on a bed of crisp, autumn leaves. The next few minutes I spent getting my breath back and hopping up and down on my uninjured foot.

Give me a break, I'm a city girl and don't spend a lot of time in the woods where tripping hazards like rocks and branches hide away under colorful blankets of leaves. Vowing to pay more attention to my feet, I missed the next ground-level obstacle and instead commenced the there's-a-spider-in-my-hair dance after making contact with a nice, sticky webs.

Yeah, I know I'm a witch, and we're not supposed to be thrown by contact with creepy crawlies, but I don't care. A spider in my hand is not the same as one in my hair or on my clothes. At least I didn't strip naked and shake those out.

I did wonder what twist of irony let the environment affect me, while leaving me a powerless observer of the fight during my last visit to the past. Then again, it was probably for the best. Time travel stories where people make tiny changes in the past and then are stuck with the repercussions when they return to their lives make for great cautionary tales. It was probably for the best I not have the option to make any paradoxical choices.

While all that was running through my mind, I spared just enough attention to the compass to follow it into a small clearing split by a worn track. Blue smoke trailed skyward from the chimney of a stone hearth I would have recognized anywhere.

According to my admittedly vague memory of the Balefire history, my great-grandfather had built the section of the house encasing the fireplace in 1782—a few months before my grandmother was born. Given the stacks of rough-hewn lumber and the unmistakable sounds of hammering coming from the back of the house, I'd landed here at the beginning of the building project and unless I was totally off on my calculations, was about to get a glimpse of Tempest, my great-grandmother.

If I haven't mentioned it before, my life seems to be taking several turns for the surreal. I've gone from knowing almost nothing about my family history to seeing some of it play out right in front of me. I've learned things that shocked me and things that saddened me with not a lot in between. Maybe today would be different.

With my luck? Probably not.

Standing in the front yard pondering the existential ramifications of time travel wasn't getting me any closer to the reason I'd come here, so I forced myself to walk around the back.

Tink, tink, tink. Not the sound of a hammer on nails as I'd thought, but of one striking metal on an anvil. The muscles in the blacksmith's arms corded and bunched with each blow, though from the back, he looked to be young, almost too young for the work, and slight enough that the power needed must have been hard to muster.

Call me dumb, but I didn't catch on that the smith was female until she quenched a curved length of iron, tossed it onto a pile of others like it, and pulled off her cap to let cool air blow through locks of hair the same color as my own.

Great-grandmother was ripped.

It came as no huge surprise when she turned, and the face that went with that hair was also a match for mine. We Balefire women share more than the witch blood that runs through our veins.

Tempest wore men's trousers—scandalous in her time—under a sleeveless shirt, also a man's by the look of it, and managed to look gloriously female in both. When she lifted her arm to rotate her shoulder, the Stone of

Blood pendant stood out against the homespun ecru-colored material.

My hand went to my chest where the pendant normally hung and only found the compass which hummed and bucked in my hand. Perhaps I'd been too quick to shun the family heirloom. Sylvana hadn't been the only one to don it, and now I felt like a traitor for not realizing how my maternal figure's shortcomings weren't necessarily a sign of the entire Balefire clan's proclivities.

Her eyes passed right over me on their way toward a man walking around the corner of the house. I felt a tingle of anticipation, but nothing more substantial until I turned around and my breath caught in my throat.

My father walked—no, strutted would be a better word—toward Tempest as though his presence had been requested by engraved invitation. The look of distaste on her face said otherwise, while one hand moved down to rest on her abdomen protectively, and the other gripped the hammer more tightly than when she had been using it to pound iron. Was he that big a threat? Could I have come from someone who would coerce a woman?

If he was carrying the Bow of Destiny on him anywhere, it had the ability to turn pocket-sized because I couldn't see it.

"What are you working on?" He cast a wide smile at Tempest, who appeared unmoved by the sunlight sparkling off his pearly whites. Then he leaned in and angled his body just a bit too close to peer into the Balefire-powered forge. "Impressive."

Sparks flew between them. Literal sparks. Ones that had nothing to do with the forge or the Balefire, and even less to do with signaling attraction between the pair of them.

Reading Tempest's body language, I suspected they were an overflow of the tightly contained magic I felt simmering just below the surface of her attempt at a placid face. I've seen that feral look in a woman's eyes before. In my line of work, you get to know the difference between a *come-hither* look and one that says *touch me, and you'll lose an appendage.*

A flick of her gaze told me exactly which dangly bit she'd have liked to relieve him of. Ouch.

"What do you want?" More than a whiff of Irish accent threaded through her clenched teeth.

"What I've always wanted. You." Smooth. Okay, not really. My father, ladies and gentlemen, the inventor of the cheesy pickup line. I'm so proud.

"Be off with you. I'm a married woman with no interest in the likes of you." Tempest let go of the hammer to place a second hand over her belly. Cupid's eyes widened, then narrowed and I could see he'd caught the meaning of the gesture. A flash of unabashed longing altered his expression, but only for a second before the tension left him and acceptance set in with a shrug of his shoulders. Could he have had more than a passing attraction for my great-grandmother?

"So you are. For now, at least. I'd like to bless the babe, if you will allow it." Voice so smooth you could spread it on toast, Cupid did not wait for her consent. "May she grow to be as beautiful as her mother and twice as wise." He turned to leave, then tossed a *goodbye* back over one shoulder.

"Good riddance," Tempest muttered to his back. "May the cat eat you, and the devil eat the cat."

Interesting mental image.

"Come along, lass. Don't be all day about it." I heard the smile in his voice before I turned to see my great-grandfather making his way toward his wife. One look and I knew he was a perfect match for her. Fiery ginger hair made a startling contrast to the robin's egg blue of his eyes. A tall man, his face reddened from the force of his labor, he moved toward her as though drawn, and enfolded his wife in a full body embrace that spoke volumes about his feelings for her, and she pulled his head down for a kiss.

It went on long enough that I had to look away because watching felt too much like voyeurism.

"I've just finished the last pieces of the circle." All business now, Tempest pointed to the pile of arced iron. "Would you put them in place while I check the crucible?"

"Aye, that I will." Cheerfully, Kenneth lifted half the pile with one hand and carried it around behind the fireplace. I moved closer to watch him begin to lay the outline of the casting circle around the star shape already embedded in the flagstones. A tiny thrill shot through me as I watched the process. How many people get to see bits of their family history firsthand?

At the forge, Tempest reached into a bucket of ore to pick out just the right piece. Curious, I angled around for a better look. Rooting through with deft fingers, she chose one and gently pulled out a palm-sized nugget that looked nothing like I expected. Dull, bronze in color, and otherwise dead plain, I decided I must be looking at some other metal. Maybe she used something else to blend with the gold.

Way to go, Lexi. Only you could go looking for gold without bothering to do any research. Salem had been right about me shirking my studies.

Tempest tossed the nondescript hunk of rock into a receptacle nestled in the bed of flaming coals, and I leaned over her shoulder to see what was in the crucible only to learn I'd been dead wrong. Molten metal glinted up at me with a liquid shine—and judging by the humming vibration from the compass hanging against my chest, I was staring at a pot of smelted living gold—the very thing I'd come here to find. The thing I had no idea how to harvest.

Not that the experience of seeing my ancestors was trivial, but if I couldn't figure out how to accomplish my goal, what was the point of coming here? My nerves began to tingle at the thought of another wasted trip. If I didn't get the gold, I couldn't fix the bow. If I failed to repair the bow, I would never embrace my destiny. And that meant more love seeping out of the world. I didn't want to picture that future, and I certainly didn't want my failure to have played a role in bringing it about.

Think logically; I ordered my brain.

Okay. Logic. Here we go. I could touch spider webs (shiver) and trip over obstacles. I could feel sweat trickling down my back from being so close to the flame and heat of the forge. Maybe I could pick up a small hunk of raw gold from the pile and put it in my pocket. Easy, right?

I probably don't need to tell you how utterly that plan failed, and while I'm thinking about it, a big, fat thank you to the universe for being way too picky about my options. Could have cut me a break for once, but no.

On top of my plan not working, the compass kept vibrating until the sensation worked on my last nerve. Finally, I pulled it out to see if there was a way to stop the annoyance, and it practically yanked me off my feet to get closer to the gold. It was like the small instrument had a huge magnet in it, and I was helpless to stop the motion as it dragged me closer to the crucible.

If tripping over a branch in the forest had left an angry scrape near my wrist, dunking my face in a container of molten gold was going to leave a bigger mark. I yanked the compass over my head and let it dangle by the chain instead, but the speed of its descent brought my hand close enough for the heat to frizzle the tiny hairs on my arm.

If it dipped any lower, I'd have no other choice than to let go, but first, I let the chain run through them until there were hardly any links left to clasp and only the tips of my fingers retained contact.

Time stretched out while my skin pinked from the

heat, my resolve began to weaken, and my nerveless fingers started to unclench. Quick as a wink, the compass dodged left toward the pile of ore waiting to go into the fire. I heard a metallic slurping sound and saw a pea-sized pebble get sucked into the compass, which went limp in my hand. Well, okay then.

Two steps back I welcomed air that brushed a cooler breeze against my brow. I'd done it. Or the compass had, but the result was the same. I could go home now.

Or not.

I'd never figured out how the ring functioned in reverse. Turning it hadn't worked for me the last time, and I'd been so keyed up from what I'd seen, I hadn't paid attention to anything else I might have done to trigger my return.

Maybe it was on a timer, and if that were the case, I'd take this opportunity to stick around—like I had a choice—who knows, I might learn a useful skill or two to take back with me.

Now that my attention wasn't so focused on my goal, I heard chanting that sounded like it had been going on for some time and stepped around the fireplace to see what was happening. Standing in the middle of the pentacle already set in the flagstones I recognized from my time in the sanctum, Tempest worked a spell that made me want to clap like a fangirl at a boy-band concert. The iron bits of the partially-completed casting circle hovered around her at close to waist height. With one hand, she slowly spun the material to orient the pieces in front of her and with the other, she forced witchlight to weld the iron securely until each section was perfectly positioned.

That would have been impressive enough, but she followed with another spell to speed up the whirling of the circle, then slowly lowered it into place. A groove opened up to accept the iron ring as seamlessly as though the stones had been made from butter and carved with a warm knife. Next, she crooked an index finger, and the crucible danced merrily through the air to tip and pour its molten gold contents over the iron ring, sealing it into place. The final component of the spell fell like a cooling balm over the living gold, which sizzled and spit before turning the bronze color I was used to seeing. If I hadn't watched it happen myself, I wouldn't have believed the unpolished casting circle had been constructed using the same material as the Bow of Destiny.

I'd just succeeded in committing the spell she used to memory so I could tell it to Salem when the ring on my finger lit and I felt myself being dragged out of there. What a trip.

"Wow," I stammered, standing next to Salem in the sanctum once more. "That was intense."

"Did you get it?" Circling in a figure-eight, Salem vibrated with excitement as if I held a dozen tuna flavored treats.

A wide smile lit my face. "Yep, I sure did. But I wouldn't have been able to without the compass." I showed him the scrapes from where I had fallen. "So, I can touch sticks and stones and spider webs while I'm there." Remembering, I checked to see if there were still strands of sticky silk in my hair, "but I can't pick up anything intentionally or bring anything back." My hair was web-free. "And, I can't fix the bow in the past, either. I thought the whole trip was a failure until the compass did...well, look."

I swept my hair off my neck to show Salem the compass, which had lifted off my chest, its arrow pointing in the direction of the fireplace. In close proximity, the living gold contained inside was drawn so strongly to the flame that the chain dug into my neck if I stood still.

"All I had to do was get it close enough, and it absorbed a chunk of living gold."

"Raw ore, you mean?" Shock raised Salem's voice to the level of a Siamese yowl. "What are you supposed to do with that?"

"Oh, ye of little faith." I'd seen my great grandmother work the Balefire like a forge, and it didn't look too difficult: heat crucible in Balefire, add chunks of living gold. After that, it was a sure bet I could screw things up six ways to Sunday. We'd have to hope luck or intuition would be enough because those were all I had going for me. I'd relied solely on instinct since I realized I wasn't going to come into my powers like a normal witch, and they had always gotten me through whatever storm I'd stumbled into.

"Didn't you say there was a crucible in the store room?" Salem maintains cats don't scamper, but that's as good a word as any for what he did.

I unclasped the chain, wrapped it tightly around my hand to ease the yanking on my neck while a wide-eyed Salem sorted through the closet, and finally returned carrying a sturdy-looking pot with long handles on either side.

"Found it."

"Rest the handles on the tops of the andirons, see how they were made just for that reason?"

"Now to add the gold." The compass strained toward the fire as if it, or the chunk of gold inside it, wanted to be given to the heat. Letting it lead the way, I strode forward to thrust the instrument, hand and all, into the fire licking around the waiting pot. Green flames tickled across my fingers, and I thanked my lucky stars for the Balefire genes that rendered the flickering tongues harmless to my skin. The compass needle spun in circles, faster and faster until it disgorged the lump with a whooshing sound.

The nugget rattled into the bottom of the pot and lay there defiantly *not* melting. Assuming I must have missed a step, I replayed the memory. Gold in crucible—check. Flaming Balefire—check. Those games where you're supposed to find the difference between two images— yeah, I suck at those. There had to be something, though.

I could have slapped myself when I saw what I'd been missing. The color of the Balefire flame was off a few shades. Gathering my magic together, I aimed everything I had at the fireplace. Like the tide runs toward shore, my legacy roared up, and through me. Tempest's words slid out of my mouth in such a jumble I only heard them myself at the moment I said them.

Flame, white and hot, traced tongues over the crucible's bowl and the lump of metal gathered itself, burst outward, then smoldered and turned to liquid gold.

"Now what?" Salem's question competed with the sudden noise in my head. The Bow knew its salvation was at hand and it wanted to heal badly enough to beg for it. Or, that's what I got from the noises it was making, anyway. More gurgled notes that sounded nothing like the tune it had played while resting on my father's shoulder as he stepped between my mother and grandmother.

Forgotten in my hand, the compass whipped back and forth between the crucible of melted living gold and the glass-covered box where the Bow of Destiny rested in pieces. A not-so-subtle hint.

Remembering how my great grandmother heated each bit of metal again before fusing them together, I chose two pieces to introduce into the fire and carefully used a set of fireplace tongs to hold them in the flame until they glowed.

The air thrummed with magic, a sensation that was by now so natural I noticed its rare absence almost as strongly as I felt its presence. Not until this moment had I experienced the two sides of my heritage working in harmony; living gold forged by a Balefire ancestor formed the five-pointed barrier inside which I placed the crucible alongside the relic created by my father's divine hands.

"I hope this is going to work." If there was an incantation or a prayer I was supposed to offer, I had no idea what it might be, so I decided to trust my instincts. Balefire to Bow.

Assuming the smelted contents of the crucible would act as a glue of sorts, I laid the bow in the center of the pentacle with the still-glowing broken pieces lined up in their correct positions.

"Here we go." The crucible weighed heavier in my hands than it should have given the tiny amount of melted ore pooled in the bottom. A hand on each handle, I strained to lift and tilt the container high enough to pour its contents without burning myself. I might be immune to Balefire, but molten metal would flay me to the bone.

I was spent and sweating by the time the gold began to ooze, shimmering as it slithered into the break I'd chosen for this first attempt—the worst break, the one in the center of the hand grip—and then solidified. A bright flash of white light sparked the air, and the repaired section flared to cast bright spots across my vision for a moment before the bow shivered once, and the compass abruptly stopped pulling.

Using the tongs again, I dropped the bow into a cauldron and wiped away the sweat from my brow as water hissed and sizzled around hot metal. I couldn't tell you if this is how regular gold gets forged, but my magic and my grandmother's expertise hadn't let me down.

When I pulled the fused pieces out, Salem crowded in to get a look.

"It worked. You can't even tell there was ever a crack there." I ran a fingertip over the formerly broken spot. "But there are two more repairs to be made, which means I've got to make two more trips to the past. So what did it look like when I disappeared."

"You just sort of faded, like a ghost. It was one of the more bizarre things I've ever seen, and that's saying something. I could see right through you, Lexi."

"Well, that's disturbing. I'm glad it was just us. Can you imagine the freak-out if Kin or the godmothers got a load of that?"

When the bow was safely ensconced in its box and the compass securely clasped back around my neck, we took a moment to study the ring.

To look at it, you would never expect the item contained such power. The simple band of beaten silver with a bit of tarnished patina looked like one you could buy in any one of the gift shops dotting the coastal region and catering to tourists. Five tiny circles, pressed into the metal, marched around the rim.

"That's odd." Salem followed me to the center of the room where I held the ring under the brightest beam of sunlight I could find. "I swear only one of those circles was filled in the last time I looked. And see how dull the metal is now?" I twisted and turned it to try and catch the light. "All the shine is gone."

Pulling the ring gently from my fingers, Salem gave it the once-over. "The two outer circles do look different." Him repeating what I'd already said made me shake my head. Hey, I'm growing, I didn't point out I'd mentioned that already. "Are you sure it wasn't like that before?"

"Almost positive. It's as if it's counting down, you know? Like when you mark off the days on a calendar." The comment triggered another thought. "Oh, I bet it is. I bet it's like a Genie's lamp. You get just so many wishes and then, poof, it's someone else's turn."

"Common enough concept in magic," Salem allowed.

"If I'm right, " and I knew I was, "that means I have three more visits to the past and only two more repairs." Ever since my trip back to the awful night I was orphaned,

I'd been imagining the possibilities. If there were any other way to repair the bow, I'd have had four more visits to the past at my disposal. Four more burning questions to which I could have gotten answers.

But maybe the gods would smile on me for once—it sure seemed like they owed me a break—and I'd get to use the last opportunity for my own personal ends. "Should be a piece of cake."

Salem regarded me through slitted lids. "You know what happens when you get cocky..."

"There's a difference between cocky and confident, Salem. Though, now that you mention it, there is something that's been bothering me. Two things, actually. The first is Serena and her motive for going after Carl and Kin at the gym."

"Revenge?" Still talking, we made our way back to the sofa.

"Certainly played a part in it, she's attempted to punish me for years over something I don't even remember doing when we were kids. But this attack was more about fishing for information—hence the truth spell —but why go after Carl or Kin? What could she possibly have hoped to learn? They didn't tell her anything because they didn't know anything *to* tell her. So, what if there's more to it and she tries again?"

"Would she be stupid enough to target Kin a second time?" Sometimes Salem forgets he's not in cat form and tries to crawl into my lap to have his ears scratched.

"Oof...Salem! Why can't we communicate when you're

small and furry? You're squishing me." His forlorn look had me switching positions so he could lay his head within easy reach of my hand and he all but purred when I used my nails on him. "Back to Serena. How good are your sleuthing skills? I thought you might be able to turn spy for me. Find out whatever you can. I don't think her state of mind is entirely sane."

"That girl was bat crap crazy before Jett got banished. Actually, I may have a way to get some inside info, " Salem mused while stroking his chin with the back of his hand, "but you're going to owe me a metric ton of salmon in return for the self-respect hit I'll have to take."

"And why is that?"

"I'm going to have to cozy up to someone I can't stand —Serena's familiar, Morana. She's always had a *thing* for me."

If I hadn't thought Salem was serious about the ton of salmon, I would have doubled over in laughter at the thought of him rebuffing the advances of an amorous kitty. The idea raised a question I'd been thus far too chicken to ask.

"And you don't feel the same way; I take it?" I received a scathing glare in response. "Is there someone you *are* interested in, Salem?" If I sat any closer to the edge of the proverbial seat, I'd end up on the floor.

I didn't realize Salem was capable of blushing, but his ebony skin took on a decidedly pink tinge, and he refused to make eye contact when he spoke. "There was. But her ninth life ended some time ago."

Oh. I felt like I'd gone on a five-mile run and then stuck my stinky foot in my mouth. "I'm so sorry, Salem. I had no idea."

"It's okay. I'm okay." I could tell he wasn't. "You know this is my ninth and final life. If there is an afterlife for beings like me, maybe I'll see her there." Salem blinked and changed the subject. "What was the second thing?"

"The second thing is related to the first, and I definitely need your help. Things have been pretty quiet around here lately, but once that bow is fixed, I'm willing to bet life will get messy again. From what little I've been able to glean, it's likely there's danger involved with being a Fate Weaver."

"You're still worried about Kin, aren't you?"

I ran my fingers through my hair in frustration, "How can I not be? He nearly got killed just following me into Shadow Hold. And now with Jett gone and the faeries hanging around all the time, I'm afraid he's developing a false sense of security. I can't always be there to pull him off the ledge, so I'm wondering what you can tell me about protection spells. Something I can use to keep him safe from magical harm."

"I'm thrilled you want to continue your training, but protection spells aren't exactly cut-and-dried. They're extremely complicated and require significant energy expenditure. And even then they're only a one-shot deal."

"What do you mean?" I asked.

"Protection spells only act as a deterrent—kind of like a sped up version of the power of three, where the karma whammy comes swiftly, and hopefully gives the victim a chance to get away. Not only that, they border on affecting another's free will. It's a gray area, and if you're not careful, it's extremely easy to step into the black."

"You don't think it's a good idea."

"Protection goes hand in hand with healing, which is, of course, useful in a pinch. Both are elemental in nature since you're altering the state of molecules to, for instance, heal a wound or create a barrier. And before you ask, barriers and shields produced in self-defense don't count in terms of karmic cost."

I raised an eyebrow, "So, it's a line even if Kin *wants* my protection?"

"That's different. And your affinity for elemental magic gives you an edge. But honestly, Lexi, if you're looking for a quick fix why not just ask the godmothers for some warning system or a resting shield charm—it would buy him some time in a full-on attack."

"No, I can't have them risking any more for me. I know they say they're content to stay out of the Faelands, but they'll want to go back at some point, and I'm not going to be the reason they can't."

"Lexi, you know they'd do it in a hot second." Salem said.

"Yes, and that's exactly why I can't ask."

"What about Flix, then? He's already got "tainted blood"," Salem made a disgusted face at the offensive moniker, "and I know for a fact he hates going to Faerie.

Plus, he's not a guardian, so I'm not even sure that rule would apply to him anyway."

Salem had a point, and it wasn't as though I didn't have enough on my plate. I'd spent twenty-five years as a helpless null, and now I never wanted to feel that way again. But Kin's safety was more important. "I still want to learn. That's a given. But I'll enlist Flix for now, just to make sure."

"I have an important question to ask you." The way Kin's strong fingers were kneading my sore shoulder muscles into submission, he could have asked me almost anything, and I'd have said yes. A combination of friction and the natural warmth of his skin teased heady scents from the muscle rub my grandmother had blended and left on a shelf in the Sanctum.

Notes of chamomile, lavender, clary sage, eucalyptus, and peppermint relaxed both body and soul as the pain ebbed away.

"Umm. Okay. But you're going to have to wash your hands first. That peppermint oil was not made for use on the tender bits."

"No, Lexi. I'm serious here. I want a drawer."

When I didn't immediately fill the silence with an answer, Kin said, "I want to keep some things here. Is that so much to ask? You have half a wardrobe at my place, and I think I deserve the same consideration."

How had he gone to the defensive place so quickly? A

split second is barely enough time to devise an answer to a question you're expecting and this one hadn't qualified as one of those.

"Of course you can have a drawer—two if you want them. I was just surprised that you were so serious about it is all. You didn't even have to ask, just pick the one you want and toss my things on the chair or in the closet."

There. That was settled. Or was it?

"There's something else, isn't there?" The look on his face simply shouted there was.

"I was wondering if you could put a…" Kin's voice dropped to a whisper, "spell on it to keep anyone from doing anything weird with my things." This was all my fault. With Twinkleberry wine loosening my tongue, I'd told him a few faerie godmother stories after our bout of fun in the hot tub the other night. Enchanting his boxers with invisible itching powder was not out of the realm of possibility, so I understood his concern.

"Consider it done."

"It's not too weird? My asking you to do magic for me?" I let the perfect opening to tell him about the Flix's protection go by.

"I'll clean out some space for you first thing in the morning. But for now, wash your hands, Mister. I want them on me." He did, and I made good use of them before falling asleep in his arms.

I fell into the dream like it was a cliff and I was wearing a parachute.

Fire. Balefire. White. The same color used to forge

living gold. Singing. I heard singing. No, not singing. A chant. I couldn't hear the words, only the rhythm. Hands. Not mine. Hers. Holding something pink. A blur that slowly faded to clear. A baby. A pink baby with tufts of dark hair and eyes of green. A bow shaped mouth the delicate texture and color of a rose petal. Fire. Behind the baby. White fire.

The chanting swelled. The hands moved closer to the flame.

No! Don't put the baby in the fire!

Too late. I closed my eyes and waited for the screaming to start.

A giggle.

They put the baby in the fire, and she laughed while she played with the flames.

Fire to keep the keeper
Flame to heal the healer

I woke up with part of the chant echoing through my head.

Some dreams feel different from the kind that are nothing more than an end-of-the-day info dump. They, like this one, take on a weight of importance that pulls at your psyche until you pay attention to the message.

What did it mean? Could immersing a baby in the Balefire provide some protection or increase her affinity for becoming a Keeper? Had I been subjected to the same ritual?

Flame to heal the healer. Something about that line made me think of my grandmother in her Clara-shaped tomb.

Slipping out of bed without waking Kin, I made my way downstairs, pulled the handle, and entered the Sanctum where I sank into a cross-legged position on the wide hearth and studied the flame. Nothing I tried would make it turn white, so I turned my attention toward the healing part of the chant.

Heal. If the Balefire could heal, maybe it could also break the spell and free my grandmother. Only one way to find out. I squirmed closer and tried to shove my injured shin into the fire. I doubt you'll ever have occasion to try and stick your leg into a fireplace, but if you do, let me give you a tip. Don't bother. It's damn near impossible. I ended up on all fours with my butt facing the flames and my neck craned around hard so I could see. Eventually, I managed, but it wasn't pretty.

The long scrape I'd brought back from my brush with a tripping hazard in the past made contact with the flame. I left it in there as long as I could hold the position—which was not very long, let me tell you. My planking skills are sadly lacking.

When I collapsed onto my stomach, panting from the effort, I didn't even need to look to know it had worked. The tingling itch of healing flesh told its own story, and I found another use for the Balefire. You learn something new every day, right?

CHAPTER

TEN

K in was already up and gone when Salem's scratchy cat tongue woke me at a much earlier hour than I usually cared to see. In fact, I'd have guessed it wasn't even light out yet, but when I opened the heavy drapes covering the big bay window across from my bed lo and behold, there was the sun.

"What could you possibly be thinking?" I scowled at him, pointing toward the night shirt I was wearing, the words *If you love me, let me sleep* emblazoned across the front.

"The godmothers have prepared breakfast, and are requesting your presence, Miss Lexi." Salem mocked over his shoulder after whooshing into his human form and skipping out the door.

"There had better be some premium coffee down there," I muttered under my breath.

Premium coffee was a given; an eclectic brunch menu was not. The after-effects of my odd dream had kept me up until the wee hours, and I'd rather sleep than test out a new party menu even if the kitchen smelled amazing.

"Why do you all hate me?" Heavy cream and double sugar went into my coffee. This was a morning for sweet and light, and the extra sugar helped kick the caffeine into high gear.

"Just drink your coffee and stop being grumpy. I added a little something extra to the brew." My hand halted with the cup halfway to my mouth, and I took a cautious sniff. Terra's definition of something extra ranged from the sublime to the disgusting. Sure, Dragolian frog snot has ten times the potency of espresso, but it tastes like...well, regular frog snot. Yuck.

"What's in it?"

"I've been working on an infusion using some of the ingredients in Twinkleberry wine, but with fewer side effects for humans and just enough euphoria to promote happiness." Terra explained.

"You know you can't serve this at parties, right?" Visions of a horde of naked partygoers taking to the streets flitted through my mind.

"Why not? Happy customers make for repeat customers. That's business 101."

Buying time to frame my comments constructively, I pulled a stool up to the counter and rested my elbows on the granite. "Twinkleberry wine ought to be considered a controlled substance, and you can't drug people against their wills, it's not polite." Most of the Fae I'd met set great store by maintaining at least a facade of civilized society. Don't get me wrong; they engaged in plenty of treachery behind closed doors all while presenting the customs of politeness in public. Offering someone a mood-lifting beverage took two giant steps over the line, then turned and spat on it.

Before I had time to form words, Terra dropped a verbal bomb, "Kin seemed relaxed and happy when he left for work this morning."

"Kin drank this? Did you tell him what was in it?" Then again, Kin had wanted to try a sip of Twinkleberry wine for weeks now; he'd probably jumped at the chance for a drink of laced coffee.

Terra sighed in that way that told me she was getting annoyed and the no-fight rule only applied to her sisters. Not only was I fair game, but she'd been denied the outlet of a good bout of magic-flinging fury for so long, a fight sounded like fun. When a tiny, localized earthquake rattled the stool under me, I took the hint and drank the coffee.

For the next ten minutes, I felt like the newest exhibition at the zoo.

"Quit staring at me. Is this what you dragged me out of bed for?" Admittedly, my post-breakfast mood probably was the best test. If her concoction could turn me into a morning person, it was too strong to be unleashed upon the world.

"No," Terra muttered and then amended to, "maybe. We're trying out some new recipes besides the coffee." She nodded to Soleil, who filled a plate from the warming oven and set it in front of me.

"There's nothing hinky in there," Soleil assured me after I sniffed the food suspiciously. Silver dollar waffles, perfect in their miniature size, formed the outsides of sandwiches, some filled with sweet ingredients and some with savory—all of which looked delicious and smelled incredible. I picked out the scent of fresh berries, sausage, and even chocolate. Candied flowers dotted the plate. "Speed dating brunch. It's the new big thing," the fire-haired faerie answered my unspoken question.

"You'll be a hit. This is so good it's almost an aphrodisiac. How did you get the waffles so perfectly small and thin?"

Stupid question, I knew it the second it left my lips. Shrinking spell.

"I wish I could send half my client list along; odds are some of them would find matches and take the weight off my shoulders. It would have been easier if Jett had concentrated on matched couples; once his influence was gone, they'd have naturally drifted back together. But no, that would have made things too easy for me." The coffee was definitely not working.

"Instead, my pain in the ass half-brother had to work some aversion magic on every unattached person he could find. You can thank him for all those speed dating parties. The jerk."

"So why don't you do that?" Vaeta's question came out of left field.

"What? Speed dating?" My voice rose. "I know you're new, but you've been here long enough to know that's not how I roll."

"Better check the mix on that coffee of yours," Vaeta

warned Terra. "I don't think it's working properly." I heard a snort from the corner where Evian was doing something I couldn't see clearly. "Seems like it makes Lexi cranky."

"There might be another reason," Evian offered. Her connection to the tides made her sensitive to the monthly ebbs and flows of a woman's body.

"Hush up, over there. After all these years, you know I'm not a morning person."

"Well, I think it's a perfectly perfect idea." Vaeta defended herself. "What is the term? One stop shopping."

"If you could find a way to invite the matches for your current client list, you could clear the backlog of first meetings all at once. Maybe not with your normal flair, but still..."

When they wanted to get a rise out of Vaeta, elemental faerie of air, they called her Airy Fairy, or Airhead—this was one of the times when they were off by a country mile. The idea not only had merit but if I could work out the one major detail, it was flat-out genius.

Without thinking, I poured another cup of the doctored coffee and slugged it down black.

"The only snag is finding an efficient way to contact all the matches. It's not like names pop out of my..." Terra narrowed her eyes at what she thought I was about to say. "...hat." I hastily amended the end of the sentence. "I call it my LPS—Love Positioning System—because it works a lot like a GPS. Once it locks on, I can follow it to my client's perfect match. I'm not sure how I could parlay that into a method for inviting people to a lonely hearts party."

"There has to be a way." Evian got up and came over to take the chair next to mine, and the four of us began to throw around ideas.

Charming stamps or envelopes was the current favorite when I came up with a simpler solution.

"Enchanted ink. Flix is always bugging me to get a computer and a printer. I think I can make ink that will only be visible to my client's matches. We'll print fliers and post them all over town. You'll handle the party, right?"

"If it fits into our schedule." Even Terra couldn't keep a straight face for that one.

There's no recipe for enchanted printer ink, so I was in new spell-writing territory and worse, I'd need to test the stuff once I finished.

I dumped out the shopping bag full of ink cartridges printed with the numbers Flix specified in his text message. It's mind-blowing how three colors and black can be combined to create every hue and shade needed in an image, and I think it's a total scam that each brand has its own type of cartridge.

"Okay, here we go. It's got to be a charm. Flix says I can't introduce any potion ingredients into the ink because that will clog the..." I couldn't remember the phrase he'd used. "...ink spewing whatsit."

"Is that an industry standard term?" I stuck my

tongue out at Salem who added, "Intention plus invocation. Concentrate, and this will be easy."

Ten minutes to come up with a proper incantation and another five to prepare myself and speak it was all I needed, and then I tooled off to work on Pinky, my backpack stuffed full of supplies.

Flix was already at my desk with a weird expression on his face. Half smug and half kid in a candy store.

"Where is it?" A folder about the size of a notebook lay on my desk instead of a laptop or worse, a huge monstrosity of a desktop computer. "I thought you'd have it all set up by now."

"It is all set up." He gestured to a new piece of furniture I hadn't noticed. A console table with a shallow, built-in cabinet fit with the rest of the furniture in the room. "The router is in here and so is the printer, see? All the convenience of an updated office and none of the clutter."

He knew me so well.

"Where's the computer, though?"

"Right there," he pointed to my desk and the notebook I'd dismissed earlier. "Check it out." Flipping the cover open, he switched on the notepad computer. "It does everything you'll ever need, works a lot like your phone so it won't be difficult to learn, and is small enough to satisfy your utter contempt for clunky electronics."

Fingers running over the screen, he pulled up the various apps he'd already installed and showed me how, with a few flicks, I could do everything I currently did on paper.

"Everything syncs to your phone, too." Great, I could become one of those zombie people always staring at their phones. Still, I wasn't about to rain on his parade and tell him I had no intention of giving up my planner anytime soon.

"Thank you; this is way better than anything I could have imagined." And it was. My office looked nearly the same as always, and now he would stop bugging me. Maybe. I hoped.

"Did you do the ink?" His hair was platinum today, his eyes a clear powder blue, and his smile wider than I'd seen it in a while.

"Yep, got it right here. Now what?" I looked skeptically at all the buttons and settings and lights I'd probably somehow scramble and turn a blinking, angry red. It's not like I don't know how to use a printer, it's just that I have a tendency to screw them up beyond repair.

"Leave this part to me." Flix pulled open a door I would have needed a map and a flashlight to find and replaced the ink cartridges with the enchanted ones from the bag. "There, they're all loaded up, and we're good to go."

"Now, where's the program to design the fliers?" Several little icons covered the screen, and I had no idea what half of them were—not even the ones Flix had shown me earlier.

Leaning over my shoulder, Flix tapped a blue box.

"This is the desktop publishing software. I already set up a sheet with some dummy text. If you don't like what I've done, all you need to do is change it to say what you want."

Easy enough. I couldn't see a thing I wanted to change.

"This is such a genius plan, if I do say so myself." With the godmothers' lonely hearts party idea serving as divine inspiration, my matchmaking gears were greased and working at top speed. "Once we decided to host the thing, the big dilemma was how to invite the right guests. If this works, it will be perfect. To anyone already in a happy relationship, the fliers will advertise a church potluck dinner from last month; only those meant for someone on my client list will be able to discern the time and location of the actual party."

That was the idea, anyway. Mixing technology with magic—what can I say, I'm a millennial witch, might as well take advantage of it.

"You're right, Lex, it's genius." Flix automatically stroked my ego. "Let's just make sure we put up enough of them. What do you think?" The printer had silently spit out a piece of electric pink card stock covered with black, shimmering ink. FootSwept's broom and stars logo sparkled across the top of the page, and Flix had picked a delicate script that was both romantic and easy to read.

"Hey, you two," the cheerful voice of Mona Katz startled me nearly out of my skin. A former client turned friend—100% unique in that description, Mona had wiggled her way into my heart. Smart, independent, and driven, her personality reminded me of the Energizer bunny; she just kept going, no matter what.

With blond hair hanging in loose waves over tanned shoulders, eyes bright and sparkling, Mona's good mood was contagious, and one of the things I appreciated most about her.

Plus, the man I'd set her up with happened to be a friend of Kin's, and since Kin was my first and only long-term relationship, I'd never been in a position to need "couple friends" before. Having friends at all was sort of new to me, and the "couple" part was a milestone I'd aspired to but never really thought I'd achieve.

"How's it going, Mona?" Flix flashed her a smile that would have made most women turn into a puddle on the floor, but she was used to it by now and too happy with Mark to give him a second glance. I couldn't tell if that irritated Flix or impressed him, but he returned her friendly, proffered hug anyway.

Mona settled into one of the comfortable chairs posi-tioned beneath two windows across from the entrance door and fingered a flier that had fallen from the stack. "Why are you printing an advertisement for a month-old barbecue chicken dinner?" she asked, a puzzled frown spreading across her face.

"Oh, that was just a test," Flix covered quickly, snatching the rest of the pages from the paper tray and making a beeline for the door, "I'll see you both later."

Mona still looked a bit confused, but I knew just the

distraction to make her forget about the incident, "Come out back with me. I just received an assortment of sandals from one of my contacts at Macy's. Want to come stake a claim on a pair of the size sixes?"

"Um, yeah, like I'm going to say no to that," I remembered when Mona had first tiptoed into my office; she'd vehemently opposed the idea of charity and questioned my motives for loaning her anything from the closet. Once I explained that the clothes were for one, basically free (traded for my services), and for two, my way of bringing some of the more apprehensive clients out of their shells and definitely *not* a commentary on my customers' fashion choices, she couldn't get enough. "I was going to ask if you'd mind if I borrowed something for my date with Mark tonight. We're going to the movie in the park, and I want it to be special."

"Of course, anytime. Here, try this on," I handed her a cherry red dress with a hemline so high that even on Mona's petite frame it would show a dangerous amount of leg, "just for fun."

"You should meet us there," Mona said brightly. "Come on; a double date would be fun."

It did sound fun.

"How do you feel about a triple? We were planning to do something with Flix and Carl later."

"Love it. Now, what do you think about this dress?"

I'll spare you the '80's montage of Mona and me trying on umpteen outfits while pop music blared in the background, but an hour later we lay amid a pile of discards, our chests heaving with laughter.

"So tell me more about you and Mark. I never get to pry into my clients' lives after they've ridden off into the sunset. But since we're friends, I'm hoping you won't mind…" I waited for her face to break into yet another grin before continuing, "Can I ask how you were so sure Mark is the one."

I know, you'd expect me to ask a better question than *that*, I mean, how many times has that phrase been uttered over the course of history? Probably some long number with the words *mega* or *giga* inserted somewhere. But can you imagine what an honest answer might mean to a person who has spent years as the impetus for the merging of souls—someone who has always been the cause, but never the target? Now, since I'd fallen in love with Kin, I was even more curious as to how my experience compared.

"Well, it was kind of like Dorothy from The Wizard of Oz—when I met Mark, my world went from black-and-white to Technicolor. I'm not going to say *love at first sight*, exactly, but there was an immediate attraction. The night of Lemon's wedding we went out for coffee, and somewhere through our second order of pie I just *knew*. All of the other men in my past paled in comparison. I think that even if, for some reason, it doesn't work out, I'll still never look back. This would be the relationship to which I compared all future relationships because now I know it's possible to feel this way, and I'd never settle for less."

I was silent for a long moment. "I think I know exactly how you feel. The first time I met Kin, I had this urge to kiss him—like it would have been natural, even though he was a total stranger."

"You totally should have; can you imagine the look on his face? Even if he were a crazy person and didn't find you attractive, it would have been one hell of a story to tell!" Mona giggled.

Our conversation continued in this nature until a thought struck me, out of nowhere, as epiphanies tend to do. I had been fostering this idea that wielding the Bow of Destiny was going to require me to acquire or utilize some previously unbeknown-to-me skill, but wasn't it much more likely that it would amplify the power I already used every day?

Maybe "Fate Weaving" was just a fancy way of describing the action of matching two people whose destinies were intertwined. I'd watched multiple outcomes of the same person's fate; seen what might happen when mates are ripped apart—and knew there were other forces out there intending to do just that.

What if Cupid's arrow reinforced fate's hold; amplified the connection between two people to ensure the longevity of the relationship and the most positive outcome? I was sure there was a much more complicated explanation, and a healthy dose of nuance thrown in for maximum effect, but I felt certain my conclusions were at least partially correct.

I still wasn't keen on shooting people in the heart with a pointy object, though.

Then again, I'd had that vision of shooting Joshua Owens which didn't fit in with this theory at all. Amplifying his current emotional picture seemed counter-intuitive to getting him happily matched. I've always assumed there were larger forces at work in my life. Something pushing the right people into my office at the right time.

None of my problem clients had ever presented a challenge like Joshua, though. Maybe he was a sign that my work was taking a new turn and the bow would be a bigger part of things from now on. No use speculating while it was still in pieces, though.

Right in the middle of pulling a cocktail dress with a flippy skirt over my head, my LPS flared to life along with that feeling of compulsion I'd occasionally been having ever since my powers kicked into high gear.

The last time I'd felt this way the god's bounty hunter had been tossing matches at me in order to get my attention. It had worked, but not quite so well as the sword she'd pointed at my throat.

Still, I could not resist the urge. Someone needed me and it couldn't wait.

Scoff if you will, but love is important. It's vital, really. Sure, there's a scientific explanation for why the world goes around, but if you ask me, the force that set it spinning in the first place didn't have anything to do with big bangs. Love drives creativity, it's the basis for books, and songs and poetry and art. It's important, I tell you.

"Mona, I've just realized I'm terribly late for an appointment. Do you mind if I give you a call later?"

"No, not at all. I can hang these dresses back up and lock the door behind me if you like." Mona offered.

"Don't worry about cleaning up, but please stay and finish deciding on your outfit for tonight. Anything you want." I left Mona drooling over a rack of handbags and raced away on Pinky without giving the enchanted ink still installed in Flix's printer a second thought.

CHAPTER

ELEVEN

"Lexi? Is that you?" Mona's cheerful voice thankfully interrupted an ongoing conversation about some boringly technical aspect of the big block Chevy motor. I'd tuned out as much as I could, but there seemed no end to the topic. Under most circumstances, I could count on Flix to provide a certain level of relief from entirely male-dominated conversation. Except when the subject turned to cars—then it was only *my* eyes glazing over.

"Hey, there you are." I welcomed the female company, and since Mona and her boyfriend, Mark, were still carrying folding chairs, I assumed they'd just been running late for Tidewater Park's weekly open-air classic movie night.

I'd been late myself, since the couple I'd been compelled to match had not only been all the way across town, but they also presented a challenge requiring me to take extreme measures. I was sure their insurance would cover the fender bender Id caused.

Tonight's offering was one of my all-time favorites starring Jerry Lewis in The Nutty Professor. "We've got popcorn and drinks," I picked a spear of grass from Mona's hair, and she blushed a pretty pink.

"We'd love to." Mona happily plunked her chair down next to mine and chose a drink from the cooler. "Sorry we're late, it's been a long day. Six tier wedding cake with an outdoor theme." She flexed fingers that had spent the afternoon squeezing an icing bag and sighed.

"Outdoor?" I tried to picture what that might entail and came up dry.

"The bride and groom topper was a couple in a sleeping bag. I had to make a tent out of fondant, and then iced the entire first tier to look like grass. First time I ever made a trout out of sugar."

"Tell me you have photos." Mona keyed them up and handed me her phone. Despite the rustic sound of it, she'd managed to create an elegant cake. "How did you get the sides on that third layer to look like birch bark?" It was so realistic you could see the pale yellow on the back of the places where the bark peeled artistically into curls. Uncanny.

"Icing sheets and edible ink."

"You have a real gift." Mona's cheeks pinked again. "I mean it; this is just fantastic. You've made a few cakes for my aunts, haven't you?" Aunts was the easiest explanation to give outsiders since the faeries certainly didn't resemble mothers. " Are they treating you well?" I couldn't come right out and ask if they'd done anything blatantly magical in front of Mona, but at least I could gauge how well the godmothers were passing for normal humans.

Mona didn't skip a beat, "They're fantastic. Some of the stuff they come up with is just epic. Did you know they rented ten hot air balloons for a wedding last week? All the guests got rides, and it was spectacular. They're certainly creating a buzz around the industry."

I bet. At least Mona didn't seem to think anything was amiss.

"Oh, by the way," Mona piped up before I inadvertently cut her off.

"Ouch!" My body jerked in response to the painful sensation of Kin's fingers tensing around mine. "Kin, that hurts. What's..." Sweat broke out on his palms, and when I turned to look, his face had gone sheet white. "What's wrong?"

Another spasm convulsed through his hand, and I yelped again.

"I don't feel good." He panted into my ear. "It hurts."

"Flix, something is wrong with Kin?"

"Got my own problem going on at the moment," came his terse reply. When I leaned forward to get a better look, I realized Carl was also a target of whatever had hit Kin.

Oh, no, not again. Why couldn't the miserable twit just come after *me*; I was the reason Flix lashed out at Jett, though if he'd stayed out of my business, he wouldn't have been banished in the first place. He'd had no right to the bow—he wasn't a Fate Weaver and as such couldn't be allowed to get his hands on it. Jett had blatantly stated he'd like nothing more than to suck all the love out of the world, and he'd use our father's tool to do it if he got the chance.

"What's happening? Do you think someone spiked the drinks," and Mona spiked hers, too, literally, into the air. Like it happened by reflex, she lobbed the bottle away from her without paying too much attention where it went. I heard a startled exclamation in the distance but didn't have time to worry about possible repercussions.

I pried Kin's fingers away from mine and wondered why Flix's wards weren't working. After the last incident, he'd insisted on protecting both his man and mine.

What on earth was Serena trying to accomplish? First information, and now a blatant attack? Salem had been very clear that if a witch tried to use magical means against someone warded with Fae magic, all she'd get was her own spell returned threefold.

It made no sense, but then again, it was Serena we were talking about.

"Probably a bad reaction to their workout smoothie. Stay here. I'll get them some Pepto or something." I ordered Mona. "Flix, why don't you come with me?"

"Shouldn't we take them to the ER?" I was going to have to come up with something to tell Mona, but for now, the best I could do was take care of the source of the problem. Explanations could wait until I had time to do them justice. A hundred years ought to be long enough.

"Let's try over the counter, first. We'll be right back."

In the dim glow from the movie screen, we picked our

way around the grassy hill dotted with clusters of people in lawn chairs or lounging on blankets. The mingled scents of insect repellent and movie-time snacks covered up the one odor I was hoping to detect: the overpowering perfume Serena habitually bathed in.

Flix and I made our way toward the screen and then reversed to circle back behind where our party of four still waited, having detected no sign of the scrawny witch we knew must be at the heart of the attack.

Shadows leapt from the handful of flame I conjured once we were far enough away from the crowd, making it harder to focus rather than easier and I quickly turned down the intensity to a low glow. The sound of moaning is what led us to a fetal-positioned Serena, who cringed even more at the sight of us.

"What did you do to me? It's like fire in my blood. Make it stop."

"I didn't do anything to you. You're the one tossing nasty magic at people under Fae protection; it shouldn't come as a shock when it bounces back. Harm none, ring any bells?"

Serena growled. "All I was doing was eavesdropping, I didn't do any spells, for Hecate's sake."

"She's telling the truth." Flix muttered through clenched teeth, "You deal with her; I'll cause a scene we can't afford."

Flix's hand landed on my shoulder for a hard squeeze; then he was gone.

Before I could blink, Serena yelled at the top of her

lungs, "Lexi Balefire is trying to kill me," changing tactics and attempting to call attention to herself—and me. My hastily-erected barrier dropped to the ground around us with an audible thud, and Serena hissed in outrage. Fortunately, the enclosure had absorbed her screaming, and every person close enough to have heard the ruckus remained focused on the film.

"Who are you to talk to me about harming none?" The gawky witch uncurled from her protective position and gracelessly regained her footing. I had to give it to her; the girl didn't give up. In the wan light thrown by my witch-fire, I could see that Serena had become even more gaunt over the last few weeks if that was possible—she'd been little more than skin and bones before. "You attacked me." Her voice rose to a squeak.

"I did not. I didn't even know you were there until you went after Kin. This is on you, and it was the worst move you could have made, Swampgrass. If anything happens to him, the only thing they'll find is the slime stain you leave behind." The witchfire in my hand went black for an instant, and Serena's beady eyes registered shock. Her momentary loss of self-control let something else slip, and I heard Kin's voice coming from somewhere on her body.

"...a weird cramp, it just cut off like someone flicked a switch. I feel like I ran a triathlon."

"You didn't cast any spells? Care to revise that statement?"

"It was just an amplification charm so I could hear if

you said anything about Jett. It wasn't hurting anyone." Not a nice thing to do, but not super aggressive, either. For once, the pain she caused hadn't been intentional.

"Kin is under Fae protection, so you'd better steer clear of him from now on."

"Get that over-moussed Fae to help me find Jett, and I'll leave you alone forever!" Serena wailed, her face screwed into one of the rawest, honest expressions of pain I'd ever seen on a person. "Jett needs to know about..." she shook her head and started again. "I have to find him, and I can't get a single faerie to help. What a bunch of jerks."

"He won't do it, Serena." Well, that wasn't true, Flix would be happy to send her along to her doom if it wouldn't have weighed so heavy on my conscience. I can't stand Serena Snodgrass, but I won't be responsible for anything that might end in her death. Sympathy for her spilled across my emotions and, apparently across my face, because when she saw my expression, Serena's turned bitter. Well, more bitter, anyway.

"I hate you, Lexi Balefire."

"Right back at you." Sensing all the fight was gone out of her for the moment, I dropped the silencing bubble. Those things take a lot of energy to maintain. "Stay away from Kin and do yourself a favor. Forget about Jett. He's not worth it."

A burst of loud static from the speakers near the movie screen distracted me for a few seconds, and when I turned back, Serena was gone.

• • •

"I'm going to have to start bottling this stuff." Terra poured a second dose of her famous tonic and handed it to Carl, who wrinkled his nose at the smell. If no one had been looking, I'm sure he would have found a way to get rid of the cup's contents that didn't involve any of the liquid touching his tongue. Nasty stuff, but it packed a revitalizing punch. On second thought, bottling it wasn't such a bad idea.

"What kind of kick-butt wards did you put on Kin that a simple charm would trigger that kind of backlash?" I chose an apple slice and a wedge of cheddar from the platter in the center of the table.

"I didn't..." Flix pursed his lips thoughtfully. "Just the standard repel and redirect like you asked. The worst that should have happened was her spell bouncing back on her."

The vigorous nods of agreement from the four sisters were unnecessary; Flix spoke the truth not only because he was mostly bound by Fae law to do so, but also because there was no reason to lie.

"Repel and redirect? This was my fault, then." Terra tossed an apologetic look in Flix's direction and then fixed her gaze on me. "I overheard you talking to Salem, and I knew you wouldn't ask me for help. So...I added my protection into the mix. Unfortunately, I went with a variation, and I guess the different energies must have generated a feedback loop when Serena's intentions triggered them."

Despite Carl not looking too happy with him, Flix

couldn't hold back a smirk. "Must have hit her like a ten-ton gargoyle on a rampage."

"You put some whammy on me without even asking?" Carl and Flix stepped outside to have an earnest conversation that involved a lot of hand gestures and dirty looks while the rest of us failed miserably at trying not to watch. They kissed and made up, finally, but anyone with eyes could see the hint of resentment still simmering under Carl's placid demeanor.

Even the faeries picked up on it, and they often miss the finer emotional strokes.

"You know what we need? A game night," Soleil bounced in place and even though I know he loves me, the sight of a well-proportioned, absolutely gorgeous hunk of Fae jiggling around in front of Kin was enough to make his eyes glaze over. I'd wonder about his testosterone levels if it didn't.

"A what?"

"You're drooling, Sweetie." I nudged his mouth closed with my index finger. How is it a man can go from being reasonably suave, with a command of the English language, to a gibbering, monosyllabic mouth-breather at the mere sight of a little jiggling flesh?

"You in?" I said to Flix. As the reigning champion from our last game night, he had a title to defend. "It's too late tonight, but Kin doesn't have a gig this weekend, so we'll plan it for Saturday—make a night of it."

"Oh, I'm in, and you're going down, Balefire."

TWELVE

K in wanted to stay, but I convinced him to go home. I had a trip to make to the past, and I wanted to get it done without any more drama than we'd already had for one night.

It had taken just under a week for the ring to recharge this time. After each trip to the past, the carvings on the band altered slightly. Tonight, two of the circles had filled in as though marked off a list and another shimmed with an inner fire.

The crossed out spaces reminded me of those exams we took in school where you had to use a number two pencil to fill in an oval for each answer. I hated those tests. Unless you sharpen your pencil every two minutes, there's no way to stay inside the lines.

"Salem." I called to him with both voice and mind, "It's go time." He'd meet me in the sanctum, which lately he'd taken to calling my *laboratory* with a distinctly Frankensteinian pronunciation.

"I'm right here," he announced as the fireplace closed behind me. "I've been waiting for you. I've completed my *mission*." I wanted to ask if his virtue was still intact, but I didn't dare.

"And, did you learn anything?"

"I did. Big news and you're going to want to sit down for it." Since I already was, I gave him the circling hand wave to indicate he should continue—well, that and a smirk.

"Serena's pregnant," and so was the pause he took after dropping that bombshell on me.

"She's what now?" It was almost too much to contemplate.

"Knocked up. With child. Preggers. Explains why she's going to some lengths to get what she wants. There was some dark magic brewing, and she's dead serious about finding Jett."

"Wow! That's all I can...I can't wrap my head around it."

"You should also know that I'm done. Do you hear me? I will not be pimped out ever again. Do you know that horrible cat of hers, Morana, wanted to do it *in human form*? It's disgusting, Lexi, and you're lucky I got away before she started trying to undress me. I refuse to go back."

So many ewws. "Um, I'm sorry?" What was I supposed to say to that? "You're off the hook if that makes you feel any better, and I'll buy you a tuna steak," I added when he continued to frown and glare at me. What more could I say? My head was spinning, and I needed a minute to process his news. Not that I had a minute right then.

Refocus, Lexi. I shook a mental finger at myself.

But that baby is going to be related to you. Myself answered back.

You shut up right now.

"Didn't you hear me say it's go time? Let's get to it; it'll make you feel better," and take my mind off other things before I lose it down the rabbit hole to Wonderland. Or worse, Blunderland.

"Okay, he sighed. But let's call it an even dozen tuna steaks. I've got the checklist." He picked up a notepad from the ottoman in front of him, and then cast a critical eye over my clothes. I felt like a teenager trying on prom dresses in front of her dad. "Sneakers? After last time? Go back and get a pair of boots and not the ones with heels. Something sturdy."

"I'm not going to trip over a branch every time." Unimpressed by my superior logic, he did the finger whirl that meant I should turn around and do what he said. "You're not the boss of me," I muttered on my way back through the fireplace.

When I returned wearing boots, jeans, and several light layers, he grinned his approval.

"You've got the compass?"

I pulled it out of the neck of my shirt along with the Stone of Blood. Salem gave me an eloquently-raised brow when he saw them both dangling from my fingers.

"Family heirloom." Having seen my great-grandmother sporting the pendant, I'd reconsidered my feelings about being connected to my past. My mother had only been the most recent bearer in a long line of them, and while she deserved no respect, I would not dishonor the Balefire name by refusing to wear the stone.

"This should be a piece of crab cake."

"Yuck. That's not right at all." And now I had a weird mental image. Thanks.

"It's cake. Works for me." Salem licked his lips with a dreamy expression at the thought.

"Besides, you just jinxed me."

"Did not." He retorted.

Before we devolved to a grade school level did not-did too fight, I held up a hand. "Enough. I'm going to go now."

Filling my thoughts with the image of living gold, I twisted the ring and let myself sink into the familiar feeling of being tugged along through the dimensional passageways. Threads of time wove around me, curling into tendrils of nothing if I reached my fingers toward them.

I landed in a white whirlwind of stinging snow and cold that felt like a monster biting at my bones. Blizzard conditions caught my breath almost before it could leave my lips and flung it back down my throat in a choking wall of frigid air. The sweatshirt tied around my waist added very little extra heat to the layers of clothing I already wore. I thanked my lucky stars that Salem had made me put on boots and that he'd stuffed a pair of gloves into the pocket of my hoodie. I should have listened when he suggested a winter coat, the dirty minx.

The sound of my teeth chattering disguised the ping

when the compass homed in on what I'd come here to find, and I could barely see it past the ice forming on my lashes. If the gold was more than a five-minute walk from here, I doubted I would make it. If I froze to death, what would happen to my body? And why hadn't I considered that particular question before I let myself get drawn into this situation? Salem tried to warn me about being prepared, and I'd let the last two trips blind me to the chance of bad weather.

Still, if my luck held, and I was, once again, in the space where Clara would one day stand frozen, I was close enough to make it to the house if I hurried. I couldn't see anything through the blinding storm, but I set off for where the compass pointed.

Five minutes felt like an hour while I struggled through the cold and a series of *what if* thoughts. *What if* the gold wasn't inside the house? *What if* I couldn't open the door when I got there? *What if?*

Each question fell away as I put one foot in front of the other and by the time I slammed into the shingled wall, I had stopped thinking altogether. The only thing keeping me going was the need to find warmth.

No one spared me a glance as I stumbled inside on a drift of snow and wind, slamming the door behind me. My feet carried me along the familiar path to the fireplace without me providing them any direction, which was good because I was long past thinking at that point. The Balefire danced blue and green and yellow while I thrust my hands toward her brilliant flame. For the first time, I knew how a flower felt when it bent its face toward the sun.

If you're going to thaw out in front of a fireplace, by all means, choose a magical one. Only a few scant minutes passed before I stopped shaking like a leaf and tuned into my surroundings well enough to get an idea of when I was.

"Clara, you're too young yet to understand this." I recognized my grandmother, mainly because she looked just as I had at her age, which I guessed to be around thirteen, though I couldn't tell if she had been Awakened yet or not. Plus, the name Clara tipped me off. She sat cross-legged at the edge of the fireplace, so close to me I could see the flecks of amber in her green eyes, which lost their sparkle at the other girl's slight.

"Stop treating me like a child. You're my sister, not my mother, Margaret; I'm nearly old enough to get married myself." Whoa, how times have changed. I knew Clara had been around two hundred and fifty years old at the time she turned to stone, and that meant I had just popped into the eighteenth century when the normal human life expectancy was several decades shorter than in my time. People married younger out of necessity.

Margaret? I had a great aunt named Margaret, and no one had ever told me? Was she dead? And if she wasn't, why hadn't she come looking for me a long time ago?

Still, there was something about the girl that niggled at my memory. The twist of her head or the shape of her jaw. I couldn't put my finger on it.

"Like anyone would want to marry *you*," Margaret replied with a sneer.

Clara's fingers strayed to the Balefire, and I watched in astonishment as she lifted one of the flames into her hand and flicked her finger. It morphed into a palm-sized dragon and let out a breath of fire before turning in a circle, lying down and disappearing. If she still hadn't come into her powers, Clara was more gifted than I had even guessed.

"My future husband is going to be gentle and sweet like Daddy was, not a freak like that *God* you love so much."

"Being sweet and gentle was what got Daddy killed, Clara. You'd be better off with someone you won't outlive. Trust me on that one."

"Oh, Mag. Don't talk about him like that. He was twice the man Cupid will ever be."

"You don't know what you're talking about, Clara," Mag replied in a tone that indicated they'd had variations of the same conversation more than once.

Mag? The Mudwitch? The same woman who had threatened to turn me into a modern-day Cinderella and then given me the ring that had brought me to this exact place and time. That Mag? Now that I knew where to look for it, I could see the resemblance between this fresh-faced teen and the fluffy-haired woman who reminded me of a grandmother and acted like a snake.

Well, isn't that just peachy? Our whole conversation on the night she'd caught me doing a bit of breaking and entering into her cottage came back to me. The way she assumed I was Sylvana, and that I'd come to make trouble; the look in her eyes when she realized I wasn't; and the way she'd pressed the ring into my hand and bade me hide it away.

Even if I hadn't known who she was at the time, it seemed as though she'd tried to help me. Still, I couldn't help feeling a bit hurt that she'd made no effort to let me in on our shared heritage. Hadn't she realized I might need some guidance? Or at least a history lesson?

Then again, what had she earned for her trouble? Sylvana could easily have been the one to go back and blast that charming little homage to Victoriana right off the roots that made up its foundation.

Now I felt even worse. When I got back, I vowed to find Mag and make sure she was all right. If I got some answers in the process, all the better.

I'd pulled the compass back out, but hardly had time to look at it when someone started banging on the front door. What idiot would be out traveling on a night like this? You know, besides me.

Tempest emerged from the kitchen, and I was surprised by the change in her. She looked older and more tired than she should, and I wondered how old she'd been when she'd met Kenneth. The family tree listed on the first pages of the Grimoire handed down to me didn't include dates, and as such had been perused with only moderate curiosity. It hadn't occurred to me that any of them were still kicking around, and since nobody had ever come to call, I'd assumed I'd been correct.

Nothing could have prepared me for who was on the other side of that door when it opened. Nothing.

No weary traveler lost in the storm, no neighbor who needed healing or help with birthing a baby; instead, it was my father's face that appeared out of the swirling flakes and howling wind. What was he doing here? Again.

Had the mere mention of his name drawn him to this place, or had he kept as close an eye on the Balefire witches as Clara had inferred?

A long wool coat draped over broad shoulders, and he wore a top hat rakishly pulled low over one eye as he stepped inside like he had a right to be there. My eyes searched his face for a shred of any trait we shared. Intuitive knowledge of lovers was one thing, but it would have been nice to see something physical that I could point to and say, *I get that from my dad.*

All I saw was arrogance, and I'm not that girl. I guess that's the difference between being a God and being half of one.

Old enough to feel the aura of magnetism he wore like a second skin, Mag cast an appreciative eye over the man who took up too much space in the room. Clara, younger by a good seven or eight years, merely stared at him with suspicion while I wrestled with similar feelings.

The abandoned child inside me insisted that this was Father, Daddy, someone I should want to know and who should want to know me. Family. Sometimes that word is more a curse than a blessing. Every little girl without a father yearns for that feeling of safety found only in the strong arms of the one man who, by reason of her birth, should be committed to keeping her safe. There are a lot of us who will forever be denied the pleasure. I needed to separate myself from that kind of thinking and see him for who he was. A god who didn't play by human rules.

"Mother?" A wealth of questions threaded through Clara's voice.

"I'm fine," Tempest reassured her daughter, but the look she gave Cupid was full of fire. "Come, you must be frozen, let me get you a hot drink." His eyes traveled over her with a speculation I couldn't define because it had more to it than sexual interest. "Girls, you'll stay here." Her tone brooked no refusal, but it didn't apply to me and, forgetting my mission, I followed.

"What are you doing here? I told you, the answer is no. Always no."

"You're still a young woman." Again his gaze took her in, "Relatively. I thought you might feel the need for some...masculine interaction."

"My husband is still fresh in his grave, and I'd not disrespect his memory by taking up with another man so soon. And should I feel such a need, t'would never be with the likes of you."

Cupid's eyes widened, then narrowed. I got the impression his thoughts were running along the lines of, *you don't want to get with all of this?*

Clearly, the answer was no, and he wasn't used to a

woman who didn't trip over her panties trying to jump into bed with him. If the whole thing didn't make me feel icky, I'd have laughed myself into a heap on the floor. The look on his face was priceless. I shook my head at the idea that someone who was clearly well-versed at playing the game could also incite lifelong love and passion, and bring true soul mates together. It didn't look to me like Father had a true love of his own, and that bit of information simply smacked of irony.

"Mother, is everything all right?" Clara appeared in the doorway, her face a study in dark worry.

"I'm fine, Clara. Go back to your sister. Our guest was just leaving."

"Think carefully about your decision. My patience is not endless. One of these days, you'll miss your last chance with me." Hah, that was about as truthful coming from him as it was from those robotic telemarketing calls that assure you there's nothing wrong with your credit, but this is your last shot at reducing your interest rate.

Tempest's lips twisted in an attempt to hold back a smirk. "Thank you for the warning."

The second the door closed behind him, Margaret burst out, "Did you see how handsome he was?"

"Handsome on the surface, but underneath there's darkness and light in equal measure without enough conscience to choose between them."

Mag sniffed at Clara's observation, almost ridiculous in its astuteness, considering how young she was then. "What did he want?"

"He wanted Mother."

"She ought to have said yes; get us out of this godforsaken town and back to Ireland where we belong. Someday, I'll get to see it, and London and Rome, too."

"What about us? You'd just leave us behind?"

Mag considered Clara's question with the jaded look of superiority every teenager since the beginning of time has learned to cultivate. I think it's part of puberty; something in our DNA—perhaps the equivalent of whatever instinct prompts all animals to venture out on their own once they're capable of surviving without a parent's care. Or maybe it's just the opposite; preparation for the inevitable loss a mother feels when her children are no longer dependent. Irritate her well and good so when you're gone relief takes the place of grief.

Fascinated as I was, it was time to get the living gold before the ring called me back and I lost my chance. The compass needle swung wildly, and for long enough that I began to worry before it finally pointed toward the fireplace. It took under a minute to verify there was no gold on this side, and I realized I would have to enter the room behind the Balefire. The room that would one day become my sanctum.

Easier said than done. When I reached into the flame for the handle to trigger the door mechanism, I came up with nothing more than another dilemma. Here I was, unable to ask how to enter the workshop, and with all the drama going on, I'd spent way too much time indulging my curiosity about my father and my family.

What was I supposed to do now? A lot was riding on this, and I had let myself become distracted.

Two options presented themselves. The first was to go outside and see if there was a second entrance. Not very appealing given the current weather conditions. Option number two it was. The Balefire licked soft tongues of cool flame against my face when I thrust my head and shoulders into the fireplace. Hands outstretched, I expected to encounter the solid rock that made up the back wall. Instead, I overbalanced and fell right through into the darkened workshop.

Any witch worth her salt can conjure enough flame to light her way, and that is exactly what I did. I'd have liked to dawdle and gawk at the changes from the sanctum I remembered, but I'd wasted enough time already, so I followed the compass and found a handful of nuggets tossed carelessly into a box on one of the shelves.

The compass did its thing just in time for me to be yanked back to the present with the familiar tugging sensation and a popping noise in my head.

THIRTEEN

This time, once I'd rematerialized in the sanctum, I wasted no time forging the living gold and repairing the Bow of Destiny. Once it was tucked back away, another damaged section having been seamlessly melded back together, I turned to Salem and described what I'd witnessed with as much detail as I could remember. His memory was significantly better than mine, so I knew he'd be able to recall all the fine points long after I'd forgotten them.

"I thought Mag was a crazy old coot, and maybe she is, but she's part of my family, and I'm worried about her. I'm pretty sure she wasn't inside the cottage when it got blown to smithereens, but she might still be in danger. And she did give me the ring, which turned out to be just what I needed. I don't think she's dark. I'm starting to think Sylvana is the only wicked one of the bunch. Speaking of which, I half wonder if she wasn't the one who tried to blow Mag up in the first place. There was some bad blood between the two of them."

When I'm worried, I tend to ramble.

"Is there anyone Sylvana gets along with?"

"Doesn't look like it." The thought saddened me, if I'm being honest. If I'm being more honest, it made me a little angry. My mother had all the things I never did, and didn't appreciate any of them. "But Mag is her family, too," I continued bitterly, "not that I'm surprised at her lack of loyalty."

"Why would she go after a harmless old witch like Mag? I can't see any purpose to it. It doesn't seem likely, and who knows how many other enemies she has—I mean, you don't wind up living in the Fringe for no reason." Salem asked the question I'd already begun to ponder. "Once again, it would be helpful to have more information."

"That's becoming our motto, isn't it?" I paced back and forth, my brain working at top speed. "Maybe there's a way to learn *all* the family secrets. From the one person who knows each and every one—Clara. The dream I had the other night got me thinking. If the Balefire has healing properties and can liquefy living gold, maybe it would also turn Clara back to flesh and bone."

"You might be on to something there. Her body is immune to the flame just like yours, so she wouldn't be harmed even if it doesn't work."

I looked from Salem to the light of the Balefire burning in the hearth. "You want to try it?"

· · ·

"Do you think we have enough?" I placed a crown of woven sticks on Clara's head and yawned. Salem and I had been up all night between the trip to the past and planning our current escapade. At some point, I'd need a nap, and soon.

Between us, we'd emptied the back yard of every dried branch we could find before clearing most of the half-acre patch of woods behind where Clara stood. The Internet says no witches were ever burned in this country, but seeing a human figure in the middle of a thigh-high pile of brush gave me a pang anyhow.

Sacrificing the rosebush growing at her feet caused me another rough moment. Ever since my first trip back in time, I'd come to equate the flowers with my grandmother. Velvety flowers with thorns protective enough to draw blood when they needed to. Hopefully, they'd be unnecessary before long.

Hands on his hips, Salem surveyed our handiwork. "Seems like it. There's only one way to find out."

I looked at him and cautioned, "Don't laugh, I just have to do this."

To Clara, I said, "Um, I don't know if you can hear me, but we're going to try something to see if we can bring you back. It won't hurt. I don't think. So you know, if you can hear me, what I'm doing, it was done out of love, okay?"

I selected a stick as long as my arm and trekked back into the house to introduce the dry wood to the Balefire, then asked Evian for her assistance before carrying the merrily-burning torch back to where Salem waited.

"What's she doing here?" He asked. "This is witch business."

"Making sure we don't start a forest fire." I'd already asked her to help Vaeta make the air thick enough to hide our activities from the neighborhood.

"Should I say a spell of some sort?" I asked once the faeries were gone.

Even if this worked, my grandmother would not come back to life screaming, but I couldn't seem to shake the mental image. I must have watched too many movies and TV shows about torching witches.

"Infuse the flame with your intention. We're in uncharted territory trying to remove a curse that originated from combining two spells. I'd say trust your instincts." Salem instructed.

"What if I don't have any?"

He shrugged. "Then I guess you'll just have to light it up and see what happens."

Sounded simple. Wasn't.

Following my instincts, as directed, I closed my eyes and breathed into the working. Inside the barriers of air and water, the stilled breeze pillowed sound and sucked at my eardrums. I cast my awareness out like fingers to rifle over the hardened stone and anchored its texture in my mind for a weightless moment of anticipation. My imagination turned the stone to soft and yielding skin perfumed with herbs and oils and love. Pressure built alongside the need to thrust the burning brand into fuel waiting for the Balefire's touch and in the moment when the first blue flame licked the first hungry branch, I became the fire.

Heal. Purify. Devour. I knew nothing else but those desires until my heated tongue tasted stone and I searched the surface for that which might require my healing touch. Finding none, I withdrew to finish my feast among the tender morsels piled upon the ground. There was no work for me there, only an offering—a meal where I could eat my fill and be sated.

"Lexi!" Salem's voice sounded frantic when it finally penetrated the buzzing in my ears. "Lexi!"

"I'm okay." I thought I was, anyway. "What happened?" It felt like I'd been on a three-day bender with a gallon bottle of Twinkleberry wine.

"Why don't you tell me?"

I opened my eyes to see why his voice sounded so shaky and found myself sprawled half on the ground and half in his arms. I did a mental catalog of my body to see if anything hurt and found that I felt wonderful. No, this was no Twinkleberry hangover.

Bit by bit, my memory returned.

"It didn't work, did it?" I scrambled up to confront the statue still standing amid a ring of smoking embers. While I watched, the badly singed rosebush lifted from the ashes and bloomed Phoenix-like in the space of seconds. In another minute, all evidence of my efforts had been erased.

"Were you trying to scare my last life out of me?" Salem demanded.

"Not intentionally. I remember becoming part of the Balefire for a minute there, and that's about it. Doesn't seem like a big deal."

Salem's mouth dropped open. "Not a big deal?" He snapped it closed again and stalked away, ignoring all my efforts to get him to tell me what had happened.

Whatever it was, I felt fine now. Better than fine. Other than the disappointment of not having broken the spell on my grandmother, that is.

"So now we're back to square one. I'd better go back to the Fringe and see if I can find Mag. I've been wondering something, Salem."

"What's that?"

"Why does Mag look so much older than Clara? She's only a few years Clara's senior. It doesn't make sense."

"That's a question you'll have to ask her yourself. Using strong magic for long periods of time could do it. There are spells that pull from the elements, and there are some that require a witch's essence. Do too many of the latter, and you could turn to dust." He explained.

"What kinds of spells? Like dark magic?"

"Some. Just as many that are light, though. You don't usually see a witch age like that unless she's been in the trenches for a long time. Light and darkness are always in a pitched battle. Most of it plays out in the day-to-day events—the choices we make, the love we find, the hurts we cause."

"Sure, but what does that have to do with my aunt's condition?" I said.

"Some are called to fight in other ways. It may be that Mag was chosen. Or, it may be any one of a dozen other reasons.

Let me go to the Fringe for you. I can track down Mag's familiar. We have sort of a network. Just don't get too used to it; I'm starting to feel a little like an errand boy. Or a bloodhound." He muttered something about fish under his breath, and I ignored it.

"Hurry back. I'm worried, and I won't sleep knowing you're out there."

Salem's face softened, "Yes, boss." He mocked lightly as he flitted into cat form and trotted away.

Once he was out of sight, and the faeries had taken down the barrier, I was alone in the clearing with Clara.

"I'm sorry. I don't know how to help you, but I won't give up. Not ever." Heady, the scent of roses filled the air, and when I reached to caress a tender petal, I nicked my finger on a thorn. Why did that keep happening? Every single time.

As the drop of blood spilled down on my grandmother's stone foot and the rose bush rustled, I wondered if it was her way of communicating her displeasure. What would I be waking if I succeeded? The gentle girl I'd seen in the past or the fierce witch I saw before me now.

I only knew I had to keep trying.

I settled down on Kin's couch, a glass of wine in my hand, and sighed when he started rubbing my feet. If I didn't know better, I'd swear he had magic hands. Things were going well, for once, and I took advantage of the moment of peace to talk about everything I'd learned and the nearly-repaired status of the Bow of Destiny. Kin listened with rapt attention, always eager to learn all he could about the strange new world that had recently opened up to him.

"What is it about the Balefire that makes it so special? It's the source of your power, it's hot enough to melt this living gold, yet I've seen you touch the fire and not come away burned—where did the Balefire come from?" Kin's curiosity was bubbling over, and I realized it was time to tell him the tale Sylvana had told me.

"The Balefire came to us through one of my great-great grandmothers, Esmerelda, a couple of thousand years ago during the Fae Civil Wars—which, by the way, featured the slaughtering of thousands of witches. It reminds me of the plot of Star Wars, with the Unseelie Fae as the dark side, and the Seelie Fae as the light—witches got caught in the crossfire, much like the innocents employed to build the Death Star. The Unseelie wanted to preserve Fae blood lines, and forbade mating with humans, witches, or anything else that wasn't quote-unquote *pure*."

"Your sci-fi nerd is showing."

"Shut up." I gave him a gentle nudge with my foot.

"Of course, near-immortals being told who they were and were not allowed to fornicate or even associate with didn't go over well, and the Seelie rose up against the dark court. Esmerelda's husband, Clarence, was a powerful wizard. He died trying to protect his sister, who was half-Fae, leaving Esmerelda and their small daughter alone and defenseless.

An Unseelie prince by the name of Oberon came looking for them. He fell in love at first sight with Esmerelda, forsaking his family and his princely duties and refusing to harm her. He turned to the light, made Esmerelda immortal, and together they rallied troops to defeat the Unseelie.

Now here's where it gets interesting, at least with regard to the Balefire family history. Esmerelda was one of the most powerful witches of her time, and she created the Balefire as a weapon against the Unseelie court. As long as it burns, no Unseelie may enter our realm. Upon victory, an accord was struck: the witches agreed to guard the Balefire flame, and the Seelie agreed to protect us while in our realm. Hence, every witch has a faerie godmother."

"What happened to Oberon and Esmerelda?" Kin's eyes were wide, and for good reason. It was one hell of a bedtime story.

"That's the same question I asked. So, Oberon became King of the Faeries, with Esmerelda as his Queen, and they knew they would have to return to the Faelands. Esmerelda insisted on raising her daughter, and so they left four Seelie princesses in charge for one Fae year. Time works differently here than it does in Faerie, so they were able to spend one hundred years in this dimension with Esmerelda's daughter, Isabeau. Oberon offered Isabeau immortality, but she refused, requesting a prolonged life instead for all of witchkind, ensuring that if the Balefire line ended, another family would be able to take its place. *She's* the one who made sure this world would always be protected from the black court.

As for the King and Queen, they're still there, ruling over the Faelands, blocked from reentering our realm by the very thing Esmerelda created to save it."

"Wow, that sounds like a fairy tale. Oh, I guess that expression makes more sense now. Every day I find out some new, unbelievable truth. Life with you is never boring, Lexi Balefire."

"I know how you feel and now, to top it all off, it turns out I've had an aunt this whole time. Just add it to the list of *what ifs* I contemplate daily. I hope Salem finds Mag. Even while she was scaring the bejesus out of me, there was this other feeling. Something familiar; I realize now it must have been the blood bond. Witches are meant to recognize their own, especially Balefire witches."

"Why don't I ever hear anything about the Balefire men?" Kin's question didn't surprise me; I'd expected him to get around to asking it at some point.

"Well, I found a few photo albums tucked into a box in

the sanctum and as far as I can tell, no Balefire witch has ever produced a son. Sylvana said her father left when she was a baby, and I've no idea whether he's still alive or not."

Kin was silent for a long moment, "I've been trying not to think about that part. Being outlived by you, I mean. I've always expected to live a normal human lifespan and then meet my maker, so that doesn't bother me so much. But you'll still be young-looking and beautiful when I'm an old man."

"Well, then I guess all the other old men will be jealous of you." I kept my tone light; we were wading into dangerous territory. At least he was saying "will" instead of "would be." I'd take that as an indicator it didn't bother him enough to leave.

Our relationship had moved at light speed, so while in terms of our time together thus far, this conversation was somewhat premature. However, given what we'd been through already—saving his soul with true love's kiss, having almost lost him to Jett's debauchery, and sharing truths that I'd never been able to discuss with another human being—it was a perfectly acceptable line of inquiry.

"I think we just have to live our lives and see what happens. You never know, right? Maybe I'll get turned into a vampire or something, even out the playing field." Kin joked. I decided a tutorial about those who reside in the shadows could wait for another time.

"We'd better get ready, or we'll be late for our reservation." I managed to breathe between the kisses Kin had begun trailing along my neckline during his crack about vampires.

"A few more minutes won't hurt..." he brushed my concerns aside.

"Just a few." I nodded in agreement, losing all will to argue.

Halfway through the day on Saturday, I started to wonder if game night had been a particularly good idea. Ominous noises issued from the backyard, and I had no clue what they meant because all the windows on that side of the house had gone dark. Twice I'd heard raised voices, which was never a good thing, and late in the afternoon, an explosion shook the foundations.

The distinct scent of freshly-turned soil perfumed the air, and I knew that meant Terra was doing some serious revamping of the terrain out back. I just hoped she remembered where the sewer line ran this time; repairing it had been a breeze, but a geyser of grossness isn't something easily forgotten.

Call me a coward if you must, but I holed up in my room with the excuse that I needed to update the RSVPs for the lonely hearts party—which took all of ten minutes and wasn't the least bit urgent. But you have to understand, this was not my first time, and the aforementioned snafu wasn't even the worst we'd ever had. As much fun as faerie game night could be, the setup was always fraught with possible meltdowns. One time we played post-apocalyptic Monopoly because Evian dripped water on Soleil's shoe and the resulting brouhaha got out of hand.

The trick to measuring the level of impending chaos was to listen for one of two things: complete silence or pandemonium. Anything in between those two extremes signaled the all-clear. Of the two, pandemonium was the easiest to deal with, because the term *silent but deadly* has more than one meaning in the Balefire household.

Since the no-arguing-while-party-planning pact was still in effect, the godmothers were having trouble remembering when a fight was allowed, and so they'd been avoiding them altogether. Good for me on a temporary basis, but I'd bet the bank there was tension building up that would eventually blow and make Vesuvius look like a pimple.

Kin says I shouldn't be pessimistic and prattles on about how new habits form in as few as 21 days. Kin has no idea what he's talking about, and I'm considering calling him when the time comes. Let him take care of the fallout for once.

I'm probably not that mean. Probably.

"It's a Candyland/Stratego hybrid with a few more surprises." The door closed so quietly behind Salem I had no idea he was in the room.

"You scared a year off my life. What have I said about sneaking around?"

"Hello. I'm a cat. Silent predator."

"Please, the only prey you're sneaking up on these days is stuffed into storage containers in the refrigerator."

Ignoring his two-toned glare, I returned to the subject at hand. "Candyland and Stratego? Well, that probably explains the explosion. I was hoping for Clue, and ...well, I don't know what would go with Clue. They didn't see you, did they?"

"I'm in one piece with no extra appendages, so I assume I got away unscathed. Nice welcome, by the way. I've been gone for days." Forgetting his human size is bigger than mine, Salem settled on my lap and rubbed his head against my chin.

"Did you find Mag?" He arched his neck like he wanted a scratch under the chin, which I declined. A fur-covered chin is nice to scratch; a naked one feels odd.

"She's alive." At least he hit the headlines first. "I found her familiar and passed along the message that you wanted to talk."

"That's it? You didn't find out what happened or if Aunt Mag was hurt?" I'd started thinking of her that way already—as family.

Rising, Salem stalked toward the end of my bed. "Jinx wasn't especially chatty." That was the last I got out of him because the next minute, he was curled up on the polka-dotted beanbag chair at the end of my bed making kitty snores.

Mag was alive, that was the main thing to remember.

I had time for a soothing bath with lavender and mint oil before Kin showed up. I nearly jumped out of the towel

I still had slung around my midsection when I stepped out of the bathroom to find him lounging on my bed.

"Hey, Babe." He gathered me up for a kiss that made me wonder if we ought to forgo faerie game night and have our own version right here. "Terra says it's game time. Everyone's waiting for you downstairs."

On the way past, I gave Salem a poke. "Game time." His response was a grumbling growl, and he settled deeper into the plush comfort. His loss.

"Whoa. This is...wow!" Pretty much the standard response to seeing what the faeries could do when they wanted to have a little fun. Kin's mouth hung open as he took in the backyard.

Gumdrop mountains rose over the peppermint stick forest and the lollipop woods, and in the distance, I saw smoke rising from the chimney of the peanut brittle house. Talk about a five-year-old child's fantasy coming true.

"Do you smell that?" Kin nudged me with an elbow. "It's the molasses swamp. I wonder if they went with the version that had some kind of plum tree in the center, or the licorice castle. Lord Licorice always gave me the creeps. Not as bad as Grandma Nut, though."

"You really know your Candyland, don't you."

Kin blushed. "I like board games."

"Well, don't worry. We had the earlier edition before they added all the characters in the eighties. It's probably the gingerbread plum tree."

"I'm not the only one who knows the game."

"Just remember, this is the faerie version." I warned. "It's not going to have the same rules and who knows what else they've added into the mix. I did tell them they need to pick a shorter game this time."

"You work too hard; it's good to have a little fun now and then." Flix stepped into the room, closely followed by Carl who wore a similar expression to Kin's. Nervous excitement.

"A little fun does not last a week." I turned to Carl to explain, "The faeries are convinced two games are better than one, so they combined Risk and Monopoly one time."

Frowning, Carl tried to imagine that particular combination.

"We set the record for the longest game night ever." I gave Flix a wicked grin, "And I kicked your butt. I am the queen of game night."

"Before you get fitted for your crown," Terra interrupted, "let me tell you the rules for tonight's festivities."

Again, Salem had been right. We would be playing a mix of Candyland and Stratego, as best I could tell. To reduce competition between us, Terra divided us into teams of two and paired me with Flix. Kin and Soleil, Carl and Evian, and Terra and Vaeta would be playing together.

Each team was assigned a colored flag (already hidden in one of the stops on the game board). The first team to pass through the board, search for and collect any opponents' flag, and reach the finish line would be the winner.

Succumb to one of the many hazards, and your team was out of the running.

"How is that fair? If you hid the flags, you have the obvious edge."

"I will be your game master for the evening." Salem appeared from nowhere. He'd probably cat-footed it in here and then turned to human form at the time calculated to give me the biggest scare. He was mean like that. "In the spirit of fairness and impartiality, I was asked to hide the flags and the bombs. Now, as game master, I will sit here on the deck, warm my face in the sun, enjoy a tuna burger, and watch the rest of you act like children."

He was one to talk, with his constant attempts at making me jump out of my skin.

"Bombs?" Kin mouthed to me from his position next to Soleil, who had poured herself into a pair of skintight yoga pants and was stretching her calves with a determined expression on her face. I grinned, shrugged, and wiggled my eyebrows. Now that he was on the opposing team, I wasn't giving him any pointers.

After Salem had tossed a pair of watermelon-sized dice to determine the playing order, team Sol-Kin stepped up to the starting line. As game master, Salem chose a card for them and shouted out their first move, landing them at the bottom of the rainbow bridge.

On our first turn, Salem drew a card with an ice cube on it. I didn't remember there being any ice in Candyland, but we dutifully moved forward until we turned a corner and the others were out of sight.

"I think that's it." Flix pointed to a marker made from a solid shaft of ice, and we turned down the short trail leading into the designated area where we might find one of the flags. His longer legs put Flix ahead of me, which is why I slammed into his back when he stopped short. "You've got to be kidding me. Is that Don't Break the Ice?"

Sure enough, a small pond lay before us; its surface divided into squares. A giant with a hammer stood on the other side.

"How does this work? Are we the red guy in the center, then?"

Before Flix could answer, the giant boomed. "Step on ice. Don't get wet. Get to other side."

Easy enough, right?

But, no. This was ice. Evian ice. We slid onto a surface that felt like it had been greased with butter and crossed the first three spaces just from the momentum. The giant hammer hit the block in front of us, and it dropped out of sight with a splash. Flix skidded left at the last second and dragged me around with him, the arc of my body sweeping one foot out over the yawning hole before he pulled me to safety.

"Do something." A second hammer blow took out another block, and suddenly, Flix was in danger. Worse, his grip on my arm would take me over the edge with him.

"Skates." I pictured them with as much detail as I could, given the amount of adrenaline coursing through me, and called two pairs from the wall on the back of the garage.

"Nice job." Flix turned the unavoidable slide into a professional-looking hockey stop when the skates materialized on his feet. I, on the other hand, did something that looked a bit like the splits and an attempt at a somersault combined into one awkward move that featured the flailing of almost every part of my body. Flix had to exercise superhuman strength and balance to keep me from taking us both down.

With the grace of a gazelle, Flix avoided the gaping holes created by the next two hammer blows, and we landed in a heap on the far shore just as the sound of an explosion echoed in our ears.

Once the echo died down, an air horn went off.

"One down, two to go." Game night bombs were never deadly.

"Was there ever an igloo in Candyland?" Flix suspiciously eyed the domed structure we'd landed beside.

"Maybe in one of the later versions. Not in the one we had, though. I don't see a door anywhere, are we supposed to break in?"

Cocking a thumb, Flix pointed out something I had yet to notice. A pickax leaned up against the curved wall.

"Looks that way," he ran a hand over a section of ice like he was looking for a weak point.

"Or that's what they want us to think." There were three—no, four—possible scenarios that might play out depending on what we did next. Knocking a block out of the igloo and setting off a bomb or finding a flag accounted for two of them. The igloo being full of something else entirely was the third option. Anything from soup to nuts might be waiting inside. Or, as a final choice, we could walk away and leave it for the next unsuspecting team. It was time to decide.

"I have an idea." And this is why I am the reigning queen of faerie game night. "Give me a boost." Flix caught on fast and nearly tossed me directly onto the top of the icy structure.

"Hey, you with the hammer. I'm standing on thin ice here." It seemed the pun was lost on him when the giant scratched his head and just stared at me. I tried another way. "Bet you can't break this ice."

A mighty roar was all the warning I received, and I launched out of the way just in time to avoid the blow. Flix snatched me out of the air and dashed for cover behind a nearby fir tree. I'd been right to go with the option five, the out-of-the-box plan. The giant set off the bomb instead of us and got the surprise of his life when a deluge of confetti showered down on him. He wasn't the most handsome giant, to begin with, but covered in blue glitter he looked like a man-shaped disco ball with blinking eyes.

Choosing discretion as the better part of valor, we turned silent laughter into tears before Salem showed up to make the decision whether we had lost or could continue. He checked us for glitter particles and, finding none, cleared us to take our next turn.

"Who got knocked out in the last round?" It was impossible to see from here.

"Carl and Evian had an incident in the Peppermint Stick Forest. It wasn't pretty. You should also know that Kin and Soleil found a flag under the Tootsie Roll-a-way bed inside the Licorice Castle." Before he could tell us anything about Terra and Vaeta, I saw a streak of light overhead and heard a noise akin to the sound I imagine a plane makes when it falls from the sky—sort of a whistling whine.

"That's not part of the game." A sense of urgency washed over me, and I set off for where I could hear Terra's voice shouting something unintelligible. Salem streaked past me in cat form, and Flix was hot on my heels.

Four faeries shot up from wherever they were and arrowed straight toward the source of the falling sound. Something was terribly wrong. Carl, red and dripping with mint-scented slime, rushed in from one direction while Kin came from another.

"What happened? Are you okay?" I ran my eyes and fingers over Kin to check for injuries.

"I'm fine." He stilled my busy hands. "I'm not sure what's happening, though. We heard a noise, Soleil looked up, and then she just took off like a rocket. They all did."

"Here they come." Flix squinted up at the sky and pointed at what looked like a strange bird. A crumpled, feminine figure seemed to float gently downward, her clothing making flapping noises against the breeze. "They're headed for the house."

We made it to the back deck just as the four faeries lit there with a fifth of their kind cradled gently between them.

"Let's get her inside." I rushed to open the door. From what I could see, the poor thing had been run through the wringer, dried in tangles, and then run through again. She was covered in scratches, had a twin set of black eyes, and her clothes were in tatters.

Under it all, she reminded me of Cinderella's godmother from the animated movie. Plump, apple-cheeked, and grandmotherly, she lay on the sofa near the Balefire. Until she opened her mouth and killed that mental image with a spate of foul language that would have landed me in time out—the magic version which has nothing to do with sitting in a chair or a corner—and then she passed out.

"What happened?"

"Who is that?"

"Where did she come from?"

A jumble of questions came all at once.

"I think I know her." Soleil squinted and tilted her head. "Yes, I'm sure I do. It's Fawn."

"Fawn? But isn't she..." Terra pressed her lips together to keep from speaking, but Soleil filled in the blank.

"Godmother to Serena Snodgrass."

Now my interest was piqued. "Serena's godmother, huh? Poor thing. What kind of bad karma did she earn to end up with that assignment?"

"Serena's not wicked; she's just misguided." Fawn

never opened her eyes. I guess she wasn't unconscious after all. "And passing judgment on those you don't understand isn't exactly virtuous behavior."

"She's too dumb to be truly wicked," I muttered, somewhat abashed, and earned myself a sharp elbow to the ribs from Vaeta, of all people. Miss Foot in Mouth herself—who was she to expect me to be nice? Fawn's comment must have taken most of what was left of her energy because her face grew even paler and took on a bluish tinge. Terra went into triage mode.

"All right now. Evian, you know where I keep the good stuff. I need that bottle of boysenberry brandy. And Lexi, get me the green tonic from the cupboard by the stove."

If she was using the green stuff, the situation was more dire than I thought. I'd only seen her pull it out once, and that was when Soleil was flying around in her mini form and got sucked into a jet engine. That should tell you how tough faeries can be.

I grabbed a glass and the tonic and handed both to Terra, who gave me a wink for the extra initiative and then poured a dollop of green liquid into the glass. A shot of boysenberry brandy sloshed and swirled into the viscous goo, and a puff of smoke or steam blew out. Before the tiny cloud had time to dissipate, Terra forced the contents of the glass down the injured faerie's throat.

Fawn let out another series of exclamations and levitated about six inches off the sofa. The wounds remained, and her eyes were still ringed with bruises, but her color came back.

"Tell us what happened." It was an order, even though Terra's voice remained gentle, and I think Fawn would have ignored it if she hadn't been so ticked off. Even then, she tried to couch her words to make Serena look like less of a jerk.

"Someone," she glared at me as though I might have been the someone in question, "taught Serena a summoning spell. I was minding my own business and the next thing I knew, I was being dragged backward through the..." Fawn blushed as if she'd been caught doing something she shouldn't have been doing, cut off the explanation, and then finished with, "...when I realized what was happening, I put the brakes on, there was a struggle of wills, and then I ended up here."

"Why would she do a thing like that?" Even before I learned a little more about how the faerie godmother process worked, I knew forcing one of the Fae to do anything was a recipe for disaster, trouble, and about six other unpleasant nouns. Serena should have known better. I already knew the answer to my query, but wanted confirmation.

As if it just now occurred to her to ask that very question, Fawn paused, listened, then said, "Her head is filled with only one thought." She paused. "Who is Jett Striker and why does she want to find him so badly?"

CHAPTER

FIFTEEN

"Lexi Balefire, as I live and breathe." Sinclair Fuller drawled from the other side of an eye-level display case housing chocolates, fudge, and a myriad of delicious confections that simultaneously made Sinful a diabetic's worst nightmare and a dream come true. I couldn't pick a favorite treat if I tried, so I always allowed Sinclair to load me up with whatever concoctions he thought I'd like—and he was always spot-on. So spot on it made me wonder if he had any relation to the witch with the gingerbread house, but no matter how hard I scoped him out, I sensed not an inkling of supernatural energy.

"Long time, no see, I know. Things have been a bit crazy at work lately. I'll take a ten today, but make sure there's a pistachio something-or-other in there; I've got a craving."

"Everything all right? Anything more than a six and I start to get worried about you." Sinclair was referring to the choc-o-meter stress scale we'd spent the last two years perfecting. An order of ten usually meant my anxiety level was through the roof. Even though I wasn't lying when I said things had been crazy, I felt more in control of my life than I had in a long time.

"Actually," I beamed, "I'm planning on sharing, for once."

"Ahh, I see," he returned my smile with an indulgent one of his own, "not just a bridesmaid anymore, are we? He'd better treat you right." Sinclair winked as he dropped a few champagne truffles into the box *gratis*. Truth be told, if I could pick out my father, he'd be just like Sinclair Fuller—sweet, gentle, and just protective enough to allow me to make my own decisions.

And the candy. Oh, the candy.

"He certainly does. I'll bring him by sometime, let you be the judge."

"I'm going to hold you to that, my dear. Oh, by the way, I saw the new business cards; you know you could have put a stack of them on the counter, right? I get loads of downtrodden singles through here, especially on the weekends."

I wasn't quite sure what to say, and for a second I wondered if someone had started another matchmaking service in town trying to horn in on my business. "What new cards?"

Sinclair's face contorted into a puzzled expression and he pulled a rectangle of familiar-looking pink card stock out from beneath the cash register. FootSwept's logo splashed across the center of the card, along with the tagline "Get Swept Away." FootSwept's address and phone number appeared on the back. I recognized the sparkling black ink immediately.

Someone had just rocketed to the top of my naughty list. I bade Sinclair goodbye and swore under my breath during the entire six-block walk to the office.

Flix sat at my desk, busily fiddling with the notepad computer I should have known would make my life anything but easier, a puzzled expression on his face. "What is going on here? Did you do this?"

"Do I look like I'm the responsible party?" I tossed him an annoyed eyebrow raise and the business card at the same time. "I've barely touched this thing, and by the way, it seems like I was right. The computer has caused more problems than it solved."

"Well, then who did?" He demanded, ignoring my completely legitimate—and not at all snarky—comment. "Someone has obviously been meddling in our business, and only one name comes to mind."

"There's no way this was her; after all, it can only increase business and Serena would never help me, even inadvertently." Flix gave me that look. You know the one that says, *don't be an idiot.* Or maybe *you are an idiot.* Either way, I thought back over the last few days, and finally slapped my head against my forehead.

"Mona. She's the only one who had access. I had to run back home, and I left her in the closet picking an outfit for her date with Mark. She said she'd lock up on her way out, but it looks like she decided to do us a little favor as well."

"She must have printed more flyers because they're circulating in a three-town radius. I think there was a mix-up with the ink, because it's not limited to the matches for your current client list. It's anyone and everyone who wants to find love. We've already had over a hundred and fifty RSVPs to the lonely hearts party, plus at least a dozen appointment requests waiting for your return call. I can't imagine these business cards are going to do anything except bring us more clients than we can handle."

I told him he was right.

"We were already in feast mode, and now we've got even bigger issues." Flix looked like he could have breathed fire, and I only hoped Mona had a cake to bake today and no plans for stopping by.

"What effect do you suppose the ink will have on the cards?"

"How the heck should I know? This was all your brilliant plan. You're the one who mixed it up and enchanted it." Salem would get a kick out of lecturing me about the proper use of magic.

"Let's figure out what to do about the party for now, and worry about the cards later."

"What party?" I hadn't heard the office door open, but I recognized the voice of Joshua Owen and rolled my eyes before spinning around to address him.

"Hello, Mr. Owen." I leveled his gaze and hoped this time he'd treat me with a bit more respect. " I was going to call you and invite you to a little soiree we're planning this weekend. The guest list has ballooned out of control, which means there will be plenty of available, *unattached* women in attendance." Making it very clear I wasn't one of them was a top-of-the-list level priority.

"Wherever the ladies are, that's where you'll find me. Consider this my RSVP." I didn't hear the rest of whatever Joshua had to say because the bow began its sad lament, calling to me even though it rested in pieces several miles across town. I could almost feel what it would be like to bend the string, knock the arrow, and weave Joshua's fate into a brilliant tapestry.

Whether I felt he was deserving of my efforts or not, clearly destiny had a plan for his future and judging by the strength of the call, our most frustrating client's future union would serve humanity in a positive way. That is if I came through in the clutch and didn't kill him first. I'd search all the realms for living gold if it meant getting Joshua Owen off the dating market and out of my office for good.

Once the man in question had been successfully dispatched, a flier in his hand more for me to ensure he was worthy of attending than to convey the date and time of the event, I broached my concerns about him to Flix.

"I've never had a client I disliked as much as I dislike that man. He's lucky he didn't ask about the church supper; I'm not about to help some Lothario get laid by preying on eager, unsuspecting women."

Flix laughed, "So you're going to turn away half your male clients, then? I can tell you that they all come in here reeking of sexual frustration. The only reason I haven't clued you into that fun fact before is that once you set them up, I can tell they're committed. You're the real deal, Lexi, and I'm guessing our handsome friend will feel the same way once he's been tamed."

"When you say it like that it sounds like a death sentence. I'm not in the castration business, for crying out loud."

"Relax, Lexi, it's not like you're the one doing the snipping. That's between the couples themselves. Trust me; they're happier than clams just to have someone to go home to every night." Flix assured me.

"It doesn't seem like I have much choice. Based on the bow's reaction, the fates want him matched, and soon—I'd love to know why, but the visions only happen when I come into contact with both halves of the couple, and there's been no sign of a signal from his mate. Maybe she's not close by? Or maybe my dislike for the man is clouding my LPS."

"Sounds like you need to put your personal feelings aside and treat him like you would any other client."

"Sure, I'll get right on that," Easier said than done.

SIXTEEN

The next time the ring flared back to life, Kin and I were curled up in my bed, binge-watching Netflix with a silencing charm blocking all outside noise.

"I hate to get up, but this is important," I frowned, kissed Kin on the lips, and hopped out of bed, "fixing the bow is more crucial than ever."

"The Sons of Anarchy will be here when you're finished." Kin really was the best boyfriend in the world. "Can I come watch?" He asked with a twinkle in his eye.

"As long as you don't get freaked out watching me turn into a ghost. Salem says it's quite unnerving." After three trips, I thought I knew the process well enough to see any possible danger, and I didn't think it would hurt for him to watch. If he was going to get a case of the witch willies, better to find out now and handle it before something weirder happened. That I was expecting weirder should say something about my life lately.

"I think I'll manage." He replied, looking a bit unsure but unwilling to admit to anything that might diminish his manliness.

I wasn't taking any chances this time, and pulled on a

set of thermal underwear, snugged a second extra pair of socks beneath my boots, and added enough layers to my torso to keep me warm but still allow for movement in case the gold wasn't easily accessible.

Kin, eyes intently focused on me, sat next to Salem. His swift intake of breath was the sound that followed me back through time.

I twisted the ring around my finger three times and felt the familiar sensation of traveling through space and time. Except for this time the only space I traveled through was the ten feet from where I'd been standing to the other side of the fireplace. I found myself in the parlor, clearly not too far in the past judging by the old-fashioned tube television set resting on top of a seventies-era curio cabinet in the corner.

Fascinated, I spun around slowly, taking it all in. There were photographs hanging on the walls; if not for the dated pressed metal frames encasing each one, I could have mistaken the child in them for myself. Well, except that I'd never looked that sullen in my whole life.

There was no doubt in my mind that the child was my mother, Sylvana. In the present, her face had been cut or burned out of every photo I could find. According to her, Clara had gone mad with the scissors, but I was willing to bet money on that being counted as another one of her lies. Sylvana would never cop to anything that might make her look bad.

Even if I hadn't already been a first-hand witness to my mother being a miserable excuse for a witch, I'd have predicted an unhappy future for the girl in the photographs. She looked like the type who would go from sullen child to temperamental teenager, torturing anyone she didn't like and blaming everyone else for her problems—a stereotypical mean girl.

I stripped off enough layers to be comfortable in the warm room and lost myself in staring at the photos until a cat with a puffed-out tail tore past me. With its fur standing on end, I couldn't tell if the cat was mad or scared. Probably a little bit of both.

"Endora," a voice sing-songed into the room just ahead of a little girl who tripped in with what I can only describe as an evil grin on her lovely face. My mother, ladies and gentleman, liar and cat torturer. She hadn't yet Awakened, so I knew poor Endora was still confined to her cat form and therefore at Sylvana's mercy.

"Sylvana Elizabeth Balefire, you leave that poor cat alone!" A woman's voice echoed from the kitchen. I followed little Sylvana through the hall and into a room that in no way resembled the space I was used to. Everything was either pink or avocado green, and the combination reminded me of one of the toads that like to hang out in the backyard near Terra's mud hut.

Clara, looking so similar to her statue it was a little scary, rested her elbows on the table, a cup of tea cradled in her hands. Mag, seated on the other side, stared at Sylvana through slitted lids. Whatever catastrophic event had sapped the youth from my great aunt's face must have taken place sometime between when she and Clara were girls and the year I was visiting now, because Mag looked exactly as she had the first time I met her in the Fringe. Fluffy white hair billowed around a lined face that I knew from experience could appear gentle and harmless until Mag had a reason to turn fierce.

"I wasn't doing anything," my mother lied smoothly, "she must have seen a mouse or something. Are you two about done chit-chatting? We're supposed to be in the workshop; it's time for my lesson."

Clara sighed and rubbed her temple. "Your lesson will have to wait until we finish with our tea. Aunt Mag gets cranky when her tea gets cold."

"But you said I could try scrying with my own crystal today. You *promised.*"

"Go to your room, Sylvana. Now." She went, but with an eye roll one of my godmothers would have smacked right off my face if I'd dared show them such disrespect.

"There's something wrong with that girl, Clara." Mag only half whispered. "And you know it."

"She's my *daughter*, Mag. You don't understand what that's like."

"Thank you for pointing out my lack of offspring, dear sister, but it doesn't mean I'm wrong." Mag waved a finger at Clara.

"We have more important things to worry about right now. *He* stopped by again. He's already looking in her direction." Her eyes slid to the door Sylvana had just exited. "It's like he can smell the power on her and you've seen it too.

She's developing more power than I could have imagined." Pain colored Clara's face, and I realized how difficult it must have been to raise a willful girl like my mother all by herself. "He's not going to simply walk away from the possibility."

I knew she was talking about my father.

A quiet giggle rang with a metallic echo in my ear, and I looked up toward the ceiling where a ventilation duct connected the kitchen to the upstairs. I recognized the scrolled pattern of the metal cover, its surface thick with layer-upon-layer of paint, various shades showing through a few chipped places.

Before the advent of forced hot air heating, two story houses weren't all that practical in colder climates. Cutting a hole in the ceiling and fitting it with a fancy grate allowed heat to pass from one floor to another. A popular solution now known to be a fire hazard.

Any child growing up in such a house could also tell you that while the heat was nice, the vents were even better for spying. Many an hour I'd spent listening in on heated faerie arguments with my ear pressed to the other side of that same grate; my—and Sylvana's—bedroom was on the other end.

"So you're quite sure that's what he's been after all this time?" Mag drained her cup, held it out for more, and nodded to show she agreed with Clara's assessment of Cupid's intentions. "A Balefire Fate Weaver would be almost as powerful as he is—and she would always have a target on her back. We can't let him succeed."

"Funny, that's not the tune you used to sing," Clara challenged.

Mag's voice quivered as bitterness crept into her tone, "Raising a powerful child was not what I wanted him for. He had other assets of interest." The veiled sexual innuendo, coming from someone who looked the way she did, made me cringe and triggered a snort of disgust from Clara.

"You know I've been over my teenage crush for quite a few years, Clara. And I'm already paying the price for my youthful indiscretions, so there's no need to rub it in my wrinkled face. Especially when we're on the same side."

"You made a choice to satisfy your wanderlust. Don't try and blame me for the repercussions." Despite her mild tone, Clara's words carried weight as she leaned forward and poured yet another cup of tea. Mag pulled a flask from the folds of a caftan-like garment made from what looked like polyester and covered in a pattern of tropical flowers. Some of the contents of the flask joined the tea in the delicate china cup, and Mag took a deep gulp before she answered.

"Are you trying to say you would have stepped aside if I decided to stay? That you would have been happy to let me be the Keeper of the Flame?"

Clara wanted to say yes, but the lie refused to pass her lips. "No, but that was never at issue. You've had itchy feet since you were old enough to ask Mother if she would allow you to walk away from the Balefire."

"And now I have arthritic ankles, so I've decided to settle down."

"That's wonderful news. Sylvana's in your old room, but we can always move her into mine." No enthusiasm colored the offer.

A shudder ran over Mag at the thought. "No. This is your place now." Her eyes flicked away from Clara's, and I got the feeling she was trying to be diplomatic with her opinion about living near Sylvana. "I already have a place."

Mag described the hut I'd visited in the Fringe and Clara gave a half-hearted argument against the isolated location.

"You could blow yourself up, and no one would ever know."

After several minutes of arguing over the merits of living between worlds, Mag deliberately returned to the previous discussion.

"Him turning me down was a blow to my self-esteem, but I'm fine with the fact I didn't show up on his radar. I've learned a thing or two over the last couple of centuries, including that Fate Weavers rarely live the long, happy life you'd want for your child. Even if there was no danger, handing out the happily-ever-afters doesn't ensure she'd get one of her own, and the work takes a toll. I don't want to see any of our Balefire daughters put in that position."

"Unfortunately, daughters are what we usually get, and we're not always going to be around to protect them.

There's a change coming, I can feel it. Can't you?" Earnestly, Clara searched Mag's face as though hoping her sister would disagree.

"I'm afraid you're right. Anyone with half an iota of power can sense the looming darkness, and maybe that's why he's so determined to make a Fate Weaver strong enough to stand beside him."

"It won't be a Balefire; not if I can help it."

Right. Never say never. You'd think a witch as powerful as Clara would have figured that out already. Thanks for jinxing me, Grandma.

All sarcasm aside, I listened closely to all they had to say about an impending imbalance between darkness and light. This was the same assumption Adriel had been working under when she teamed up with the faeries to fight a demon that had turned out to be Vaeta in disguise. From the minute I heard the word danger, I wanted to learn as much as I could about my possible fate.

There's no handbook for Fate Weavers, and I've never met another one, so everything I knew about that side of my heritage had come from Vaeta. She professed not to know anything useful but spouted random facts as though they were common knowledge. Delta, a supernatural bounty hunter whose attention had been more on finding the Bow of Destiny than instructing me in how to use it, had also been of little help.

No one knew exactly where my father had gone, and the only other person who had been there that day and might be able to provide a clue, well, she wasn't talking.

Not with lips of stone, anyway. All this talk of fate-weaving danger seemed melodramatic. I'm putting happy couples together, not fomenting thermonuclear war and I don't see how one of those could be connected to the other.

The compass interrupted my meandering thoughts by sending a couple of vibrating pulses against my chest. Caught up in the conversation, I'd forgotten my mission. This should be an easy retrieval. I already knew where great grandmother used to keep the living gold. Or I thought I did. Somewhere between my last visit to the past and this one, the fireplace had been fitted with the handle I knew from my own time.

I tiptoed (yes, I know they couldn't hear me or see me, but I couldn't help myself) over to the fireplace and reached into the flame. The conversation continued behind me as I stepped into the sanctum. One question I'd like to ask my grandmother—if and when I finally release her from her granite state—is who made the rules about these visits to the past. On my way to turn on the lights, I barked my shin on a haphazardly placed trunk, then danced my way into the back of a chair that wasn't where I remembered it.

How could I run screaming through a room and no one would hear me, open the Balefire without anyone noticing, but still trip over a trunk full of books? It made no sense.

With the lights finally blazing, and my shin throbbing, I checked the shelf where I'd seen the gold before and came up empty. The next ten minutes I spent ransacking the place until the compass buzzed me again.

Oh, right. I was supposed to *use* the compass. Duh.

After the familiar whirl to orient itself, the needle pointed right at the Balefire, which meant the gold was probably in the parlor. I could have saved myself a barked shin, and I didn't grumble when I flicked off the light and avoided the trunk on my way back out. You can't prove otherwise; no one was there to hear me.

On the other side of the fireplace, the compass directed me back into the kitchen where it pointed toward Clara and when I circled the table, stayed oriented on her instead. I stopped breathing, probably out of reflex, and panicked a little. Was I supposed to grope her and expect she wouldn't feel it? And if she was carrying the gold, wouldn't she notice when it went missing?

After invading her privacy by running my erstwhile gold detector around her for what felt like forever, I was pretty sure the amulet dangling around my grandmother's neck was the source of the living gold, and just as certain I didn't have a shot at pulling off a retrieval.

However, with the ever-present buzz of the bow chiming in the back of my head, I knew I had to try.

Once I got a good look at it, I'd have bet my birthday tiara that Tempest had been the smith behind the work of art. Egg-shaped and wrought from pure silver, the amulet featured our family sigil, a tree with Balefire branches. I'd have loved to go back and see what method she used for creating the design in bas relief.

Waiting until Clara leaned forward to snatch a cookie from her sister's plate, I saw the heavy pendant swing free, and yelling, "Sorry." Even though she couldn't hear me, I made a desperate grab.

The ring flashed just as my grasping fingers went right through the metal. All I felt was a tingling chill, and then a stomach-lurching feeling of being dragged back to my own place and time. Empty handed.

Drat.

SEVENTEEN

My hopes for a journey to a moment in the past of my own choosing (not, mind you, that I had any idea precisely when I'd like to go) having been burned to cinders and the ashes scattered to the wind, I turned to Kin for solace. It didn't occur to me that this meant taking another step toward my future, seeking comfort outside the arms of my godmothers for the first time in...ever.

Five women living in close quarters made for a lot of amplified emotions. The party planning pact seemed to be quelling the annoyances that normally brewed to boiling. Since I'd come into my magic—and after the initial fallout sparked from the worry I might not need them anymore—things with the godmothers had calmed to a simmer, and now I doubted you could even poach an egg in it.

Preoccupation with the lonely hearts party that was just days away left hardly any time to work up a good critique of my life or my choices. We'd reached a detente: the godmothers would treat me like an adult and support my relationship with Kin, and I'd include them in my life and keep them informed of anything dangerous coming down the pike.

Not that supporting my relationship with Kin could be considered a hardship; I mean, the guy treated me like a princess and the godmothers like queens. What more could you ask for? He had wormed his way into their hearts, so much so I was starting to think they liked him more than they liked me.

Tonight the two of us were enjoying a magic-free, plain old camp fire in Kin's backyard oasis. He'd arranged two beautiful Adirondack chairs around a graduated semicircle of stacked, reclaimed bricks in a range of colors and a variety of patinas. A set of soft cushions covered both chairs, and several throws draped over the arms would keep us warm and comfortable long into the night.

The air smelled of citronella and eucalyptus (because banishing bugs smacked of personal gain, so I used old-fashioned oils to keep them away), and twinkled with the light of at least a dozen darting fireflies if I squinted against the flames and stared into the relative darkness beyond the patio.

Port Harbor is a fairly small city, but the lights are still bright enough, even on the edge of town that unless you were allowed entry into my faerie enchanted backyard, you'd never mistakenly think you were out in the country.

Most of the time, that fact didn't bother me. It meant fewer mosquitoes on nights like this. Where some people needed to commune with nature—remind themselves they're part of a great cycle—to feel in touch with the universe, I find my reassurance in the faces of all the people I interact with every day. Tonight, however, I was happy to limit communing to just one other participant.

Kin stoked the fire and then disappeared into the kitchen to return with a large wooden cutting board filled with graham crackers, marshmallows, and several of my favorite kinds of chocolate, including peanut butter cups and a dark variety he'd seen me sneak into my purchases during our last trip to the grocery store.

"I know it doesn't compare to the wonderland outside your terrace door, but I think it's pretty cozy back here," he grinned, pulling a couple of long, clean wooden skewers from someplace behind my chair. I'd already settled into the cushions and begun to let the detritus of the day slowly dissipate.

"It's perfect," I replied, spearing two marshmallows at once and expertly, patiently, toasting them over the edges of the licking flames. Smoke wafted into the night, the caramel scent of molten sugar on its back. Shadows danced against the brick, now and then coalescing into recognizable shapes like clouds on a hot summer day— twin hearts, Falkor from The Neverending Story, and a pointy witch's hat—before flickering into obscurity.

Kin and I talked for hours after I'd abandoned my chair in favor of curling between a fuzzy blanket and his warm chest. The chemistry between us was palpable in the air and in the lingering fingers that stroked an errant lock of hair from in front of my eyes or wiped a smudge of chocolate from the corners of his lips.

I did my best to capture the moment clearly in my

mind's eye, encase the memory in bulletproof glass, and preserve it forever.

At some point, the air turned cool against the sweat we were creating, and I allowed Kin to lead me by the hand to his bedroom. A respectable amount of time later I finally fell asleep, wrapped in his warm embrace, completely sated.

When I sleep, I'm pretty much dead to the world, which is why I so despise waking up in the morning. It's also why my office hours start significantly later than most businesses. It always takes a while before I feel like myself again, even with a generous amount of caffeine thrown in for good effect. Clasped in Kin's warm embrace, completely spent and more relaxed than I had felt in months, I dived into unconsciousness with abandon and welcomed the beginnings of a dream.

Everything was pitch black, but I could hear chanting in my ears and feel warmth on my skin. Warmth, and something else. A hand cupping my bottom, and one supporting my neck. My body felt more compact than usual, like I'd shrunk and was being carried by a giant. The sensation made more sense when I cracked open an eye to see Clara's face swimming in front of me at what felt like twice its regular size.

Fire to keep the keeper

Flame to heal the healer

The words echoed in my ears like a promise.

Clara smiled down at me indulgently, her mouth forming the *O* most adults make when entertaining a baby, and her green eyes shining with love and affection. Peace crept into every pore, every muscle, relaxing me with safety.

I'm sure there was more happening outside my field of vision, based on the number of voices repeating the mantra that had been running on a mental loop ever since my dream visit to a similar ceremony from an observer's perspective.

Held snugly in the crook of my grandmother's elbow, and due to that whimsical quality dreams have of rendering you completely unable to control your body, I couldn't look around. Whether this was an actual event I was reliving or a constructed memory based on the vision from my last dream I couldn't be sure. But I felt the heat from Clara's hands and saw the white light of the Balefire flickering in my peripheral vision, and it certainly felt real. This time, *I* was the infant being offered to the Balefire flame.

Without warning, I went from basking in the warmth of the flame to being thrust among its brazen tongues, the notes of the chant pounding in my ears, the fire tickling at my toes.

Every nerve in my body tingled as energy bubbled below the surface, rushed over my skin, and was reabsorbed over and over again until it compressed into a pinprick of immeasurable power within my breast.

As I was pulled from the fire, the energy dissipated, but the feeling of fullness in my heart remained long after I woke in a daze and snuggled closer to Kin. I couldn't sleep with all the thoughts swirling around in my head. Finally, I slithered out of bed and slipped downstairs quietly, making sure not to wake Kin.

In the kitchen, I brewed a cup of green tea, doctored it with a dollop of honey, and padded out to the patio to curl up in one of the chairs Kin and I had abandoned a few short hours before. The campfire had burned down to a few blackened pieces of wood, something the Balefire would never do as long as its Keeper maintained the flame. And I knew I would fulfil that role until the last breath left my body. That spark of energy still thrummed in my heart; connecting me to the Balefire. It had always been there, a tether to the power of the flame—but now I knew exactly what it was.

No matter what the other pieces and parts of me could or wanted to do, the Balefire could never be denied.

I also knew, somehow, that Clara's connection had broken the second she'd turned to stone. What I couldn't work out was how to get it back; the Balefire could penetrate her granite form with no more success than the first spell I had tried. Possibilities swam through my consciousness until my brain grew tired and my eyelids began to droop. When I woke, once again snuggled close to Kin, I couldn't be sure if I had walked back up the stairs myself, if he had come down to retrieve me upon waking to an empty bed, or if I had flown back in on the wind.

EIGHTEEN

Dressed to the nines, I moved through the lonely hearts party like a ghost borne on a cushion of lovely music.

Kin's singing voice is sunset and kittens and a baby's cheek—colorful, sweet, and smooth. Sexy is what it is. Turn-your-knees-to-water sexy. His gaze pierced mine from across the room and made me want to peel him like a grape and slurp him down in one delicious bite.

He'd agreed to play one set before passing the baton to Mona's boyfriend Mark, who would spin tunes in his role of DJ for the rest of the evening.

Warm bodies packed the place from wall to wall, called to us by Mona's cards and the fliers posted all over town. Hopeful energy wove in and around the room and pulled me to where I was most needed.

Thanks to the faeries' event planning skills, I hadn't stepped foot inside the warehouse venue until a couple of hours before the first guest arrived. Glamoured to the hilt, the four of them buzzed around the space putting on finishing touches while I watched, unneeded, from the sidelines.

Evian, naturally, manned the bar with her usual flair while the rest of the godmothers spun through the crowd serving guests like total pros. I could not have asked for more seamless teamwork. All in all, the event was a smash.

In contrast to the industrial bones of the building, they'd chosen a romantic, but still chic decorating theme. White linen draped tables covered with fragrant roses in every shade of pink and red Mother Nature could produce (and a couple that I'm pretty sure only appear in the Faelands). Black wrought iron sculptures rose from several points around the room, their bases draped with even more roses.

My favorite decoration, a stylized heart with two curlicues protruding from its point, was the faerie's idea of an inside joke. The emblem, called a Sankofa, symbolized the idea of using what you'd learned in the past to guide you through the future. Good advice for new couples and the personal significance didn't escape my attention either.

To keep the decor from being too girly, guests sipped frothy brews from sturdy glass mugs resembling mason jars with handles. Making their way around the space on simple silver trays, fifteen kinds of appetizers disappeared between smiling lips. Drink menus and descriptive labels picked out in white script against a gunmetal gray card stock punctuated the mix of masculine and feminine opulence.

Strands of twinkling Edison bulbs crisscrossed the space beneath the ceiling, creating a soft glow over the dance floor and bar, carving out more than a few dim corners where couples might retreat for a bit of privacy. And canoodling; there was a lot of that going on. I witnessed several lip locks sweet and steamy enough to eventually lead to a true love's kiss, binding the couples together for life.

Sexual tension clashed with nervous anticipation and, in some cases, outright desperation. I couldn't tell you how many little black dresses and carefully chosen neckties were in attendance, but it would have been obvious even to an impartial bystander that this was a pick-up party—and a damned successful one at that.

Left with zero event-related responsibilities, I extricated myself from the unapologetic people-watching (and judging) Flix and Carl were enjoying and embarked on an evening full of what I do best: matchmaking. The queen of *have you met so-and-so*, I flitted around the space pulling couples together.

"Hey, Elizabeth, how are you enjoying the party? Oh, and by the way, have you met Todd Sweeney? Hey, Todd, this is Elizabeth Walker, she's a swim instructor at the Union Street YMCA. Oh, you were both on your college swim team, how about that?"

Several variations of the same conversation later, four more new couples were cozied up to quiet tables on the outskirts of the festivities, discussing shared interests between furtive glances from beneath lowered lashes. Two more took advantage of the impromptu garden space just outside a pair of sliding doors. It wouldn't be a proper party unless Terra landscaped—her motto, not mine.

Amid the hum and buzz of voices, the bow pitched muted tones against the fine bones of my inner ear. Each time I spotted a pair of soul mates, it warbled a babbling song that slowly increased in volume as the night wore on. When a couple broke from the crowd and began to focus solely on each other, the noise turned softer, becoming a hum of approval. I still couldn't tell if it was singing or trying to talk to me, and after an hour or so, I wasn't sure I wanted to find out. How was I ever going to get anything done with all that noise?

Sure, I knew weaving fates affected the world beyond that of the specific couple in question, but what would happen if I abandoned my responsibility remained a mystery with ramifications I wasn't able to predict. Just like the power of threes, love has long-ranging conse-quences.

Experiencing that many matches coming together at once prompted a *what if* moment for me, and I imagined what might have happened if I'd let the fallout from Jett's actions simply work itself out on its own. I'm sure some of the couples would have come together without my help, but a good percentage would have been left adrift. Would the absence of the positive effects of those unions create a vacuum of negative energy instead?

Be nice if I had a clue, but I couldn't see a downside to putting people together.

Right in the midst of me giving myself a mental pat on the back, Flix, his arm draped around Carl in a protective manner, drew my attention to a situation developing across the room.

"Well, would you look at that?" Flix banged his glass on the table. "Ten bucks says he goes after the redhead at the end of the bar."

"Double or nothing says her perfect match comes back from the men's just in time to swat Lothario like a bug." Carl challenged.

I turned to look at the object of all the betting and wished I hadn't.

Joshua Owen was about to win Carl a crisp twenty and probably earn himself a trip to the ER, besides. The redhead in question had been hanging off the arm of a mountain of a man with biceps nearly as big as her head —her perfect match. Joshua, for all his swagger and bravado, was the next best thing to a hundred pound weakling in this scenario.

The man closing in on Joshua swayed to the left on his way to the end of the bar, as if he'd had a cold one too many.

The noise in my head took on the tone and volume of a large cage full of chattering parakeets taking turns on a squeaky swing. The bow had an opinion, and it demanded I listen.

Whatever The Hulk dished out, Joshua would have

earned, judging by the way he leaned over his quarry and chatted her up. Until he was firmly matched, the idiot stayed on my list, so I muttered a few choice words from the faerie's naughty-naughty-no-no category and hurried across the room to see if I could intervene.

Before I made it halfway there, it was already too late. Dropping seemingly-friendly hands on Joshua's shoulders, the flinty-eyed guy insisted—bodily—on taking things outside. A bit over-the-top, considering he'd just met the woman, but it takes all kinds, I suppose. Or maybe the magic in the air ramped up his protective instincts.

The redhead looked positively thrilled at being the object of the fight, and I searched the general area for some backup. None of the hired help were anywhere to be found, and I made a mental note to give my godmothers the name of another, more reputable service. Throwing a pleading look back at Flix, I fell into step behind the redhead and gained the parking lot just in time to see the big guy's arm pull back for a first punch.

"Dude, stop." An otherworldly level of command amplified Flix's order and made it echo across the narrow sidewalk. "The little fellow meant no harm. Look at him; he just wants to buy you a beer. Why don't you go back inside and have a laugh about this." It worked, too. Some Fae mind meld let the air out of the confrontation, and it fizzled into nothing while we all watched in astonishment.

"Nice work. Ever used that trick on me?" Flix's face betrayed nothing.

All he said was, "Idiot lost me a bet."

"I'll duck backstage and see if Kin needs any help." After I sneak him into the shadows and kiss him silly—that part I left out. "We'll meet you back at the table in ten." Just inside the door, we parted ways.

Romance rode heady on the air. I had Kin's lips on mine, my hands in his hair, and my body straining to plaster itself to his when I heard Flix speak with an edge of panic.

"Lexi, Carl's gone. I've covered every inch of the place, and I know he wouldn't have left without me. He was having too much fun." Tension practically zinged off him as Kin and I pulled our clothes back into place and followed him through the crowd. Flix restlessly scanned the faces surrounding us, and I did the same, pushing through the throngs of people until we'd circled the room twice and came up empty.

"Mark's running sound tonight; he has a good view of the entire place from the booth. Maybe he noticed something. I'll go ask him." I gave Flix's arm a comforting squeeze that failed to relieve the tension I could feel rolling off his skin. He ran a hand through his hair without mussing the carefully arranged waves that reminded me of a Ken doll's molded plastic head. "You two make another pass around the perimeter, I'll catch up to you." I also added a *don't worry*, but I could already tell it was too late.

A spiral staircase that looked suspiciously like petrified wood wound its way up to where the sound booth occupied a caged-in balcony section above the bar. Some of Terra's work, no doubt. From that vantage point, Mark had a clear line of sight to the table where Carl had last been sitting.

"Hey, Lexi. Tell Kin I said he sounded great tonight." Mona bounced off a second barstool where she'd been sitting next to Mark. "Everything okay? I saw you and Flix take off like you were on a mission."

"One of my clients has a flirting problem, so we went outside to help make peace. You didn't happen to see where Carl went, did you?"

Mona tilted her head and gave me a confused stare. "Did you hit your head during the confrontation?"

That sounded mildly insulting for some reason.

"I don't..."

"You and Flix left, and not a minute later you came back in, spoke to Carl, and then the two of you went out the side door by the stage."

"I did?"

Mona tried to pull me toward the stool she'd just vacated behind the sound board. "You're not having another one of those episodes, are you?" Having been present for a series of strange events that were witchy in nature, I'd explained away the oddities by telling Mona I was prone to anxiety attacks. I could weather the short-term humiliation better than the aftermath of revealing my magic to her. "Or one too many cocktails?"

I knew I hadn't been the one to leave with Carl, which left very few alternatives. Or actually, just the one. Someone was using a glamour to look like me, and there was only one person who would be that stupid. Serena Snodgrass. Which meant Serena had gone after Carl and left Kin alone this time. I couldn't help but feel mildly relieved, an emotion immediately supplanted by those of disloyalty and shame.

"I'm okay. Thanks, Mona. Kin's waiting for me." I turned and practically flew down the stairs—no easy feat in heels, mind you. Spiral staircases were designed by a sadist! Ask anyone. I hit the bottom going way too fast and nearly fell, but Kin grabbed me and set me back on my feet.

"Serena has Carl, I'm sure of it. Mona saw him following *me* out the side door, and since we all know where I was at the time, she must have used a glamour to lure him away." Stealing my face? Really? Retribution would be swift and merciless. Any remnants of sympathy I may or may not have harbored toward Serena quickly vanished as I realized just how diabolical she'd become. Perhaps I'd been wrong in my assessment of her as a weak-willed dingbat.

We detoured back to our table on the way out so that I could grab my purse and the keys to Pinky, my beloved scooter. Kin had come straight from work, and I'd been late getting home, so I'd chosen to ride instead of walking to the party. Not surprisingly, my purse was gone; in its place sat a blank white envelope.

Flix snatched the note from the table and was reading the contents inside of a second.

"She's going to harm Carl if I don't deliver Jett to this address by tomorrow at midnight." Flix handed me the piece of paper, and I recognized the location—a lightly populated area to the west of the city central.

I caught a glimpse of Mona anxiously watching while Kin escorted Flix to the side exit and flashed her a *don't worry about it* smile. At some point, a more detailed explanation would have to be given, especially if I wanted to remain friends with Mona—which I did. She was my only new friend in years, and I knew from personal experience how much damage could be done by keeping large, complicated secrets. Which reminded me, there was something about Serena the others didn't know.

It turned out my purse and Carl weren't the only things Serena had made off with; Pinky was gone, too.

She died a dozen horrible deaths in my head, and I felt better for shuttling anger into imagination instead of letting it out with magic.

"She's got at least a ten-minute head start on us. Give Kin your keys, Flix. Are you getting anything at all from Carl?"

"Nothing."

"Even Serena isn't stupid enough to kill a person." I felt a little mean voicing Flix's greatest fear. "Shouldn't you be able to sense if he's in danger?"

"Only if someone uses magic on him. She used you—

your face anyway—to get to him, and that means the only magic she used was on herself."

"How did you find me that day in Shadow Hold?" We reached the car, "Let Kin drive." I reminded as I gently pulled the keys from Flix's hand because I didn't think he was in any shape to concentrate.

"Where to?" Kin asked.

"My place. We'll need a few things and some help from Salem to put together a rescue plan. That's what we're doing, right? Going after him now before Serena figures out we won't be pulling Jett out of the hat." I climbed in next to Kin.

"We're going to do whatever is necessary. And you were screaming in my head." I'd forgotten I asked by the time Flix answered.

"And the call button in the office?" More than idle curiosity drove the question. Flix was my oldest and dearest friend, but he kept a lot of things private, even from me. I'd long suspected him of having a supernatural level of empathic power because he always just seemed to know what I needed. In that respect, he was a much better friend to me than I was to him.

Being open about his abilities might be crucial to rescuing Carl, but I could tell Flix wanted to do what he always did: shove the topic back into the shadows and continue hiding his most secret thoughts. "You can tell me anything; you know that, right?"

Was that true? What if he said he could read minds?

Would I ever be able to look at him the same way again? Hot blood beat a patch to my cheeks. I'd had thoughts about him. Embarrassing ones. Best friend or not and despite his sexual preference, the man was gorgeous. No woman could look at him and not wonder about certain...things.

"I'm tuned to your vibrational frequency."

"What does that mean in normal speak?" Kin whipped the wheel to turn onto my street. He was learning the fastest routes home from anywhere in the city—the benefit of my vast knowledge. Garmin could call me for directions.

"Can you read my mind?" There, I'd asked him flat out.

Flix paused long enough that I felt an embarrassing answer coming on.

"Not as such." Phew. No, wait. What did that mean, exactly? "It's more that I can read your emotions. Sad, happy, annoyed, whatever you're feeling, I can tune in and tell." He didn't mention aroused, but I assumed it was on his list. Nice.

"Can you do it for Carl, too?"

"No, and even if I wanted to, I wouldn't. That would be cheating."

Sounded right to me. There's no sense of adventure if you already know the outcome, and that's especially true in new relationships. Does he like me? Does he want me to like him? Losing the thrill of discovery in the early days of romance would take all the drama out of the emotional highs and lows. Falling in love, or even in like, is always a gamble—that's half the fun.

"I'm still not sure I understand. Even if you can tune in to whatever Lexi is feeling, how did you know where to find her when she was in trouble?"

We were getting to the heart of how Flix might be able to find Carl before Serena...well, I wasn't sure how far she was prepared to go. I added that to the list of topics to explore next. Killing him might not be an option, but there were plenty of spells she could use that would make him wish she had.

"I just followed the echo of her screams, and I know that doesn't help you understand what I mean, but it's the best way to describe it. Whenever Lexi needs me, I will come." Now I was sure I'd gotten the better end of the deal when Flix and I became friends. Whatever it took to bring Carl home, I would pour my heart and soul into the effort. Serena was never going to win a prize for brainpower, but going after Carl was beyond stupid.

"And it doesn't work with Carl?" Kin continued to allow his questions to flow, oblivious to Flix's frustration until it boiled over.

"No. It doesn't." He snapped. "Don't you think if it did, I'd have flown in, grabbed him, and returned in a hot second?" Kin was smart enough not to ask any more probing questions.

"Whatever it takes to get Carl back, we'll do it," I vowed. "There's something else you should know. Serena's pregnant."

"And how did you find that out?" Flix probed.

"Salem heard it from Serena's familiar."

"You're sure about this?" I nodded my answer. "So that makes you…"

"Aunt Lexi." I supplied ruefully.

"Right. And you won't let me do anything…"

"…that might put the baby in danger? No, of course not." I was reasonably sure Flix wouldn't have crossed that line anyway.

"Terra, I need you." That she would come without hesitation, I'd long since realized, was something I should stop taking for granted. Some families are born, others are made by cobbling together the pieces wherever you can find them. Mine is a patchwork, and I wouldn't have it any other way. Yelling for Terra, I knew, would bring immediate results. By the time we hit the kitchen, she was already there. So was Vaeta.

"Do you have any sort of magical tracking on Pinky?" I demanded without preamble. A long shot after the tantrum I'd pulled about her treating me like a child a few weeks back, not to mention the additional hissy fit I'd pitched about the spell she'd put on Kin.

"We've got a party going on, and you pulled me away for that? Who knows what Soleil will do while I'm gone. And why aren't you there? This is your party, you know."

"Can you just answer the question?" I snapped, regretting the irritable tone as soon as the words left my lips.

Her hands shot to her hips and her chin lifted. "No, I don't have any tracking on your scooter. You made your position quite clear. You're an adult who no longer needs our protection." Her back, when she presented it to me, was ramrod straight. Clearly, I had not been completely forgiven, nor would I be allowed to forget my error in judgment, no matter how trivial the request had seemed when I made it.

"I'm sorry, but this is one time when I wish you would have ignored me. Serena put on my face and when our backs were turned, lured Carl away from the party. She stole my purse and my ride to do it. She hasn't used any magic on him." Not wanting to state the obvious in front of Flix, I didn't mention that she could be harming him through purely physical means.

Terra's eyes widened, then she looked down in chagrin for her snappy comment.

"I'm sorry, Flix, truly. She's trying to force your hand and get Jett back?" Terra's question was more of a statement, cutting through to the heart of the matter and zeroing in on Serena's motive. "Maybe we should just give her what she wants."

"I would if I could." Flix turned haunted eyes my way. "But there was a thing, and that thing led to another, and even if I knew exactly where to find him now, I couldn't go get him."

Vaeta's eyes narrowed, and she spat, "Tell me where you sent him. I'm still welcome in most parts of Faerie."

Flix grimaced at the suggestion, and we both spoke at once, "No way."

"It sounds to me like you're both too stubborn for your own good. There's a perfectly good nexus I could drop him into, and Serena as well. Problem solved." Vaeta rubbed her hands together twice quickly to accentuate her point.

My toes curled in pleasure at the thought of the two of them trapped together, but ethics overcame desire. While Jett might deserve it, Serena probably didn't. Incarcerating the pair felt too much like vigilante justice, and something told me I didn't want to be on the receiving end of that blowback.

Plus, there was the baby.

I can count on one finger the number of times I've taken Terra completely by surprise. Telling her about my impending aunt-hood doubled my previous number.

Flix's conscience kicked in hard. "I can't ask you to go; it's too dangerous." He said something in a language I'd never heard him use before and Vaeta cocked an eyebrow at him, before giving him a crooked smile.

"That's not your call to make, my dear. I'll be back before you know it; give me five minutes."

Vaeta winked at Flix and disappeared. While she was gone, he paced a line back and forth between the kitchen island and the refrigerator, frustration seeping from his pores. I'd seen it happen a time or two with my godmothers when they got angry enough to let the mask slip and show his inner emotions.

Vengeance on a faerie is still beautiful in a terrifying blend of sharp angles and burning eyes. Flix carried more than just Faerie blood in his heritage, which made his angry Fae-face all the scarier. Remind me never to get on his bad side. Stupid Serena.

If anything happened to Carl, I might end up having to save her from Flix. I'm not sure whether witch law covers being an accessory to murder or not, and I don't want to find out. Granite gray isn't my color.

"If she hurts him, I'm not sure I'll be able to…"

"She won't. She's not that stupid." I hoped—prior evidence failed to support my claim. "She'll keep Carl safe because she knows you won't give her what she wants unless she does. Promise me you won't go after her by yourself if whatever Vaeta's doing doesn't work out. You'll need our help, and you know it."

"Fine. I promise you can all watch me get Carl back."

Kin wisely stayed out of it. This was between Flix and me since it concerned both of us.

"Help you, not watch you." Specifics count when making deals with faeries.

"I promise to let you help me. I swear." He added, crossing his fingers and whipping them into a complicated gesture I assumed was the Fae equivalent to the phrase *cross my heart and hope to die.*

A somewhat disheveled Vaeta popped back into the room, her eyes wide, and her breath coming in shallow inhalations. "I guess I'm not as welcome in some parts of Faerie as I thought," she huffed, "and our little friend managed to hitchhike his way out. Hasn't been spotted in a while, and nearly got himself killed while he was there.

Shot his mouth off in front of a naiad. They can be right mean if you cross them."

Flix just about blew a gasket, "How the hell did he manage to get out? And where did he go?"

"That I don't know, but I don't think he came to this realm. I have a feeling he's gone to ground, or he's found someone else he'd rather terrorize. Either way, Serena doesn't seem too high on his priority list, and he probably doesn't know about the baby."

"Then we're back to square one." Flix, rendered helpless for the first time in what I imagined was a good long while, deflated quickly.

"We'll just have to find them first. No waiting, forget the twenty-four-hour deadline. We just track them down and safely neutralize Serena. Problem solved." I voiced the solution I'd known, deep down, we'd wind up employing. If you've ever watched one of the umpteen cop shows all over the television nowadays, you know you're not supposed to give in to the demands of kidnappers. Or adult-nappers, same difference.

"That seems unlikely. How are we going to find her if she's not using magic?"

The answer was head-slappingly obvious, which probably meant it wouldn't work at all. "I can scry for him, but I need an item to use as the focus. Serena herself is a no-go; she'll have warded against all locator spells. But she can't ward Carl without alerting Flix, and she knows it. Do you have anything of his on you?"

Flix rifled through his pockets. "Not on me, I don't think."

"What about in the Jag?" Kin suggested. He was probably thinking about the things of mine that had started turning up in his car; hair ties, an emergency lip gloss in the glove box; that type of thing.

"That's genius. I'll look. And if there's nothing I'll just flit back to my place and look for something there."

"I'll go with you." I wanted a moment alone with Flix. "I'm sorry for dragging you into my problems. I never meant for any of this to happen. Ever since I got my magic, things have gone to another level of weird. I mean, really. I'm going to end up sort of related to Serena. I can't even…"

"Magic creates more problems than it solves." Flix's bitter note tugged at my heart.

"I'll do whatever it takes to find him. We all will. I owe you that much for helping me save Kin's life, but that's not why. I know the mushy stuff makes you uncomfortable sometimes, so I'll keep it brief. You're my best friend, and I love you. Even if I can't read your emotions the way you read mine, or hear you crying in my head, I know you're feeling a hundred different things right now. We'll get him back before the sun rises. That is my vow to you."

Something, whether you want to call it an onus or a geis, laid its weight over me like a curse. I bore it willingly.

"Never make a promise like that to a faerie, not even a half-breed. Who knows what lengths you'll be forced to go to keep it." I shrugged off the warning. No Fae promise-keeping mojo was necessary in this case.

"Did you find anything?" I circled around and opened the driver's side door so that I could help search.

"Not yet. Check in the back."

"You two spend a lot of time in the back?" My attempt to lighten the mood only put images in my head that I would rather not have seen. "Never mind."

Face flaming, I conjured witchlight into my palm and leaned down to look under the seat. Something was wedged into the spot where the front seat bolted to the floor. It was just far enough back that I had to crawl until I was half in and half out of the vehicle and reach as far as I could. I pulled out...wait for it...a dirty gym sock.

"Euw."

"What, did you find something?" Flix asked, his voice intense.

"Maybe. You'll have to tell me if this is his or yours." I held out the stinky sock.

"It's Carl's. You know I don't wear white socks."

"You've been wearing a lot of new things lately." Lumberjack shirts. Mental head shake.

"Shut up." I got half a smile out of him. "Will it work?"

"Should do. It's definitely got his...essence." Essence. Stink. Same thing, right?

• • •

In his eagerness to see the results, Flix bumped my elbow and sent the quartz pendulum swinging wildly.

"Sorry. Sorry." He backed off a little, but not enough to keep from breathing down my neck. Between his eagerness, the pressure to find Carl quickly, and the distraction of holding someone's filthy sock, my concentration was shot. Salem pressed in on my other side, and between the two of them, I couldn't have found Carl if he'd been in my backyard. Thankfully, Kin could tell I was in focus mode and gave me the space I required.

"That's it. Both of you go over there," I waved vaguely toward the other side of the sanctum. Terra and Vaeta, after much discussion, had returned to the party. It had taken all my powers of persuasion to convince them I'd think better if I didn't have that worry riding me, too. "You're vibrating at a very high frequency, and I need a minute of peace." Maybe I should have sent them to the kitchen instead.

"But I..." I glared at Flix.

"Okay." He raised his hands in a gesture of submission and backed away.

With a bit more elbow room and a few seconds of calming meditation under my belt, I set the pendulum in motion again. Crickets. Four more times I scryed, and four more times the crystal spun around and around, never touching down.

"It's not working. And he hasn't been harmed, or

you'd know it." I directed at Flix. "Salem, a little help here?"

Salem sighed but knew better than to begin a diatribe about my studies. "She must have concealed him somewhere impenetrable. People can be warded, but so can places, like this room for instance."

Another epiphany hit me square in the face, though I carefully concealed my optimism in case this idea was a bust, too.

"She took Pinky. I've got an extra key. See where I'm going with this? It didn't occur to me before, but maybe the key will act as a link. It does sort of *belong* to Pinky." They all nodded in agreement, and Salem morphed into cat form and scurried to my bedroom to retrieve the spare I kept in my jewelry box.

The suspended hunk of quartz touched down almost immediately. Bam! Results.

Confusing results. The crystal wavered and fell on its side.

I angled my body between the table and the spot where three anxious men were staring at me with nothing but questions and desire for vengeance in their eyes. I tried a second time, shooting Salem an annoyed frown, "Okay, *you* can come back." A familiar's primary job is to help his witch, and I needed his calming presence.

"What's happening?" Flix was ready to blow a gasket. I motioned for them to take a look at the map.

"She's moving. Thankfully, Pinky can't go that fast, but it's still enough to mess with your results. The upside is, we won't have trouble finding her in Flix's Jaguar." It wasn't appropriate to defend my mode of transportation right this second, but I wanted to point out that had I traded up to the Harley Flix suggested, Serena—and Carl—would be much harder to find.

See, I'm growing as a person.

"Flix, you promised we'd do this together. We'll take the pendulum and the map, and we'll ferret her out. She'll have to stop eventually, and then we'll swoop in. Okay?" If I were expected to uphold my end of the bargain, so would he.

"Yes, yes, I agree."

Flix kept his oath and didn't go tearing off on his own, but he did utter all the words on the godmother's naughty list and a few I'd never heard before. Kin echoed several of Flix's sentiments. It occurred to me that he and Carl had become better friends than I'd realized, given their experience with Serena's truth serum.

Brutal honesty either wreaks havoc on or reinforces friendships. I think grudges and past slights act as a good portion of the glue holding Terra, Evian, Soleil, and Vaeta's relationships together, and the phenomenon isn't exclusive to otherworldly beings.

"Ugh." Kin spit bubbles. "What the..."

"Saliva soap. Terra's way of washing your mouth out."

"I don't even live here. What's the deal? How come Flix didn't get whammied?" Another silvery orb slid out from between his lips and floated toward the skylight. At any other time, I would have been howling with laughter.

The staccato beat of Flix's shoes tracing a path between the Balefire and the casting circle bore witness to a rising fury that threatened to unleash once again the vengeful Fae resting just below the surface.

"Enough," Flix roared. "Kidnapped boyfriend, kind of urgent. Let's get this show on the road." He stalked toward the fireplace entrance, the formidable set of his shoulders somewhat diminished as he ducked under the low doorway. Seconds later, we heard the Jag's engine revving and the blast of a horn and scurried after him.

Scrying in the sanctum was one thing, but scrying in a moving vehicle was quite another, and the tiny sports car seats weren't conducive to my efforts either. Serena had been tracing a path back and forth across Port Harbor's historic district, the easternmost section of the city that hadn't yet been completely swallowed by modern convention.

When the town had been no more than a fishing and trading port, a large interior cove protected residents and ships from the blistering winter winds. Now, its cobbled streets buzzed with the activity of vendors, quaint shops, and some of the best restaurants in the state. I'd zipped past muttering truck drivers attempting to maneuver through the rough roads to their desired destinations on more occasions than I can count; you either walked the streets of East Bay or you found a vehicle better able to navigate in confined spaces.

My scooter was perfect, and Serena was taking advantage of the fact that if pursued by car, we'd never stand a chance of getting close enough to spit on her, let alone reverse direction if we were spotted.

Salem peered around the front seat from his position next to Kin in the back and watched as the pendulum twirled and set down a bit further into the cove each time. "There's no rhyme or reason; no pattern. She just seems to be zig-zagging through the side streets. Thank goodness your windows are tinted. Maybe she won't recognize the car, and we'll be able to sneak up on her." I uttered nervously.

"She clearly knows we're coming, or she wouldn't be traipsing all around the bay. If this is a trap, I swear..." Flix trailed off, and I didn't want to hear the rest.

"We're getting close. She's two blocks west and heading this way." The words were hardly out of my mouth before Serena, astride my beloved scooter, raced out from a narrow alley to our left, crossed the street two cars ahead of us, and continued in the direction of the coastline. A spell fluttered to my lips from some instinctual place deep in my witch's gut, and I did what I could to clear a path. Flix laid on the horn to my dismay (not very stealthy) and we careened through a gap barely wide enough for the Jaguar to take advantage of the brief break in traffic I'd conjured.

Unfortunately, Serena either had some magical way of detecting our presence—or maybe she was just that paranoid—and caught sight of us as we thundered behind her.

A beautiful hedge of blooming Cupid's Dart flowers crunched beneath Pinky's tires as Serena attempted to cut across a courtyard positioned between two 19th century apartment buildings.

We heard a bang, and Flix screeched to a halt before—thankfully—hopping out and racing around the corner with the three of us at his heels. Salem went catty while still inside the vehicle, and streaked ahead of us at light speed.

"Nooo!" I shouted at the sight of Pinky smashed into a tree, both tires flat and the rearview mirror hanging at an odd angle against the crumpled front fender. Of course, my scooter was replaceable, and we were after a live human being who was in danger, so I turned my attention back to the matter at hand while inwardly mourning the loss. "Where is she?"

Salem sniffed, looked me square in the eye, and tilted his furry little head to indicate we should follow him. Three blocks later, in the depths of another dark alley, Salem looked around surreptitiously and poofed back into a man with wide eyes.

"I know where Carl is. Serena's *lair*, for lack of a better term, is in that direction. One of her father's old warehouses downtown. She's got the place warded to the hilt, so we'll need to either draw her out or find a weak spot. I might even have an idea."

"And you couldn't have come up with that idea *before* she did this?" I waved a hand to indicate poor Pinky and he had the good sense to apologize.

Serena had Carl holed up in the one place where she had the upper hand and had probably headed back there because she was reaching the far edge of desperation. No self-respecting witch would risk luring an enemy so close to where they practiced, and she knew we were on her trail. You can bet your rent money Serena never expected us to find her there, much less to attempt a rescue. Salem's recent romantic experience with her familiar was about to provide some useful information. We had intel, and we had to move quickly.

"How hard could it be? Serena's not what you'd call a criminal mastermind. We go in; we take her down." Kin slammed his fist against his palm.

"You don't understand. Now we'll be on her turf. There's no telling what sort of defenses she's installed. I doubt she'd show any measure of mercy."

"Okay, I get that she's large and in charge, but how does that change things?" He asked.

"Breaking through a powerful warding is a big deal." Flix had put plenty of them on our own office. When Delta, the bounty hunter who helped put me on the path to find the Bow of Destiny, had first started sniffing around, I'd felt the need for one place in the city where I could go and not be followed by anyone with ill intentions. "It's all about the intent. The stronger our desire to do her harm, the stronger her wards will become."

"Naturally..." Kin's eyes rounded when the implications hit home. "...but it's different for you. Witch rules don't apply to Fae, right?" The question was directed at Flix, who continued to pace back and forth impatiently.

"Karma is a mean mistress and not limited to witches. If we go in with aggression, it will come back on us all. It's okay if you want to sit this one out."

"You go, I go," Kin said with finality. "But there's a back door, right? Lexi's mother got into her house without Terra knowing." Kin tried to puzzle it through, and Flix was growing more impatient with every passing question; a squiggly blue vein at his temple throbbed in time with his heartbeat.

"You forget one thing.." Salem puffed out his chest. "I'm irresistible."

Before Flix turned into a steaming puddle of angry, I quickly explained how Salem had graciously taken one for the team when I'd asked him to turn spy for me. I laid it on thick because he'd need the ego boost if he were going to do what we were about to ask him now.

Armed with all the information at our disposal, we laid out the bare bones of a plan that centered around Salem's skills with the ladies. Or with the lady cats anyway.

"Okay, let's go. I'll drive." Kin offered.

"Too slow, and I need to grab something from the house. Flix can you…" I'd never asked him to transport me before. I knew he could move from place to place like the godmothers, but I wasn't sure, being only half Fae, what his limitations were.

"Yes, I can take you. Just hurry up." Tension turned his expression stony as we all clasped hands.

In under five minutes, the four of us landed in a parking lot not too far from Serena's current position. Kin looked a little green. Flix managed the shift with speed, but he lacked Terra's ability to provide a smooth re-entry.

"Hold still, Salem." The sharp command quieted him long enough for me to tie a couple of Evian's favorite toys onto his collar. "Okay, go." I gave him a little scratch behind the ears first. He hadn't even asked for extra tuna for doing this, and I knew how much of his pride was on the line. "You're the best."

Salem didn't need words to convey his reaction to my comment—the speed of his turn and the twitch of his tail told me all I needed to know as he melted into the darkness. My heart thumped double time while Salem made his way alongside the building. On quiet paws, he scaled a dumpster to get to a ledge that provided him access to a windowsill and then up the fire escape where he disappeared into the shadows.

Silence filled several tense moments as we waited.

Kin wobbled over and whispered in my ear, "See anything yet?" He slung an arm around me and leaned in while I angled the compact-sized mirror connected to the much smaller version dangling around Salem's neck. Two-way water mirrors were one of Evian's specialties, and I'd happened to have a set tucked away in my dresser drawer. Flix, whose Fae-enhanced night vision picked up more than ours, drew in a hiss of breath.

"He's heading for the roof."

The mirror showed a blur of dark against darker when Salem lifted a paw over the edge of the rooftop. Morana must have sensed his proximity because she practically oozed through an open vent near the heating ductwork. A minute before, I'd been thankful for the nearly full moon that rode low in the sky, but what happened next made me want to scoop my eyeballs out with a spoon.

"Meow." Infused with need, Morana's entire body quivered at the sight of Salem, and her butt went up in invitation. I felt his shudder of distaste, but bless him; he played the part. Thankfully, the conversation rolled out in howls and murmurs of cat language; I had no desire to hear the details. Didn't matter anyway, my imagination supplied enough to make me cringe.

"Hey, big boy. Come and get it."

"Rawr. Why don't we go inside where we can be a little more comfortable."

"I want you right here, right now."

"Inside. Please. I'll give you what you want. I'll give it all to you."

Okay, Salem probably didn't say that, and by now, I needed a gallon of mind bleach.

"He did it." Kin distracted me from the horror. "He's in. Lexi, go."

"Sorry. I was...never mind." Shaking my head to dispel the last of the mental images, I spoke a sleeping spell into the tiny shell. Immune to my particular brand of witchcraft, Salem remained alert while Morana slid into a peaceful slumber, and then he moved deeper into the warehouse.

A moment, or a lifetime later, the mirror in my hand lit up like Christmas. What I saw were feet.

Two of them wearing shoes that looked a lot like a pair I usually kept in the office in case I needed to change for the gym. I rifled through my memory for the last time I had worn them and came up with a vague vision of having nudged them deeper under my desk during the first wave of new clients. Brushing aside a fleeting resolution to work out more frequently than bi-monthly, I searched my memory for clues as to when Serena might have hatched this diabolical plan.

She could have walked through the front door and taken my entire desk without my noticing her during the past few weeks. I'd spent a lot of time ferrying hopefuls in for a consult with Flix, who plied them with good wine and his special brand of stress reduction. I'd given so many tours of The Closet I was already anticipating the arrival of fall, feeling the urge to rescue all the boots from a boring summer spent indoors. Serena could have watched and waited for me to retreat into the back room, and then—the wards were down during business hours—ransack the front office.

Barely whispering, I spoke into the other item Evian supplied; a simple-looking seashell, "Lean up or something, all we can see are feet." Salem complied, and Carl's earnest face swam into view just as a burst of speech came through the shell.

"I'm trying to think, Lexi, but that's all I remember. Are you certain Flix went to the same place he sent that Jett guy?"

"Yes, of course, I am, or I wouldn't have dragged you out of the party to come here and look for clues to where he might have gone."

Have you ever had two wildly opposed emotional responses at the same time? The sight of Serena's—or more technically, my—face and the sound of my voice fired every ounce of mad I could muster while the sight of Carl, unharmed, sent relief flooding over me. Furious me controlled the blood pressure, which shot up to an alarmingly high rate. Relieved me preferred caution to action.

Landing somewhere in between, I cupped my hand, raised the shell to my lips, and directed Salem to initiate phase two. As helpless as I felt at that moment, I had no idea what inner resources Flix was pulling from to remain so calm. Twenty-some-odd years living with faeries had taught me plenty of lessons, chief among them that the quieter the faerie, the worse the havoc they will wreak. Calm and cold fury are not the same thing; one means peace, the other can be deadly.

"Where are we, anyway? What makes you think Flix would have come here?"

Serena mentioned something vague about portals to the Faelands being in strange places.

"If we don't find anything here, you must have the key to his place, right? You're practically living together."

"What? You know we're not at that phase yet." I heard

the puzzlement in Carl's voice. "You don't seem like your-self right now."

"How should...I'm sorry, in all the excitement, I'm all mixed up. Where could he have gone?" A hint of Serena's usual shrill tone crept into her—my—voice.

"You're distraught, and I'm so worried about Flix I can't think straight. Shouldn't we be calling in the faeries by now? I'm sure they'd be more help than roaming around abandoned buildings looking for I-don't-know-what. This just isn't like you."

Carl sounded impatient and suspicious.

"Hurry, Salem," I urged. Not that I needed to tell him, he could hear for himself that things were about to go bad.

"You're right. I know I should be asking for help. I'm just so worried about Flix I'm not thinking clearly. If I could just go back to that day in Shadow Hold and hear the spell he used on Jett, I would know where to look for him."

"Tell me he doesn't know about..." Halfway through the hissed question to Flix, Carl answered it triumphantly.

"But you *can* go back in time. Just make a wish and twist your ring three times like Dorothy and her shoes." Not quite how it worked, but close enough to have me shooting Flix a dirty look. How did my secrets turn into his pillow talk?

"Twist the ring, and I can go back in time." Serena turned the question into a statement at the last second. "How do you know about that?"

We were running out of time. I clutched Kin's hand tighter and glared at Flix.

"Was I not supposed to?" Carl sounded surprised and hurt.

"We'll talk about this later," I assured Flix through clenched teeth.

"It's okay; I'm sure Flix tells you lots of things." I heard the twist of bitterness in the voice that sounded like mine as it faded into the distance. Salem had gotten past her and was headed toward the door. His human voice sounded loud when it issued from the tiny shell.

"Hurry up; I think she saw me." It turns out we didn't need to break her wards; we only needed an inside man. Or cat. Well, you get the idea.

"Doesn't matter now." Flix hit the door like an avenging angel and never looked back to see if we were behind him. A tiny, but wicked voice in the back of my head urged me to let him have his way with Serena, but I tamped it down and, staying ahead of Kin, followed Flix inside.

The rescue of Carl was a bit of an anti-climax. As soon as she saw us, Serena let the glamour slip and began taunting Flix with how easy it had been to kidnap Carl. Watching my face turn into hers gave me a major case of the heebies. Watching Flix's face turn to scary faerie was worse.

"Laugh all you want, Serena, but you failed." Forgetting all about the baby, Flix raised a hand to do something horrible, and when I jumped in to stop him, the ring on my finger flared to life with perfect timing.

Carl handled Flix before I could get to him.

"Don't. Not for me, not like this. She's not worth it."

I should have seen it coming, it's not like Serena ever managed to pull off subtle, but because my focus was on Carl, I wasn't paying attention when she lunged at me. The bony witch took me down. I'm not proud of it, but that's how it played out. She took me down and in the process, wrapped her twig-like fingers around the ring and twisted it faster than I'd ever seen her move before.

TWENTY-ONE

The gut-lurching sensation of moving through time hit and I hastily fixed the image of living gold in my mind. It was my only chance to get the last piece I needed to repair the Bow of Destiny, and I hoped against hope that Serena's touch hadn't messed things up and stolen the opportunity right out of my bare hands. It was my ring, after all, it should take its cues from me and not my arch-rival.

Locked in a battle for control with the ring burning a brand into my finger, we fell through time for so long I started to think we might be stuck in the nothingness forever. The last person in the world I wanted to be confined to the place between times with was Serena Snodgrass.

And still, we fell.

And fell. For what seemed like eons, but was probably seconds or perhaps no amount of measurable time at all.

It had been this way between us for years, Serena and me. Both wanting to be on top, neither giving an inch. I tried to tell her how important was my need, but no words could penetrate the vacuum of time. We were on the edge of becoming lost because neither of was willing to give an inch. The fight had been our truth for as long as I could remember and it was insanity—literally—as we continued to repeat the same pattern all while expecting a different result.

I thought of all the people I'd already helped without the bow—Lemon and Harry Tart, Mona and Mark, Mrs. Katz and Dr. Cooper, and scores of other couples walking around, making babies thanks to me—and all of the people I could still help in the future. That is, unless I gave into stubbornness and self-pity, and allowed us both to become trapped in the void forever. I thought about my godmothers, Kin, Flix, and Salem, and all of the other beings I'd die to protect, and decided I couldn't just let them watch me disappear.

I stopped fighting. For the first time, I let Serena win.

We landed hard enough to knock my teeth together, and I felt a bony elbow slam into my ribs.

"No," Serena moaned. "No, this wasn't supposed to happen."

I shoved her off me and sat up to look around. We hadn't gone back to Shadow Hold if that had been her intention—and I guessed it had been. If not for him being the father of her child, it was extremely pathetic that Serena would choose to revisit the loss of a louse who would have traded up if given the option. A mere few moments would show me just how wrong that assumption was.

"Where are we?"

"You did this." A bony finger waved in front of my

nose, and I knocked it away with more force than I needed to use.

"No, Serena, this is all you." A vague memory surfaced. Our first-grade year I'd had my first—and only—sleepover in this house. Serena's house. I remembered Terra dropping me off and the feeling of excitement tinged with terror over doing something new, being somewhere different, and not knowing if I could fit myself into a new routine. I'd never been to another witch's house before; Serena was the only one I'd known save for the older women who passed through the parlor with uncomfortable looks on their faces every Beltane.

I might have been able to pull more out of my memory banks if Serena had stopped wailing long enough for two thoughts to come together. Television and movies teach us that the appropriate way to deal with someone having hysterics is to slap them across the face and snap them out of it. A lesson I was only too happy to employ. Yes, I enjoyed slapping Serena. Sue me.

"What were you thinking?"

"I'm not going to defend myself to you." Serena sniffed and rubbed the cheek that bore my hand print in reddened flesh.

"I didn't mean it that way. What thought did you have at the moment when you twisted the ring?"

"Oh, just that I wished I could go back and fix the worst thing in my life. I thought I could stop Jett's banishment to wherever he is. He needs to know about..."

"The baby," I finished for her.

"How did you find out?"

"I have my ways. The ring doesn't work like that, so you've wasted your time and ruined my mission for nothing. It looks like Jett leaving wasn't the worst thing that could have happened—no great shock there since he's a the biggest D-bag of all time—and even if it was, you can't change the past."

"Then why have you been using the ring to go back?"

"*That* is none of your business." Not that what I was about to see was any of mine. "It works like this..." Before I could finish, the front door flew open, banged against the wall, and made me jump. Facing the door, Serena never batted an eyelash when her younger self entered the house. In fact, I think she stopped breathing altogether.

Eleven-year-old Serena's silky brunette hair looked like it had been cut by a six-year-old with safety scissors. The dress she wore, though clean, was at least a size too small, its hem frayed in places. Some of the stitching along one shoulder had unraveled and been inexpertly sewn so the seam puckered and red thread showed through the simple white cotton. None of that managed to take the shine off her beauty. Eyes clear as cut aquamarine traveled around the room as though trying to get a feel for the atmosphere, and set off the sweetest of faces I'd ever seen on a child. Serena had looked like an angel, how had I forgotten that?

"If there's nothing we can do to change things, why don't we leave now? The last thing I need is you seeing parts of my life that are none of your business." Serena snapped at me.

"Sorry, it doesn't work that way. Each trip lasts a certain length of time, and when that time is up, back we go. I have no control over it."

"I'm home," Young Serena called out. "It's report card day."

"Get your chores done." A sharp voice screeched from the kitchen.

"Okay, Mama." Neither the sharp tones nor the snarled order dimmed the girl's cheerful smile. She passed right by us on her way up the stairs. "I made the honor roll again."

There was no answer from the other side of the kitchen door.

I was still friends with Serena at this age. We'd begun the process of cutting our ties when we were eleven or twelve and severed them totally at fourteen. I still couldn't remember what the fight had been about, but I was starting to remember how Serena had moved around the classroom with a light grace. She *had* been beautiful at one time.

"You were so pretty," I swear I didn't mean to sound shocked, it just came out that way.

"Thanks, your opinion means just everything to me." Adult Serena's tone suggested the polar opposite was true. "I'll cherish the compliment forever. It matters so much coming from you."

"So what happened to you?" And that was just mean, but it was Serena, and I really didn't like her.

She burned me with a look then turned her back on me and the scene playing out in front of us.

"Look, invading your privacy wasn't my idea. You're the one who dragged me into this, so let's just make the best of things. You asked to go to a time when you could fix something that would affect your whole life, and now we're stuck here for however long it takes to see what that was. Even if you can't change the past, you might learn something useful, so pay attention."

I got another hot glare for my trouble, but she did turn around and watch as the day played out—and so did I. Not having experienced what you'd call a conventional upbringing—my faerie godmothers were so far outside the box they'd need a map and a flashlight to find it—I'd always been curious what a two-parent family might look like. Even more curious how witches with mothers lived. This didn't seem like either of those things.

"I'm going out." Serena's mother—who comes to my house every year to collect some of the Balefire and I can count on one hand the number of words she's ever said to me—grabbed a string bag off the back of the closet door and without so much as making eye contact with her daughter, sailed out of the room.

"Coven business." Even now, Serena covered for her neglectful parent.

I'm not sure why, but I'd always fantasized about being part of Serena's family. She had everything I didn't:

a mother to come home to at the end of the day; a father to take off the training wheels and run alongside shouting encouragement when she learned to ride a bike.

Okay, most of my ideas about family life come from TV. I guess it just never occurred to me that other people's mothers and fathers might not live up to those fantasies. All the time I'd envied Serena, she'd been living a lonely life.

At least she shut up long enough for me to take in more of my surroundings. The kitchen was what you'd expect from a witch house: potted plants crowded on wide shelves that ran across a big picture window; herbs drying on a string suspended over the central workspace; a couple of cauldrons stacked in a corner. But the living room was so typically American husband I half expected Al Bundy himself to walk in, plop onto the beaten recliner, and then fall asleep with a beer in his hand.

Alone in the house, Serena changed out of her school clothes and proceeded to scrub the kitchen to a sparkling clean, even though something told me her mother could have done the same with a mere flick of her finger. Serena was in her room doing homework when the front door slammed, and she looked at the clock in surprise. Eager excitement lent a bounce to her step as she raced out of the room.

"Daddy, you're home."

Adult Serena's face lost color, which was hard to do since her normal skin tone was pasty, to begin with.

"Haven't you punished me enough? Take us out of

here, I beg you. I'll never bother you again." She pleaded, her eyes now the pale gray color of a stormy sky and full of pain.

"There's nothing I can do." Curiosity, of the morbid variety, pulled me out of Serena's childhood bedroom to view the moment when, if we had been able to change the past, we could have made a difference in her life.

"Where's your mother?"

"Coven business like always." Young Serena's statement felt like an echo. "Daddy, I got my report card, do you want to see it? It's all As and Bs, I worked really hard this term, and I got a good grade on my history project. You remember, right? I made a diorama of the Alamo."

Serena's father picked the newspaper off the hall table, rolled his eyes, and sat down at the table.

"Jeez, Serena, don't you ever do anything besides talk? Why don't you heat up the oven and cook me a pot pie? Do something useful for a change."

Her face falling, I watched the last spark of childhood and laughter and confidence turned black and cold and insecure. It couldn't have been the first time he treated her with such contempt; certainly not the first time a parent had brushed her excitement aside. I imagined her dreams and aspirations had been similarly snuffed, and it was suddenly clear to me that Serena's turn toward the dark side hadn't had anything to do with me at all. A blow to my ego that I could totally live with.

Sympathy flooded up from my gut, slammed into the

logic born of all my memories of Serena, and turned my emotions to whackadoodle soup.

"I can't believe I'm saying this, and if you ever tell anyone I did, I'll deny it until my face turns blue, but that was totally uncalled for. The way they treated you wasn't your fault. You know that, right?"

"Shut up, Balefire. Just shut up." Holding back tears lent Serena's voice a husky quality. "I'd rather be hung up by my toenails than have you see what you just saw."

"Don't worry; I wasn't planning on hugging it out with you. I'd rather eat a scab."

"That could be arranged." She slammed a shoulder into my arm on her way past me.

The physical contact triggered one of those visions I'd been having lately. Or maybe it was a series of memories. Serena at eleven in her little pink dress, then at twelve wearing black from head to toe. By fourteen, the sour expression had settled so totally on her face that few would remember the bright and shining girl she'd once been. I was as guilty of that oversight as anyone else.

Suddenly, shame joined sympathy in an over-whelming surge of emotion I tried to shove back down. I *deserved* to feel bad; every spell she'd ever winged my way had been infused with pain and suffering, and I chose to turn a blind eye. And every retaliatory strike of my own carried harmful intent, as well. I'd blamed Serena for hurting me, but I'd never done anything to deserve her confidence, and I certainly hadn't attempted to repair the breach when I had the chance.

No wonder things weren't working out for me. I was finally getting what I deserved, having set events in motion long ago. That the ill-intentions of my past were coming back to bite me in the butt now, when I needed a bit of good karmic return, wasn't all that surprising. After all, it makes the most sense. Serena was no angel either, but her debts weren't my concern, and her actions didn't justify my own.

Wouldn't Salem be proud of me for owning up to my mistakes? I thought, just as our time ran out.

TWENTY-TWO

Sheer pandemonium met my ears as Serena and I tumbled back to the present and became corporeal again, to be interrupted by a few moments of silence before resuming at a decibel that should have cut glass.

Salem and Kin lunged for Serena, who leaped off of where she'd had me pinned to the ground and scuttled across the floor to cower as far away from Flix as she could get. I didn't blame her; Carl's lack of bodily harm hadn't softened his expression or mitigated his need for vengeance. Something of a suicide mission—Serena knew if she didn't succeed, she probably wouldn't be walking away in one piece.

"I need to find Jett." She screamed, attempting to pierce Flix with a withering glare, but his Fae was showing through, and the diatribe ended before it could begin. The sob she let out next, combined with what I had just witnessed regarding Serena's past, pierced my heart, "Bring him back, please." The fact that she was willing to sacrifice her dignity for someone who cared so little about her was the worst part.

How is it possible to despise someone and feel sorry for them at the same time?

"I'm happy to send you to join him, witch, but if you think I'm going to help you after the stunt you just pulled, you're even more daft than I thought you were." Flix retorted. I doubted a sledgehammer would be enough to smash through Flix's hardened heart; not that I could blame him. I'd spit fire after Jett almost got Kin killed, and nearly killed Serena myself during one of our encounters; somehow, it didn't feel so righteous anymore. "Besides, your precious Jett isn't even in the Faelands anymore—he escaped, and didn't care enough about you to even check in."

"Flix, please. Nobody was hurt; Carl is fine. Given her condition, I think we need to let this go."

He turned his head slightly in my direction and raised an inquisitive eyebrow over an arctic gaze, "You're siding with her?"

"You shut your mouth right now, Lexi Balefire! I don't need you to defend me. And I definitely don't need your pity." Serena spat in my direction while getting back on her feet and facing Flix head on, "Do whatever you're going to do. But remember the rule of threes. Faeries aren't immune. Maybe I deserve to be punished, but at least I'll have the satisfaction of knowing you'll be held just as responsible for my fate."

Carl stepped up and laid a hand on Flix's arm, "Please, babe. Let it go. She wasn't going to hurt me." Conviction ran so strong in Carl's voice that I gave him a probing look. How could he know what was in Serena's heart with such certainty? "Besides, being pregnant, it was probably a hormonal thing."

He might have been willing to tick me off by ignoring my request, but Flix wasn't about to argue with Carl, especially not after the harrowing experience he'd just endured. "Fine. I'll leave it alone," he promised, turning to Serena, "but if you *ever* show your face in our office, our homes—or, better yet, within a five-mile radius of any one of us, not only will you wish you'd never met me, you'll wish you'd never been born."

"Too late," Serena muttered under her breath before beating a hasty retreat through the door and down the stairs.

Kin's arms were around me the second the door closed behind her, and for the next several minutes we took turns hugging one another and making sure Carl was, indeed, just fine.

"Carl, I'm so sorry you got dragged into all this. And I'm sorry she used my face to trick you." I'd need about fourteen showers to cleanse myself of the image of Serena pretending to be me, and another several to wash off the smell of sordid past.

"No, I'm sorry for accidentally telling her about the ring. I had no idea, although I should have. Something was off—I thought maybe you were a little tipsy from the bar or something. I should have known better." He repeated, accepting my hug and insistence that not realizing someone who looked exactly like me wasn't me, after having only known me for a few weeks wasn't a major crime.

"How could you have? It's not your fault. But it is a problem. Flix, please fill Carl in on all the details. He's one of us now; he should have all the information. Not that it matters, anyway. Serena blew my last chance." I held the ring up so everyone could see its darkened surface and the five newly-filled circles indicating full deactivation. "There's no way to get the living gold, and that means we can't fix the Bow of Destiny. I've failed."

"Um, Lexi, I have an idea. I tried to tell you before—Mag's familiar, Jinx, sent word through the grapevine that your aunt wants to see you. I think she might be able to help."

A spark of hope activated my magical adrenaline, and suddenly I felt that sense of intuition I'd always relied upon so heavily in the past. This was the answer, I could feel it—practically taste it. Clara's necklace held one last piece of living gold, and I could only think of one witch I'd trust—or even feel comfortable confiding in—and that witch was my Aunt Mag. The new name still felt strange on my tongue; I'd never referred to anyone else as Aunt before, except the faeries when no other explanation had made sense, and that didn't count. Now that I knew she wasn't resisting contact, it felt all the more real.

"Well, where is she? How do we get in touch with her? I've tried scrying—no dice."

"Jinx gave me this," he held out a gold coin stamped with the family crest, and when I took it in my hand and flipped it over, it felt warm to the touch. The entwined letters "MTB" scrolled across the flip side—Mag's initials, I supposed. "It's almost like the witch version of a pager—she'll be able to find you if she wants to answer."

"Let's get back to the house. I need to fill the godmothers in, and we should at least warn them we might be expecting company." Plus, I wanted to see how the party had turned out after I'd dropped the ball by taking off in the middle. And I needed to call my insurance company about Pinky.

Flix obliged but continued treating me coldly all the way home and sped off with barely a goodbye. One more item on the list of things I'd screwed up lately. Some days I feel like a firebug trying to put out fires. Something circular in my nature creates more problems than I solve. Flix would come around. I hoped.

CHAPTER

TWENTY-THREE

"Here goes nothing," When I held my breath and pressed the side of the coin with Mag's initials on it, a fleeting rush of air whipped my hair away from my face. Before the last strand settled back into place, the doorbell rang. Terra, Evian, Soleil, and Vaeta stayed in full-on faerie mode, dropping their glamours out of respect for my Aunt Mag.

Their response to my desire to contact her was night and day from their reaction to my mother having shown up. I assumed either they were making leaps and bounds in their attempts to remain neutral and allow me a chance at a relationship with my only other known living relative, or they'd decided an aunt wasn't as big a threat as a mother and it might be best to let it go.

Leaving Kin, Salem, and the faeries in the kitchen, I took a deep breath and made my way to the front door with butterflies—or, since the sensation was sharper, bees flying complex formations—in my stomach. *Come on, Lexi. She's family, how hard could it be?*

Common sense might be the voice of reason, but I was past reason and in the front seat of what might become an emotional roller coaster. It was time to either shoot my hands in the air and enjoy the ride, or close my eyes and hang on for dear life. Given the course of recent events in my family, I'd probably end up exercising both options.

"Hello again, Alexis." Mag's eyes glimmered with unshed tears, and I could feel wetness beginning to form in the corners of my own as we gazed at each other across the threshold. Anxiously, I checked her over for signs of injury after the destruction of her home, but she looked about the same as the last time I'd seen her. She stood a good six inches shorter than my own five-and-a-half feet and wore one of those fluffy shawl-type things over her shoulders. Mag's pink cheeks peeked out beneath dark eyes that held immense power. Now, they were also full of emotion. "I'm sorry you've been alone all this time. I truly wish I could have come to you sooner, but there were circumstances."

Maybe I should have been mad, but if my recent excursions to the past had taught me anything, it was that one event could cause a ripple effect, and to dwell on whether things would have turned out better *if only* this or that had or hadn't happened was naive. Serena's life hadn't turned sour at the very moment she'd wished to return to; the events of that day were the culmination of her spending years feeling neglected and abused. Hindsight might be 20/20 in theory, but it also had a way of playing tricks on you.

Hope for a future spent with more family than I'd ever expected to meet erased any animosity I could have directed toward Mag, and I vowed to start being more grateful for the things I *did* have instead of lamenting what might have been.

"It's okay; I forgive you. And I was never alone. Would you like to come in and meet my family?"

Mag swallowed hard, nodded in assent, and followed me inside. Each of the godmothers took turns introducing themselves, and when Kin offered his hand in greeting, Mag covered it with her own and tossed a knowing grin and a mischievous wink at me over her shoulder. Salem received a pat on the head and made the rumbled purring noise that sounded more than a little strange coming from a fully grown man.

We were all here for a reason, and it wasn't just about family bonding, but one thing I've learned in the short time since Awakening to my full power is that you never know what the next adventure is going to bring. Clara had been encased in stone for years, and despite the insistent noises it made in my head, the Bow of Destiny could wait just a little longer for its final repair. This meeting was well past due, and I needed to make the most of it.

Surprising us all, Mag sincerely thanked the faeries for having gone above and beyond their job description. "I wish I had been in a position to take care of Alexis myself, but I was...otherwise occupied." She turned to face me before continuing, "Time folds in on itself sometimes. One day you were a tiny baby and the next, you were all grown up, and I'd missed it. I planned on approaching you, even visited Clara a couple of times, and observed you from across the street.

"You seemed happy and healthy, and I had no idea what to say after all that time had passed. I'd have told you about our connection that day you magicked yourself inside my hut, but you were with Sylvana and I wasn't sure if I could trust you. I'm sorry for scaring you, but I couldn't resist having a little fun. Took it like a champ, you did. But the look on your face, I tell you."

Mag looked around appreciatively, "Anyway, I can see you were far better off with your faeries than if you had been raised by an old hag like me. I hope you can forgive me for keeping my distance, Alexis."

"I'm not angry, Aunt Mag," I repeated the sentiment. "I'm just glad you're here now." And I was. I'd always thought of myself as an orphan, but it turned out that I had more family than I'd ever imagined. Some good and some bad, just like the dysfunctional families I'd seen on television. "Let's not lose each other again."

"Agreed. Now, I'm guessing you had another reason for hunting me down." Mag indicated it was my turn to explain myself. "I'd wager it's a long story, dear. Let's have a seat and sort it all out. Your friends are welcome to stay." Her manner had taken an 180-degree turn from the night I stood in her living room thinking I was invisible to her wise eyes. Don't get me wrong, I wouldn't recommend going up against her, but for today at least, she'd softened into the sweet little old lady I'd taken her for the first time we met.

Evian filled the kettle with a flick of her finger, and Soleil set it to boiling while Vaeta whisked the old Balefire family tea service into the parlor. Terra gave me a quick squeeze and suggested giving me some alone time with my aunt.

The room seemed quiet when we were left in it alone (Salem opted to curl up on the hearth and pretend to fall asleep, even though we both knew better), but when the two of us settled around the hearth Mag's shoulders finally relaxed.

"You gave me the time travel ring, and I've been using it to collect living gold from the past, to fix the Bow of Destiny, which got dashed to pieces by a bit of inadvertent Fae magic." I knew the godmothers felt incredibly sorry for having caused so much trouble, but if they hadn't gotten the bow from my mother, who knows where it would have wound up by now. "Sylvana betrayed me—I'm sure you're not surprised—and I had to choose between the bow and Kin. It was an easy choice, and I'd make it again in a hot second, but it certainly did throw a wrench in the works."

I explained how the bow had fractured when the faeries stopped Sylvana from making off with it, and how I'd needed three deposits of raw ore to repair the breaks.

"I got to see this house when it was still just a tiny cottage, and I watched Tempest forge the casting ring. That's how I mended one of the cracks. Then, I saw you and Grandmother when you were teenagers. There was still gold in the sanctum then, but there's none left now."

"That explains how you figured out who I am. I'd wondered where your travels with that ring would take you. My own were exceptionally interesting. Pity you only get five journeys. I tried for years to figure out a way to either trick or recharge it, but it outsmarted me every time. When your turn is over, it's final."

"So it's hopeless, then. I failed to get any gold on my last two trips back, and if I can't make it work again, the ring is nothing more than a bauble."

"Oh, no, do not mistake it for that. That ring is still very powerful. Belonged to King Solomon, it did. Legend says it's what he used to trap the Genie in the lamp, thousands of years ago. Just because it doesn't work for you, doesn't mean it won't work for someone else. I'd wager we don't have the time it would take to recharge enough to accept a new master, and I'd be careful with it lest it winds up in the hands of someone unworthy."

I nodded, silently vowing to consult the Grimoire for a cloaking spell. "Lamiel said all the living gold has been gathered up and taken to Olympus. There's not another known deposit left in this dimension, save for one. Unless I can figure out how to access that one or get to Olympus, I'm screwed. You'd think the gods would lend a helping hand—or even a pinkie finger, but it seems they're leaving me to my own devices. If Grandmother wasn't encased in stone, I could use the gold from her amulet."

Mag reached for her throat and pulled a recognizable necklace from beneath her collar—an exact match to the one coiled around Clara's neck. "If I hadn't already had to use my own cache, I'd give it to you. What about your fifth chance? You only mentioned four transports—the two where you were successful and the two where you failed—what happened during the fifth one?" Mag raised an eyebrow, her shrewd mind proving itself once again.

"That's another reason I wanted to see you. The first time I activated the ring was purely accidental. I was playing with it and wishing I knew what happened on the day Sylvana disappeared, and grandmother turned to stone." The scene replayed in my head.

"Clara didn't kill anyone."

Without missing a beat, Mag replied, "Well, of course not, dear." If she'd had a skein and a pair of needles in her gnarled fingers, she'd have kept right on knitting.

"What do you mean, *of course not?*"

"You didn't think I bought that pile of steaming horse manure the Snodgrasses tried to spread around, did you? My sister would never have harmed another witch, much less her daughter, even if the little wench could have used a good swatting. There's no love lost between your mother and me, lass, I won't lie about that. Tell me what did happen. Perhaps there's still hope."

I obliged, calling on Salem to fill in the specifics of the spell that bounced between Sylvana and Clara.

"Black witchfire. Always was one of Sylvana's favorites, and damned hard to counter or reverse. I'm assuming you've already tried?"

I nodded. "Reversal, and then I tried something else. Maybe it was stupid, and it didn't work anyway. I thought maybe my prophetic abilities had something useful to say about bringing her back, but I was wrong. See, I've been having these dreams. I'm not entirely clear on what they mean, but there's something there." I described both dreams in detail, while Mag's mouth formed a gentle smile.

"These are the types of questions you'd have needed a Balefire to answer. Again, I'm so sorry I wasn't there to help you. What you saw and felt was the Balefire Blessing. We all received one as an infant; we were all bathed in flame, our hearts infused with the essence of the Balefire. Flame feeds witch, and then witch feeds flame; that's how Esmerelda designed it."

One question niggled at me, "What made you decide not to become the Keeper of the Flame?"

"Ah, so you didn't see that part of my past. Fate called on me for another kind of work, and I embraced a different future because chose adventure over being forced to stick close to home. There was a big argument, and Clara and I didn't speak for years. Your mother felt the same way about tending the flame, which is why, I'm guessing, Clara passed the torch along to you. Your mother and I are more alike than I wish we were. It's probably why we don't get along."

"Was she the one who blasted your hut in the Fringe?"

"Oh no, dear, she won't come around to see the Mudwitch again—her little nickname for me." Mag chuckled.

"So what did happen? Are you safe?"

"As long as I remember to wear my glasses when brewing potions. The hut's current condition is my fault,

I'm afraid. Luckily, I listened to Jinx and got outside before the place went up in flames." Mag's cheeks flushed a bright shade of red, and I made sure to stifle the giggle threatening to escape my lips.

Mag swiftly changed the subject. "You said you've had dreams that aren't just dreams before? It's clear you have a great many skills at your disposal. You'll be quite the force one day. I believe there's a way to get the living gold out of Clara's amulet using, of all things, a tool forged from the same material. My mother had a chisel that would slice through even the hardest stone."

"You mean like chip away the granite without harming Clara? Couldn't we use the chisel to free her, then?" If this was a possibility why wouldn't Mag have come forward before?

"No, child." She must have seen the dismay written all over my face. "I would never leave my sister trapped if I had the means to help her. It's going to take both of us, speed, and precision to release the amulet. The granite will reclaim it if we aren't careful."

After seeing the way the stone had eaten Clara the first time, I considered that a valid assumption.

Between us, we mapped out a plan.

"The uses of living gold are plentiful. It's a shame those greedy gods are hogging it all. Now, open the hearth and let's see if Mother's chisel is still where she used to keep it."

"Aunt Mag, can I ask you one more personal question?" I gathered all my courage and prepared for either response.

"You want to know why I look like this, don't you?" she asked, running a gnarled, bony finger over her cheek, caressing skin once soft and rosy but now wrinkled and worn to leather.

"Yes," I answered softly, averting my gaze.

"That's a story for another time, lass, but it has nothing to do with your mother if that's what's worrying you. I promise to tell you more than you want to know about my adventures, but not until after we sort this all out." Mag winked, inciting exponentially more curiosity than her response had quelled.

TWENTY-FOUR

I did as I was told, pulling the lever and following Mag across the threshold of the fireplace and into my sanctum. Except that the minute she entered, it didn't seem entirely mine anymore. It was as if the room was welcoming her home by bending to Mag's will. In a flurry of motion that happened so quickly I had trouble following, several pieces of furniture rearranged themselves, and the shelves produced a number of items I'd never seen before.

The tufted settee I usually lounged across for a late afternoon nap maneuvered itself to the other side of the room and hunkered under a porthole window that hadn't been there before. Two Georgian armchairs upholstered in tattered, gaudy brocade that must have dated back to the sixteenth century—judging by the odor of mothballs and mold I'd whiffed before stuffing them into a closet several weeks prior—had emerged from the recesses, looking almost unrecognizable given they were now in perfect condition.

Between them sat a low, round, equally antiquated table draped in lush crimson velvet, at the center of which squatted the large, clear quartz crystal gazing ball I'd come to think of as my own. Jealousy flared up and painted the backs of my eyeballs green for the few seconds it took to recognize how uncharitable was the emotion. This had been Mag's place long before mine.

Mag puttered over to the alchemy lab, which quickly arranged itself into what I guessed was her preferred configuration, and pulled a cigar box from the shelf beneath the table's edge.

"Why didn't the room do this when I brought Sylvana here?" I blurted before it occurred to me that my mother might not be a good topic of conversation to bring up at that precise moment.

Something about Mag's laugh echoed familiar to me, though I couldn't ever remember hearing it before, "because your mother never showed her environment enough respect for it to cooperate. You get out what you put in, never forget."

She flipped the cover to reveal an exquisitely worked case hidden inside the simple cigar box. A tiny lock held the case closed. "Okay, this is it, but we need the key. And for that, I'll have to brew a potion."

"What now?"

"The Enchanter's Ruse." Salem piped up. I hadn't realized we'd been followed until I turned around and saw all four faeries, my familiar, and Kin standing near the Balefire. In my haste, I'd forgotten to close it behind me.

"It's a way of hiding things using a series of fail-safes. I'm guessing the potion's not all you need." He directed the last bit toward Mag as the six members of my motley crew found places to settle in and sate their curiosity. Mag didn't seem to mind, so neither did I.

"You are correct. Lexi's carrying another useful item," Mag pointed at my chest.

"The Stone of Blood?" That made sense.

"No, the compass." She retorted with a look that made me think she might be wondering just how bright I was after all. "We need something already made of living gold. That was Mother's caveat. Their wedding bands—hers and Daddy's—were made of it, so she knew she'd always be able to get to her tools. The bow might have worked too if it were still in one piece. In a pinch, I can use the casting circle, but it's awkward."

I didn't want to sound any stupider than I already felt, so I refrained from asking another question, even though I was nearly biting my tongue off with the effort.

"Then what?" Kin asked with unchecked curiosity. Sending him a silent *thank you*, I awaited Mag's response.

"We get the chisel, use it on my sister's amulet, extract the nugget, and fix the bow." Well, duh.

Fascinated, I perched on the edge of an old cherry red and chrome chair right out of a diner in the 1950's and doubled as a step stool if you lifted and pulled the bottom two rungs from beneath the seat. I didn't want to miss one second of watching a Balefire witch at work. My aunt looked much more vital while spellcasting; her arms whirling around as if conducting a bizarre orchestra while ingredients and tools marched or floated from various shelves and crevices around the space.

The only thing missing was a sprightly tune playing in the background.

A fat black cauldron dislodged itself from the bottom of a pile stacked precariously on a rickety wooden shelf, but couldn't quite make the jump from the floor to the kettle stand. I swear, it looked chagrined as it stopped moving, raised its handle to the upright position, and allowed Mag to heft it into place before Kin or Salem could offer a bit of manly assistance.

I noticed how she commanded her tools to do her bidding, but handled each ingredient with care, chopping neatly and measuring precisely when necessary. So different from the faeries, who were already so closely connected to the elements their magic often seemed automatic and devoid of any underlying intent. I'd long ago guessed that wasn't the case, but watching a trained witch made me see where the similarities between the two brands of magic ended.

Two unicorn tail feathers, a tablespoon of moose snot, and a few other seemingly random ingredients later (Mag provided the required *scream of an old hag* herself), my aunt held up a neon purple test tube and declared herself ready to proceed. I handed over the compass with carefully masked difficulty, reluctant to allow anyone else to touch it. Even armed with the knowledge that Mag had done nothing so far but help me, and that she probably wanted Clara restored even more than I did, handing over the compass felt a lot like losing control, which didn't sit well with me.

Did I mention I have trust issues?

"Here comes the unpleasant part." Mag grimaced as she poured the contents of the beaker down her throat. Euw, moose snot. Even though I'd known all along she was planning on drinking the concoction I wanted to gag when I saw it happen. Mag's entire body began to heave as though she felt the same way.

Quite unexpectedly, a tiny, ornate silver key popped out of her mouth and landed in her outstretched palm.

Looking no worse for the wear, Mag grinned and held it aloft for everyone to see. You can bet your butt I would be choosing a new location for the little key—sans the gross—as soon as I could. Unless, of course, Mag decided to take the chisel when we were finished harvesting the living gold. She had more right to her mother's tools than I ever would.

I added dousing the key with disinfectant to my list as well. Essence of stomach acid. Ugh. Not my thing.

Fitting the key into the lock, she turned it and surprised me yet again when I expected her to come up with the chisel and music came out instead. Hey, other than it being a tool of some sort, I wasn't entirely sure what a chisel even was, how was I supposed to know how big it might be?

Wordlessly, but with a wink in my direction, she strode over to a bookshelf across the room and picked up a chest about the size of a shoe box. It was so ordinary I couldn't tell you whether it had been tucked between the spines of *Curses and Maledictions For Special Occasions* and

The Varied Uses of Graveyard Dust, Volume 4 before Mag entered the sanctum or not.

It might have appeared ordinary, but the plain wooden container veritably hummed with power as Mag set it down beside the music box and made a few painstaking adjustments to line the two up in perfect proximity, about a half inch apart. She touched a hidden spring, and I finally got my soundtrack.

Waving the compass over the pair in an intricate pattern, Mag whispered, "Apertus."

A sparkling mote of light zigged and zagged down the space between the two boxes, then circled them twice. I could see why using the casting circle would be Mag's last ditch choice. Duplicating the complicated hand gesture while holding the boxes in perfect alignment might be enough to drive a witch off the deep end.

Light with a delicate purple tinge flared from under the simple, wooden lid which popped open on its own. Mag reached inside and pulled out a slender shaft that was flat on one end and tapered to a point on the other. With a triumphant smile, she clapped the lid closed again. Yeah, I definitely would have noticed if that box had been here all along, humming at me.

With the compass lending its weight to my neck once again, I was able to relax and begin worrying about the next stage of the plan. Mag had handed it over easily enough, though I could have sworn there was a nanosecond of hesitation before her fingers released the chain. I chalked it up to arthritis and decided I could forgive the curiosity any witch would feel regarding an item forged by the gods.

"Are you ready, dear?" Mag asked. She was already halfway out the fireplace entrance before I could reply. I guess the question was rhetorical.

"I want you four to promise me you won't interfere and get yourselves shut out of Faerie for even longer." I put on my best serious face and cornered the godmothers at the front door while Mag, Salem, and Kin filed outside to gather around Clara's stoned form.

"Alexis Penelope Balefire, we can take care of ourselves and make our own decisions." Terra retorted, brushing off my concerns with a wave of her hand. "You will not stop us from protecting you if the situation gets out of control. Like before, with the eaf—"

"Stop reminding me about that!" I swear, you let one rampaging Faebeast in the house, and you have to hear about it forever.

"Remember how it nearly killed you and Salem both? We'll take every precaution, Fae laws be damned, and that's final." The other three nodded in agreement.

If she was using my middle name, I knew Terra meant business, but I'd sooner eat a basket of Carl's dirty gym socks than cost them any more than I already had.

I heaved a sigh. There was no use arguing if the faerie's minds were made up. I'd just have to make sure everything went off without a hitch, leaving nothing to tempt them into the fray.

A yowl from Salem let me know people were waiting, so with one more useless warning look over my shoulder we made our way to the clearing and gathered around Clara's effigy. The faeries paid me the courtesy of maintaining some distance from the center of the action, positioning themselves at the four corners—north, south, east, and west—aligned with the element they each commanded. Kin was the only one who remained outside the circle, and that's where I preferred him to stay—safely out of harm's way. And if he did end up needing help, not only would I accept the blame for the godmothers angering everyone in the Faelands, I'd insist upon it.

"...always uses far more power than she needs to, and this is a delicate operation..." I overheard Salem speaking to Mag as I approached.

"You think I'm not up to it, Salem?" I challenged, giving him a look that clearly said he'd be eating kitty kibble for weeks if I wasn't happy with his answer.

Salem stared intently at his shoes, tracing a line in the dirt with his toe, "Of course not, Lexi. I'm just filling your Auntie in on the ways the lack of close family affected your training." The insult to Mag was mildly offered, but no less pointed in its intent. "You can't deny your touch is a little heavy handed at times."

"You mean you're airing out all my dirty laundry." I pinned him with a narrow-eyed glare.

"Hush, now." Mag implored, stepping between Salem and me, "let's begin."

I waited for her to start some kind of spell but all she did was pick up a fist-sized rock.

"You'll have to be quick," she cautioned. I nodded as if I had the first clue what she was talking about and leaned forward. What good I thought that did, I couldn't say.

Mag laid the chisel into the ridge where the amulet rested against Clara's bosom and lifted the rock. Tink. Tink. Tink. The sound rang out, and the chisel slid through the granite like butter.

"Get hold of it now, girl." Between clenched teeth, Mag issued the order and I rushed to do her bidding. She was fast for a woman of advanced age, but the granite was faster; by the time the chisel made its way around to finalize the cut, the stone had already begun to heal.

Breathing hard from exertion, Mag lifted a tear-stained face and showed me a smear of blood along the sharpened edge of the tool. And now I understood why the chisel was not the way to free Clara.

Laying the back of her hand against her sister's stoned cheek, Mag whispered, "Sorry, Sis. I didn't mean to hurt you."

Whether Clara heard the apology or not, I couldn't face another bloody attempt. My hands quivered and shook.

"I think we're on the right track, but we're not trying again until we refine the process." If my voice also shook a little, it was probably from issuing so strong a statement to a senior witch.

Honestly, I thought Mag looked a little relieved. She sank onto the nearby bench and contemplated her sister gravely. The personal agony Mag experienced while causing her sister pain raised my aunt higher in my estimation and dispelled the last notion Sylvana had planted in my head.

I joined her on the bench and waved for the others to go back inside to give us some privacy. Clearly, nothing dangerous had happened, and it was best to let us sort this out on our own. Salem tossed me a dirty look when I indicated he should follow the others, but went without argument. I'd probably get to hear his opinion later, though.

"Too slow. These old hands aren't what they used to be," Mag's fingers set the fluttery wisps of white hair on end. "You think you could handle the chisel? I can teach you how."

Nope. That was the last thing I wanted and the look on my face must have been enough to tell Mag so.

"Is there another tool? Like a knife that has more precision? What if I used one of the arrows?"

"No knife and the arrows are meant for piercing, not cutting. It would be like sawing at a steak with a butter knife." Mag shook her head emphatically.

I shuddered at the memory of the crimson-stained chisel.

"Well, do we have to get the amulet off of her?"

Mouth dropping open, Mag jumped up and took a closer look. She must have liked what she saw because she did a dance around her sister that Michael Flatly would have appreciated. Who would have suspected she still had it in her?

Then she pulled off her own amulet and set about experimenting on it. I think a semi loaded with lead could have run over the thing without making a dent, but Mag persisted until she found the single weakness she'd been searching for.

"Look, Lexi. If I hit straight on the hinge, it will pop open like a clam shell. Then I think I can run the chisel around from here to here," a claw-like finger indicated the stopping and starting points, "And if the granite is thin enough, I should be able to pry it open far enough for the compass to access the gold. You'll have to be fast, and it might take a few tries, but we won't be causing her any more pain."

I agreed, and we set to work.

Sun beating down on us relentlessly, sweat trickled down my back and moistened my brow. Half an hour later, amid a rush of activity, I heard the sound a chunk of gold makes when it hits the inside of the compass and let out a shout of relief that made Mag jump and toss a reflexive spell. Two bushes and a rock exploded into flame, and we had to call Evian to put them out.

But, we had the last piece of living gold, and something Mag had said was still squatting in the back of my mind while I rode the high of a job well done.

With the living gold safe inside my father's compass, at last, I wanted nothing more than to retreat to the sanctum and repair the Bow of Destiny; to hold it in my hands and for the very first time hear the call of countless fates just waiting for me to seize my destiny. After discovering just what that entailed, I'd mulled and agonized over exactly what it would mean to be a Fate Weaver; how to reconcile the two halves of myself. I'd wondered whether carrying on Cupid's work would make me less of a witch—less of a Balefire.

When I'd first gone searching for the bow at Shadow Hold, I'd had to mash both visions of myself together. Witch to God. Inherited power to inherent. But how closely linked those two halves were had never hit home quite so poignantly as right then, with my grandmother's final cache of living gold captured inside Cupid's compass.

By now, the process of repairing the bow was second nature to me. Its response to the final repair, however, went a bit over the top. A wet finger run around the rim of good crystal makes it sing with a clarity so pure it sets camp in the bones behind your ear and rattles them silly. Two seconds after it started I wished for it to stop.

I didn't sign on for having a living weapon carrying on a constant conversation in my head, but what was I going to do? Complain to the Annoying Sentient Item of Power Bureau?

Can you tone it down a bit? I sent the thought in the general direction of the noise which took a feat of mental gymnastics, but if we were going to share head space, some of us were going to have to develop decorum. The din reduced by several decibels and softened to an up-tempo piece I took to mean the bow was happy.

"Be nice to have a clue how this thing works. I mean, I know how to shoot an arrow, but am I supposed to carry it around with me all the time? Because that's not going to be good for business. I'll be the whackjob with the golden bow—that's what they'll call me. Goddess knows I don't think I thought this through." The adage of being careful what you wish for was taking on a new meaning in a hurry.

It was one thing to know I would have the privilege of wielding Cupid's bow—despite the family dysfunction—and quite another to strap that puppy on my back and walk around town on a daily basis.

"I'm sure you'll figure it out, and something tells me you already have a pretty good idea what you need to do to restore my sister."

Did I?

Leaving the bow where it sat, I paced the room while the others, blessedly, remained silent. The task was for me alone to complete, and it seemed the godmothers were willing to let me work it through by myself. This adulting thing isn't as easy as it looks.

Images from my dreams played against the chime of the bow. The Balefire blessing had to be significant somehow. What was it Mag had said? The Balefire infuses the heart of a witch.

Suddenly, and with an indisputable ring of truth, I

knew what I had to do. It had been staring me in the face all along, and as with seemingly every other problem in my life, the answer involved doing something that made me feel shaky inside.

"I have to infuse an arrow with Balefire and shoot her with the bow, don't I?"

"That's the only logical conclusion I can see," Mag agreed with me.

TWENTY-FIVE

ull of purpose, I picked up the Bow of Destiny, and that was the moment I realized during all this time and talk and worry about firing arrows at people I didn't actually have any to fire. Sometimes I think I'm nothing but a crap magnet in a room full of fans.

Maybe I expected them to just materialize after the final repair. They didn't.

"We have a problem." Quite an obvious one, and I guess I wasn't the only one who missed it. I'm not sure if that made me feel better or worse.

"What? You have the bow, let's do this." Kin, like most normal people, had a fascination with watching someone perform real magic.

"Right, I have the *bow...*" I emphasized and trailed off to make my point.

When it landed, I started giggling at the sea of dismayed faces staring back at me. In fact, the whole thing hit me funny, and the giggles turned to belly laughs and sent me stumbling toward the sofa when the hilarity sucked the strength from my muscles.

Unfortunately, I was the only one finding humor in the situation. The dismayed faces turned to concerned expressions, and that made me laugh harder until tears rolled down my cheeks, and I had to clutch my aching belly. That much hilarity makes your face hurt, too.

"Come on; you don't think this is funny? All this work, and what do I have to show for it? A magical bow that won't stop singing in my head and no magical arrows to go with it."

"I think she's hysterical." Salem looked like he was thinking about slapping the laughter out of me like I had done to Serena, and I gave him a warning look until he backed off.

"Not hysterical, just...I can't help it. I think it's funny."

"What do you remember about the day when Clara shot Cupid? Where did she get the arrow then?" Mag asked the question after everyone had settled back onto chairs and the couch. We weren't going anywhere until I figured this thing out.

My eyes dropped closed while I cast the mental image against the backs of my lids and watched the whole thing play out one last time. I vowed to lock the memory of that day away and never think about it again, just as soon as Clara was free.

"Cupid has the bow slung over his back. I don't see a quiver, but when he pulls the bow forward, there's an arrow. How the..." I replayed the scene and paid closer attention to what I hadn't noticed the first time.

"The bow isn't complete," I said.

"What do you mean it isn't fixed? Look at it, it's perfect," Salem purred the R in perfect.

"I didn't say it wasn't fixed; I said it wasn't complete. There's a piece missing up near the grip." And still, the bow was singing its happy song in my head, and the string hummed in my hand.

"Do we have to go back to Shadow Hold?" Kin looked a little green at the thought; he'd almost died there the last time, and yet he was willing to go back. Love for him rushed right up into my throat and made it hard to speak.

"No. I don't think so. Can you all clear out and give me a few minutes alone?" All the pieces of the puzzle were there, my bones told me that much, but this was Fate Weaver business, and that meant it was a job for only me.

Each reluctant backward glance received a smile of reassurance as fake as a bad toupee, but they went.

Once I was alone, I picked up the bow and mimicked the motions I remembered my father making. A burst of noise jangled through my head—a happy noise but with a plaintive edge.

"Listen," I talked to the bow as if it could hear and understand me. "This is all new to me, and if there's anything you can do to make it easier, I'd appreciate a little help here. I'm not Cupid, as I'm sure you've noticed."

The sounds turned even more plaintive. The bow missed Cupid. Now, there's a sentence I never thought I'd say.

"You're stuck with me, at least for the time being. Can you help?"

In answer, the bow went completely silent. Funny how you can get used to something so quickly that when it's gone, you're thrown off balance. As the quiet echoed through my head, the same plaintive song piped from somewhere else in the room. My ears led me to the compass, abandoned near the fireplace where I'd emptied it of its cache of gold.

"Oh, you did this before, didn't you?" The compass practically jumped into my hand and strained toward the bow. Since no one else was around, I could beef up my part of what happened later, but really, I didn't do anything other than move my hands closer together. The bow and compass did the rest.

Writhing in my palm like a snake shedding its skin, like a living thing—well, duh, *living* gold—parts of the compass folded, stretched, and morphed. The changes happened so fast it was hard to focus on any single aspect of them before the generated force clapped my hands together.

Joyful song boomed through my skull, both from within and without. Its high-toned clarity was more than my humanity could bear, and I slumped to the floor, the bow with its newly formed sight slipping from my nerveless hand.

That's where they found me an hour later. Knocked out cold with a huge grin on my face.

Amid the well-intentioned hubbub that followed, Mag went from amused to impatient, and I was right there with her.

"Drink your tea, Lexi." Terra thought I couldn't taste a healthy dose of her favorite tonic.

"I'm fine. Let me up." While Kin's strong fingers kneading my arches felt amazing—he'd cuddled down with my feet in his lap as I stretched out on the sofa—I had things to do, witches to unstone. "No, I mean it. It's time."

"I still don't see any arrows." Vaeta was the one you could always trust to state the obvious.

Patting Kin on the arm reassuringly, I pulled my feet away and rose to collect the bow from the floor where the faeries had wisely left it. My hand closed over the grip, and a powerful sense of oneness straightened my spine.

Half witch, half demigod. Those were the parts that made up my whole, and I accepted them.

I was a Fate Weaver. This was my moment to shine.

And I did shine. Pink fire colored my vision as I brought the bow to bear in a left-handed grip. Instinct drove my right hand, and I drew the arrowhead from the living gold of the bow like it was being born from the metal.

The heart-shaped head needed a shaft. That's where I came in. Drawing on everything that made me— humanity and witchblood, maybe even my soul—I poured myself into the form. The whole thing happened in the time it took my hand to cross the space between the grip and where the fletched end fitted against the bowstring.

It looked like magic. It was magic, but it was more than that.

With a triumphant smile on my face, I lowered my

hand and showed off my weapon of choice. The shaft looked like solid pearl and shone with an iridescent glow.

I might have underestimated the impact of pink eyes on the crowd. Expressions ranged from Kin's shock to Mag's wide grin. She let out a whoop that bounced off the skylight and echoed back to us.

The biggest life changes sneak up on you like a panther stalking prey. Sly and sleek, you almost never see their magnitude until the rush of attack that comes in the moments before you know nothing will ever be the same again.

Pulling an arrow from the Bow of Destiny took a vital part of me, but it also made me into the most epic version of myself. Even if only for that single moment before I settled into the newness and made it comfortable around me.

The moment begged me to say something profound.

"Look how pretty." Decidedly not profound, but completely *Lexi*.

In a flurry of activity, we rounded up one of the smaller cauldrons to carry a bit of the Balefire with us and left the workshop with hope in our hearts. It seemed like things had been happening *to* me for months now, and, finally, it was time for me to step up and be the catalyst.

I could do this, right? What if I missed? What if it didn't work? What if it did? How would the faeries react when the true owner of their home returned? Was I about to set off a nuclear faerie bomb? Shuttered expressions told me nothing of their thoughts, and all four of them remained uncharacteristically quiet. Never a good sign.

My brain revved up to full throttle while my body calmly went about the business at hand. If I let the multitude of questions pick away at my resolve, I'd never go through with it. Shooting an arrow, even one you're reasonably certain won't draw killing blood, at anyone is a tricky thing. The only way I could do it was to find that feeling again, the one I'd had not ten minutes before. Funny how confidence comes and goes.

A semi-circle of family formed behind me when I infused it with my will and thrust the tip of the arrow into the Balefire. Eyes closed, I centered myself and called on the Fate Weaver within. Pink flames shot skyward, enveloped, and clung to the arrow.

Doubt fled. Calm certainty filled me, and in one deft motion, I assumed shooting stance. Elbow cocked, bowstring taut, my eye locked on the newly formed sight. Using the bow on Joshua would be a piece of cake after this. Breath whooshed from me, and the world stilled. I was as ready as I ever would be.

I let the arrow fly.

Pink flame arced and sped toward its target, pierced stone, and lanced into Clara's heart. For half a second, nothing happened, and it was as though the world took a breath.

You've seen Lexi tackle family secrets, magical matchmaking disasters, and a sentient bow with an attitude. But trust us— she's just getting started.

Stick around for No Chance in Spell, where Lexi faces a danger even the Balefire flame might not be able to snuff out.

QUICK AUTHOR'S NOTE

If you weren't already aware, ReGina and Erin are a mother/daughter writing team, and yes, that means we mix family and work - with all the ups and downs you might expect, but since we're best friends, too, we let that stuff roll right off our backs.

When we started writing To Spell & Back, we knew it was time to delve deeper into Lexi's tangled family history.

Time travel is always a fun challenge to tackle, but exploring the lives of her ancestors—and how their choices shaped her own destiny—added an extra layer of intrigue. Love and legacy are such integral parts of Lexi's journey, and this book let us play with how far she'd go to protect both.

Of course, repairing Cupid's Bow of Destiny was no small task, and neither was imagining how the bow itself would become a character in its own right. We loved exploring the mystery of this powerful artifact and how it connects Lexi to her father, her family, and her fate as a Balefire witch.

Then there's Serena. We wanted to push her rivalry with Lexi to new heights, bringing even more chaos to Lexi's life and showing just how dangerous Serena can be when her ambitions take over. And let's not forget Kin—because every cinnamon-roll musician boyfriend needs a moment to shine (or worry about his girlfriend's life choices). This story gave us plenty of opportunities to explore Lexi and Kin's growing bond—and test its limits.

But as much as Lexi learns about her family's past in To Spell & Back, her future is still full of surprises. In No Chance in Spell, Lexi will face dark forces, old wounds, and a danger even her faerie godmothers can't predict. If you thought things were complicated before, you won't want to miss what's coming next.

If you've come this far with us and not decided we're complete and total whackadoodles...and especially if you have, we're offering a chance to sign up for our newsletters— the best place to get new release updates, sales notifications, and other fun content.

You can sign up for ReGina's newsletter and/or Erin's newsletter, and as a thank-you gift for hanging out with us, you'll also get a FREE novella that isn't available anywhere else. And of course, we promise not to SPAM your inbox!

Love, hugs, and happy reading,
ReGina & Erin

P.S. If you enjoyed this book, it would be great if you could leave a review or recommendation at your favorite store, GoodReads, or BookBub.

Your reviews help indie authors sell more books!

EXCERPT FROM NO CHANCE IN SPELL

FATE WEAVER - BOOK FOUR

CLARA

People—even witches—find great comfort in telling their secrets to the dead. Or, in my case, the not-quite-but-assumed dead.

Not that I could fault the theory. I had, after all, been turned to stone. Most people wouldn't survive the experience.

Why confess their hearts to a witch with a heart of stone? Because no matter how petty were the crimes of my sister witches, they paled in comparison to mine—to the worst sin imaginable. I stand (because I cannot do otherwise) accused of killing my own daughter. A gravely-mistaken assumption, but who could blame them for jumping to the conclusion? The punishment for killing another witch is being turned to stone.

No one knows by whose hand the sentence is served, only that it is swift and irrevocable. Kill a witch, become a living monument: an effective warning against falling prey to the destructive side of the power that runs through the blood of our kind. All the evidence was against me.

Not having murdered anyone before, I'd had no idea if

stoned witches remained awake inside their prison for all eternity. In the middle of a heated discussion with my daughter—a fight, if you want to be technical about it—my binding spell crossed with Sylvana's ball of dark magic, picked up some of her intent, mixed it with mine and slammed us both with the result.

Nothing remained but a burnt scar on the earth and me, fearful I'd destroyed my own flesh and blood, forced to stand watch over the scene of my own destruction. Wanting to cry and not being able to shed a tear is the worst feeling in the world.

I'd resigned myself to an eternity of listening to the transgressions of others while wishing I'd eventually die inside my cocoon—that is, until sly Sylvana showed up very much alive and well. And with no intention of releasing me from stasis.

When word of her miraculous resurrection spread, the number of huddled confessors decreased dramatically.

Since then, witches pass me by with a look that says they hope I never heard a word of their transgressions and if I did, that I never have the chance to speak of them out loud. But I've smelled the dirty laundry flung around my feet, and I remember the stench of every tiny tidbit.

Lexi stands before me now with fierce determination in her eyes and a longing to set me free so strong I can feel it in my granite bones. She's tried before and failed, but third time's the charm. So they say, anyway. A pot of Balefire sits at her feet; the Bow of Destiny rides her hand with an arrow aimed at my heart. It's a good thing I'm virtually frozen, because my instincts are screaming for me to duck.

I can't duck. I can't look away. Nothing is left but to stand (as if I had any other choice) and listen for the twang of the string, wait for the burning sting of the barb, and hope that her aim is true.

Looting my stoned grandmother with Cupid's bow and a flaming arrow. What was I thinking? There are a hundred ways this could go wrong.

Determined, I pulled the bowstring back, forced trembling nerves to rock steadiness. Hushed calm flowed like water to fill me from the bottom up, pushing out my breath on a sigh. There would never be a better moment than now.

I let the arrow fly.

Time slowed to a crawl, and crystalline clear vision focused on the burning arrow crawling through the air toward its target. The golden barb picked up light and magic until it passed the halfway mark and time fell back to normal speed.

Pink flame arced straight and true, pierced stone, and lanced into Clara's heart. For half a second, nothing happened, and it was as if the whole world held its breath.

My heart tried to punch a hole in my throat.

A lifetime of longing for blood family—for the mother of my dreams—hadn't come to much once Sylvana finally appeared. Wicked witches make lousy parents, and you can't trust them as far as you can throw a unicorn. Don't try that, by the way, unicorns get stabby when you pick them up. Especially the purple ones.

The pressure popped my ears, my stomach plummeted into my shoes, and the Bow of Destiny slipped to the ground. Nothing else moved in the cotton-heavy silence—not a bird, not a bee, not even me.

Failure.

I'd been so sure my plan would work. Turned to stone in a freak accident involving wicked witchery, my grandmother's statue guarded the clearing near my house for as long as I could remember. Once I'd learned her stoning wasn't a lifetime sentence for killing another witch, I'd searched high and low for a means to set her free.

Salem and I had put our heads together—my familiar used his human head, not his cat one—and hatched a plan to use my newfound Fate Weaver abilities and my father's bow to infuse Clara's heart with the mighty power of the Balefire. It's a good thing tending the magical flame is only one of my legacies, because Cupid's bow—technically mine at the moment—turned out to be the pivotal part of the plan.

It would propel an arrow made from living gold and the essence of myself—don't ask how that works because I'm a little hazy on the details—through the stone encasing Clara's body and into her heart. Dipping the arrow in the Balefire would, if all went as planned, inject enough of the fire's healing energy to bring her back to life.

Sounds like a long shot, I know (no pun intended), but it made sense when we came up with the idea. I am Lexi Balefire: Keeper of the sacred fire; maker of matches; weaver of fates. Shouldn't I be able to weave one for my grandmother that didn't involve eternal punishment for a crime she didn't commit?

Sound rushed back to a world I'd already forgotten had gone silent. The first thing I heard was the sound of my breath hitching as I cried. I glanced behind me at the grave faces of my companions and tried to accept my failure.

A sharp crack rent the air.

No Chance in Spell is available now, or if you'd rather save money, you can grab the box set of books 4-6 in the series for a discount. Keep reading for a preview of the FREE novella you'll get for subscribing to our newsletter.

A FREE STORY FOR YOU

Enjoyed meeting Lexi? Not ready for her story to end?

Sign up for either or both of our newsletters and you'll receive *A Snowball's Chance in Spell*, a prequel novella featuring characters from the *Mag & Clara Balefire Mysteries*, the *Haunted Everly After Mysteries*, and the *Psychic Seasons* series.

Christmas is canceled! Lexi Balefire's faerie godmothers didn't mean to knock Santa Claus and his sleigh out of the sky, but now his reindeer are missing, and it's up to Lexi to find them all before time runs out and Christmas is ruined!

EXCERPT FROM A SNOWBALL'S CHANCE IN SPELL

Lightning flirted in shadows of the dark clouds hovering over my house when I came home from work the afternoon before my twenty-second Christmas Eve. Nothing unusual there. With three elemental faeries living in the house, weird weather happened all the time. Or rather, every time my temperamental godmothers mounted some sort of snit.

The godmothers idled at snit.

Going back to work wasn't an option. I'd cleared the last match of the year—a lovely couple with a shared affection for online gaming—and I was no coward. When it came to diffusing faerie fights, I consider myself an expert, and this one didn't look like it rated more than a two on the volcano scale.

Yes, you heard right. I measure faerie fights on the scale of whether or not a volcano might erupt in my backyard. Living with faeries is never boring. Occasionally dangerous—especially because I have yet to come into the magic that is my birthright, but never boring.

A quick check proved they'd contained the madness to the inside and/or the backyard. The two feet of snow on the front lawn was still there and still white—you try explaining black snow to your neighbors sometime. I didn't see any winged denizens—fae or otherwise—dotting the roof ridge, or hear any ominous sounds. If not for the fact that lightning is rare in Maine during the winter, and rarer still when confined to a single area, I'd have thought it was a quiet day in the household.

In my head, I downgraded the threat to a level one, and went inside.

For the most part, my place looks like an ordinary, New England style home. Built by my great grandparents, it's the oldest house in a neighborhood that grew up around it when the suburbs expanded into what was once a rural area. Because, I think, the faeries wanted to give me a normal upbringing, they left the house in mostly the same condition it was in when they came to take care of me and only added on a wing for their own use.

I stepped into the front hall expecting…well, just about anything. Did I mention the faeries love holidays? Maybe they don't have them in the faelands, or maybe they do and go overboard there, too. I can't say since I've never been, but I could tell at a glance there were more decorations than there had been when I left.

"Terra!" I yelled, but got no answer. Terra, faerie of earth, held sway over all the flora and fauna found on dry land. She would be the one responsible for the pine boughs twining over anything that held still long enough. Fire faerie, Soleil, contributed by setting sparks of faerie light to twinkle inside the delicate ice bubbles crafted by her sister, Evian, mistress of water. The effect was lovely, but not as lovely as the three women could be when their faces weren't twisted, as they were now, with rage.

I came upon them in their favorite fighting grounds: the kitchen. It looked like I'd caught this one early since there was relatively little damage done so far. Steam rose from a puddle of water at Soleil's feet which I assumed had come from Evian. Vines snaked from between the kitchen tiles to twine around Evian's ankles, and there were a few smoking embers dotting Terra's hair. Nothing more than a minor spat.

Keeping it casual, I asked, "What's going on?" There's no rhyme or reason to what will settle a fight or send one into the red zone.

Terra turned one granite pink eye in my direction. "This doesn't concern you." The fingers of her left hand twitched and the vines slithered from Evian's ankles to her knees.

Retaliating, Evian conjured a gush of water from thin air, and doused the smoking embers. The scent of pine boughs couldn't compete with the stench of burnt hair, or the pungent funk erupting from the flowers that burst into bloom near her feet.

"Now look," I pointed out to Terra before she conjured something worse. "Evian is trying to help."

"Was not." Evian snapped her fingers and turned Terra's wet hair white with frost, except because the vines were now questing higher, she overshot the mark and doused a few of Soleil's decorative sparkles.

That was the moment I lost control.

Oh, who am I kidding? I never had control.

Soleil let out a screech and lobbed a fireball at Evian, who encased it in a ball of water and batted it toward Terra. I felt scoured clean when Terra called all the dirt and dust in the house to form a layer over the bobbing ball of doom which now resembled a small planet whizzing back toward Soleil.

It might have ended better if I'd have kept my mouth shut, but I didn't.

"You're going to put an eye out with that thing."

The ire of three faeries is a potent thing, but not as potent as a flaming mudball. I ducked, rolled, and hit the latch on the patio door in what I'd like to think was a graceful move. Probably looked like a seal rolling off a rock.

The flaming fireball arced over my head, its warm breeze tossing my hair, and rocketed off into the sky.

Crisis averted. Except, it wasn't. I should have known.

A Snowball's Chance in Spell is only available by signing up for one of our newsletters here:
https://reginawelling.com
https://erinlynnwrites.com

OTHER BOOKS

If you'd like to meet more people who live rent-free in our heads, here's a list of other series we've written. Our books are all set in fictional towns in Maine, and some characters like to flit back and forth between series. The cast of Psychic Seasons hangs out with Everly and also with Lexi Balefire from the Fate Weaver series. Mag and Clara Balefire are Lexi's grandmother and aunt!

The Psychic Seasons Series
Four women, four love stories, and a whole lot of supernatural surprises. In the quaint town of Oakville, Maine, psychic visions, ghostly whispers, and fate itself conspire to change lives—and hearts—forever

The Haunted Everly After Mysteries
Everly Dupree came home for a fresh start—not a full-time gig solving ghostly murders. But when the dearly departed start demanding justice, what's a reluctant medium to do?

The Ponderosa Pines Mysteries

Nothing bad ever happens in the weird little town of Ponderosa Pines...until someone dies. Now it's up to best friends Chloe and EV to solve the mystery—before the town's secrets bury them too.

The Mag and Clara Balefire Mysteries
Sister witches Mag and Clara Balefire move to a sleepy Maine town for a fresh start—only to find themselves conjuring up trouble, solving murders, and keeping their magic under wraps in this charmingly witchy cozy mystery series

Laurel Haven Witches
Four witches, destined by blood and magic, must embrace their power, battle a dark legacy, and surrender to the love that could break the curse—or bind them to it forever.

Nell Page: Accidental Investigator
Nell Page owns a bookstore, drinks too much coffee, and has a habit of noticing things she probably shouldn't. With warmth, wit, and an accidental talent for investigating, Nell tackles mysteries that don't always involve murder—but always matter.

www.ingramcontent.com/pod-product-compliance
Lightning Source LLC
Chambersburg PA
CBHW061101190726
48286CB00006B/1829